THE PATRON SAINT
OF RED CHEVYS

a novel by

KAY SLOAN

THE PERMANENT PRESS
4170 Noyac Road
Sag Harbor, NY 11963

Library of Congress Cataloging-in-Publication Data

Sloan, Kay.
  The patron saint of red Chevys: a novel / by Kay Sloan.
    p. cm.
  ISBN 1-57962-104-X (alk. paper)
  1. Blues musicians—Crimes against—Fiction. 2. Women
singers—Crimes against—Fiction. 3. African American
teenage girls—Fiction. 4. Murder victims' families—Fiction.
5. Gulf Coast (Miss.)—Fiction. 6. Berkeley (Calif.)—Fiction.
7. Mothers—Death—Fiction. 8. Sisters—Fiction. I. Title.

PS3659.L544P38 2004
813'.54—dc22

                                                    2003065550

Printed in The United States of America

THE PERMANENT PRESS
4170 Noyac Road
Sag Harbor, NY 11963

For Signe and David

PART ONE

MISSISSIPPI 1963

Chapter One

"I'm going to kill you." This was what I told my mother when I was five. She had insisted I finish eating my green beans and carrots, or no peach cobbler for dessert.

"You'll be a motherless child," she said, and plunked a freshly-washed dish into the drain. Her back was turned, and I couldn't tell if she was smiling. She wore an orange house dress, one of her favorites. Its bodice made her breasts look pointed and formidable, not like the two soft cushions I liked to snuggle against at night. "You won't have me around to do everything for you."

"I can handle that." I tilted my chin up so that it was even with the edge of the table.

She handed me a sponge and nodded to a puddle of milk I'd spilled on the table. "Then start practicing." She picked up the other dishes from the table and began to sing "What A Friend We Have in Jesus," giving it a bluesy spin to change the mood. I mopped up the milk and finished eating my vegetables. It was her voice. Everybody surrendered to Mama's voice, soft and hurt-sounding. She sang as if every wound in the world was in her heart, but like she was healing the pain at the same time, soothing it with her voice.

When she saw me eating my carrots, she launched into an old jubilee song, "I Wouldn't Take Nothing for My Journey Now," one she'd heard at a hand-clapping gospel festival at one of the black churches. For Mama, music could be a powerful celebration. She'd even named me Jubilee.

That was the first time I threatened my mother, only to surrender to her. The second was in the early spring of 1963. I came home early from band practice in the seventh grade and overheard Mama talking on the princess phone in her bedroom. At first I thought it was Daddy she was talking to, since she called him "sugar muffin." But I'd never heard her call him that. It was always "sweetie pie" for Daddy.

"It doesn't matter what folks say, sugar muffin," she was saying. "I love you. But it doesn't matter what you say, either. I love Harry and my girls, too. We both have too much to lose."

Her voice sounded different than it did when she talked to Daddy: excited but gentle, the way she'd whisper during the national anthem before a big baseball game — hushed, reverent, something on the verge. She loved sports, especially the Washington Senators.

Daddy used to say she liked the Senators because she liked politicians in general. She'd fallen in love with Daddy when he was a leader in the Biloxi, Mississippi Shriners in 1949. I have a photograph of the inaugural speech: Daddy jabbing his finger in the air, his broad shoulders thrown back so that he looks taller than his five and a half feet. He could be so eloquent, Mama said, and just look at that thick hair, she'd tell us, tapping at the glass in the picture frame. It was black and wavy, combed straight back from his forehead.

Standing on the stage behind him, Mama looks like

Rita Hayworth, in a slinky dress that hugs her waist and pushes up her bosom. She's only sixteen, but she's wearing her red hair in a French twist, with a pout on her lips, like she doesn't appreciate playing second fiddle, even to the new head of the Shriners, a man as handsome as Daddy. The Shriners had asked her to sing, and that was the night she and Daddy met. Mama was never a white-gloved Southern lady, Daddy said. Hell no, when she sang, she smoked.

So second fiddle wasn't a role that came easily to Mama. When she was young, her smoky blues voice was famous around town. In high school, she sang every week-end at the Green Lizard Lounge in a town called Libertyburg near Biloxi. That was her regular gig — she drew a big crowd there — but she'd also performed as far away as the French Quarter in New Orleans once, sneaking away on a bus so my grandparents wouldn't know. When the Biloxi Shriners asked her to sing at their campaign reception, she sang her first song, a torchy version of "My Sweetie Went Away." *I'm like a little lost sheep, I can't sleep, and I keep trying to forget...* Daddy said every man in the place went crazy, including him. She and Daddy never took their eyes off each other. Or so Daddy's legend has it. Mama would always smile like the Cheshire cat while she listened.

She must have sung the song differently, years later, to my sister Charlene and me at bedtime. It was soothing and gentle then, not sexy and hurt, and it would put us to sleep in a minute. We would snuggle under the covers on our twin beds, the quilts pulled up to our chins against the cool of the oscillating fan, stirring the air as if a fairy-tale wizard were there, breathing wishes into our dreams while Mama sang.

Charlene and I were Mama's only audience as she

sang us to sleep with funnier old songs like Bessie Smith's "Kitchen Man", about how wild she was about the way her 'kitchen man' warmed her chops, how she couldn't possibly do without him. . . I didn't understand the sexy stuff then, or the way she'd make eyes at Daddy when he'd appear in our bedroom door, listening to her.

"Sing the one about the pork chops, Mommy," I would chant, long after Charlene had caught on. Charlene would look at me, her upper lip curled in the disgust only an older sister can give. But catching my eye, Mama would sing as if it were just another funny song, then kiss us good-night. Her musky perfume would trail on the air after she closed the door. "Ambush," the label on the bottle said.

When I was thirteen and overheard her on the phone, I caught on to something a lot bigger than the sex in Mama's old songs. The next day, when Mama and I were in the kitchen washing dishes, I worked up my nerve. "Who're you calling sugar muffin on the phone, Mama?" I asked.

She scrubbed at a dish, holding it to the light as if some creamed corn were stuck there, but I could see it was perfectly clean. Then she slid it onto the counter and turned to me, frowning so that her blue eyes looked more intense than usual. "Sugar muffin? When did you hear that?"

"Yesterday. Band practice ended early for the trumpets, and I heard you on the phone."

"Why did you end early?" she asked. "They shouldn't be giving the trumpets all this preferential treatment. You need your practice."

"Practice? Don't you hear me every day? You've always said a girl can do anything, even play trumpet, if she works hard." When I first heard Miles Davis play "Old

Devil Moon," I'd asked Mama what that purple sound was. It carried me away, like a velvet magic carpet, and Mama saw it in my face. For my tenth birthday, she bought me a trumpet in New Orleans. At first, the noise was a zoo of squawking creatures, and I'd been banished to the garage for practice, but now the sound was smooth, sometimes even purple. It made me feel holy, like god was blowing his breath through me, even as I stood in the garage, trumpet pointed to the spider webs in the ceiling.

"You're being sassy, Jubilee," she said, an edge in her voice. Sometimes, she liked it when I was sassy, but not then. The checked curtains above the kitchen sink were parted, and the late light slanted across Mama's face, making the creases around her mouth look deeper.

"All I did was ask a question. I just wondered who was on the phone yesterday."

"Sugar muffin," she said it like she was thinking it over. "You're sure you heard me say that?" Mama wasn't a bad actress, and for a second I wondered. But then I caught the flicker of guilt and fear in her eyes, and I felt a terrible sorrow.

"Maybe I didn't hear right," I shrugged. I stood on tiptoe to slide the dry dish into the cabinet, so I wouldn't have to look at her. Fear wasn't something I was used to seeing on Mama's face, and it made me feel like I didn't even know my own mother.

She picked up another wet dish. "You and Harry," she said, meaning Daddy. "You two ask the funniest things. Did you hear Daddy and me talking last night?" She slid me a look and I shook my head, wondering what I'd missed. "Well, I tell you what. There's nobody I love more than your Daddy. Or you and Charlene." She put the dishtowel down and hugged me. I could feel her heart thumping through her apron.

I felt awful. But as long as she loved Daddy, that was all that mattered.

But on an April morning a month later, somebody – maybe Mama's "sugar muffin" – put a knife through her heart while she warmed up her pick-up truck. She was getting the motor ready to drive me to school.

That same spring morning, the police reported that Levi Litvak, our TV weatherman, was found burned to a crisp in the wreckage of his blue Thunderbird convertible on a swampy back road near Picayune. The car exploded into flames when it hit a giant cypress tree, and they had to pry the smashed engine away from the trunk. He'd hit the trunk so hard that his false teeth were knocked out. It was hard to imagine that his even, white television smile had come from dentures, but later it started to make sense, like nothing about him had been what it seemed.

Daddy and I didn't know anything about Levi Litvak when we found Mama, lying there in the truck, her face chalky, her breath rattling in her throat, a pulse Daddy's frantic fingers couldn't find.

It was a clear, crystal morning. Dew spotted the begonia Daddy had planted in the flower box outside my bedroom window, its blooms red. I had been lying awake in bed, my arms folded behind my head, thinking about a choral group from the Mobile blind school that had sung at our assembly the day before.

They were just kids, like us. We had filed in and slouched in our seats, ready to be bored. When the choir director said the cue, the blind kids began to sing, a sudden rhythm of open mouths: *Walk right in, sit right down, Daddy let your mind roll on. . .*

Shocked into silence, we'd stared: it was their eyes, the circled sockets, hollow and dark, too young for comfort. *Everybody's talking 'bout a new way of walking . . .*

Broom-makers, whispered a boy named Grady Pickens, but no one sneered.

We applauded wildly when they finished, as they sank their hands into their laps and smiled at the noise we made. We surged to our feet like a heaving beast: beating our hands madly, cheering our luck, pounding our guilt through our palms.

Call it a premonition, but as those blind kids nodded and smiled into their darkness, I felt as if I'd lived all my life on the light side of the moon, and never even known a dark side existed until that day. Early that morning, I was already feeling strange, like I knew that something even more foreign would happen, soon, to put me on the moon's dark side for a long time to come.

The bus always came early for Charlene, to take her to the high school, and that left me plenty of time in the bathroom. On the bus to Tallulah Junior High, two boys had been pinching my rear every time I'd get off, and when Mama complained to the principal, he laughed. "Just boys bein' boys, that's all," he told her. "It's nothing serious."

"I'd like to pinch his fat butt with a pair of pliers," she stormed to Daddy, outraged. "Or someplace else."

"Now, don't get carried away." Daddy flinched.

Mama ignored him, into her own fantasy. "'Just girls bein' girls, that's all,'" she imitated the principal's voice, her fingers working a set of imaginary pliers. "Honest to goodness, I feel like taking Jubilee out of that school." She stopped when she saw me standing in the door. But when she realized that the only other option was the Catholic parochial school, with its nuns and rulers and regulations, she decided she'd personally drive me to Tallulah's front doors every morning. "No hooligan's going to touch either one of my daughters," she told me. I was embarrassed, but I loved her for it.

That morning, I was putting on Charlene's neon green eyeshadow when Daddy came knocking at the door.

"Jubilee, hurry up. Your mama's warming up the truck, and you haven't even had breakfast yet. You're going to make her late to her lesson." The choke had started sticking. It was an old truck, brand-new back in 1948, when grandpa had bought it to haul hay on the farm. Now, Mama kept it in great shape, and its red hood gleamed in the sun. From underneath the hood came a high-pitched whine that sounded like a desperate animal, the motor hysterical in the driveway while Mama tipped the toe of her high heel against the gas pedal. But she knew how to handle it, and after frantic complaining, the motor would suddenly yield and make a sound like *awright awright awright*. Mama had glued a little plastic hula girl to the dashboard, and that's when she would come to life, shaking ever so slightly with the vibrations beneath the hood.

Mama had been letting the engine run in the morning before she drove me to school. She always dropped me off at Tallulah Junior High before she went to give singing lessons in people's homes, to old ladies who wanted to perform better solos in the church choir, and to girls who took voice lessons along with their tap, baton, and ballet, so they could compete for Miss Mississippi someday.

"Miss Mississippi!" Mama had sneered, after Mississippi had two Miss Americas, one right after the other. For years, everybody made a big fuss about it; it was the only good thing about the state in the national news. No one could believe the fortune that had smiled on Mississippi when Mary Ann Mobley crowned Linda Lee Mead in 1960. Fireworks spluttered and exploded in parks all over the state, and every year, flyers plastered telephone poles, announcing new pageants of all kinds. "Little Miss Biloxi" was for toddlers younger than three. All the girls started using their middle names. Carol Johnson was Carol Fay Johnson and Kathy Holliday became Kathy Sue Holliday, just like all the Southern competitors in the pageant every year. Girls signed up for every kind of lesson under the sun, not to mention charm school at the Y.

But Mama wasn't impressed. "You might as well use a cookie cutter on those girls."

Daddy tried to agree, chiming in about how it wasn't that the girls were outstanding in Mississippi. The male judges, he said, just knew how to pick them. That made Mama furious.

"Yeah, you men are the ones who invented the cookie cutter! *Playboy Magazine!*" Then, with Daddy bewildered, she raced off in her truck, with the license plates that said "Mississippi: Home of Two Miss Americas!" For years, prisoners at Parchman State Penitentiary up in the Delta stamped them out for ten cents an hour.

But the two Miss Americas had given Mama a lot of new business in her singing lessons. Statues of Mary Ann Mobley and Linda Lee Mead went up in the rotunda at the State Capital in Jackson, alongside Senator Theodore Bilbo, who wanted to send black people to Africa. Every mother thought her daughter had a chance of winning the national tiara and being put on permanent display in the Capital.

On the days when Mama didn't have lessons to give, she'd work on one of the solid oak bookcases she made to sell in the Sunday want ads. It gave the family some extra cash, so that Mama could stop sewing and buy our clothes instead. She was a lousy seamstress, and I dreaded wearing dresses with crooked seams and loops of loose thread. Charlene and I would cover our ears against the awful click-clacking and cursing whenever she sat at the sewing machine, but it was fun to watch her make bookcases. In the garage, I'd watch her sand the wood and rub lemon oil into it, using strokes so sensual she might've been massaging the wood. Then she'd inspect it as carefully as she would her fingernails after a manicure, turning it and buffing it with a chamois cloth. It was the bookcases that started the whole mess.

When school was starting in the fall, the television weather forecaster, a handsome man named Levi Litvak, had called the house about her bookcase ads. I answered the phone that evening. "This is Levi Litvak," he said, in that deep voice I heard every night on TV. He sounded foreign, no trace of a Southern accent. "From WLOX," he added, as if I didn't already know. "I'm calling about a bookcase."

My heart started thumping. No one else was home, so I made the appointment for him to come. Levi Litvak! People all over town talked about him, not so much for his weather forecasts, though he'd made an instant name for himself by predicting the first white Christmas for Biloxi, right after he'd been hired. It drizzled instead, and everybody made jokes about him, even my Sunday school teacher.

At first I thought it was all in good fun, but it wasn't long before the name "Levi Litvak" turned people ugly. They said he was a Communist sympathizer or an anti-Christian Jew, part of a Soviet plot to take over the South by mingling the races. The Klan put out a special death list just for whites, with Levi Litvak third, right under a Catholic priest in Mobile and some college kid who'd dated a black woman in Pensacola. Mama adored watching him predict the weather. A brave man, she said.

Before Levi Litvak came over, Charlene and I teased our hair into a style called a "bird's nest" and bobby-pinned little velvet bows in front where the middle of the nest was supposed to be. We stared at him when he came, from the cuff in his narrow creased pants to the wave in his pompadour.

Levi Litvak bought one of the biggest bookcases Mama had, then stayed to watch the football game with her, sitting in one of the dining chairs that Mama used to round out the living room furniture. His back was straight, the way he sat on TV. In the kitchen, Daddy was canning tomatoes from the garden, clinking cans and cursing the steam.

He winked at me when I asked for his autograph, even though Charlene glared, like I was being too forward. That was what she said later, but I tried not to care.

"Your momma's tee-rific," he grinned at me. "A beautiful lady who can make bookcases and knows the football plays!" Then he handed me his signature, with a little swirly line beneath the letters "tv" in his last name."It's an unusual name, Litvak. What kind is it?" Mama asked. His face colored. He crossed one ankle over the other knee and twitched his foot. Penny loafers with yellow socks. "My dad's from Lithuania," he told her, with a tight smile that seemed apologetic.

"Lithuania. It sounds like a place from a fairy tale," Mama whispered, and Levi's mouth relaxed, showing a row of even white teeth. "I'll write a song about that place."

"You're the singer!" Recognition flashed in his eyes and he snapped his slender fingers. "I've heard about you. Bernice. . ."

"Tattershall." She glanced down at her fingernails and looked back up at him under her lowered lashes. "At least, that's who I was before I got married." The look on her face said it all. "I'll sing you a song sometime, Mr. Litvak."

15

"Call me Levi," he said, smiling with those television teeth.

Then one of the Redskins made a touchdown, and they went back to watching the game. But something had eased between them. Levi Litvak's foot had stopped twitching so much.

During half-time, Mama excused herself. When she came back, her lipstick was brighter and I could tell she'd given herself a new squirt of her Ambush perfume. She sat on the sofa and smoothed her hand over the cushion seam that had just begun to split. You could see the foam rubber inside, and she pushed it back with her finger.

"When's that sometime?" Levi asked after the game ended. "I'd like to hear you sing."

While Mama sang, Levi played the piano, his fingers rippling out chords that seemed to dance with Mama's voice. They were watching each other, even when Daddy came in and applauded after they finished. Mama introduced Levi to Daddy, and though their hands gripped and both of them smiled, their eyes watched each other carefully. Daddy's blue eyes glinted a little, like he was trying to see past the sheepish look in the brown of Levi Litvak's eyes.

But Mama didn't seem to see. She turned to Levi Litvak, her face glowing. "You're some pianist. Beautiful piano hands. You sound sweet as a sugar muffin."

"You're the one who's sweet," said Daddy, and kissed her, right in front of Levi Litvak.

Months later, I thought it was all my fault. If only I hadn't answered the phone when Levi Litvak called about Mama's bookcase.

16

Chapter Two

On that April morning when Mama died, she had to give a singing lesson at nine at Loretta Holliday's house. She was the soprano at Saint Sebastian's, the Catholic Church.

"How late is it, Daddy?" I put the neon green away and tipped back my head to stroke my mascara on. It was a way I had of stalling for time, because Daddy never wore a watch. He didn't believe in them. He and Mama both grew up on farms, and he wanted to be able to look at the sun and know the time. Not that he could; it was just his idea of himself, because his father had been able to.

I could hear his footsteps down the hall and then back. "Eight o'clock already," he answered.

His footsteps rapped down the hall. He'd just had taps put on his shoes, and they made a ringing noise on the hardwood floor. Funny, how you remember things like that, every sound and motion on a morning when your life changes. Daddy was wearing elevator lifts in his heels, he always did, even in his house slippers. They brought him up almost to Mama's height, and it made him feel powerful. Even if he'd been six feet tall, Mama would still have dominated. But elevator shoes were the only way he'd have even an appearance of power over a woman like Mama. She always had her own way. At least until that morning in April.

Daddy was coming down the hall again, but this time there was a different, urgent sound, his footsteps coming faster and harder, like a capgun popping.

The door to the bathroom flew open. Daddy hung there, holding on to the doorknob, his face looking like a rubber mask that had melted.

"Daddy?" I froze, lipstick at my mouth. "What is it?"

"Bernice. Bernice is in the pick-up." Both his hands were clasped on the doorknob, one on top of the other, and he pushed himself away as if it took all his strength to move. "Call the hospital, Jubilee. Now! It's your Mama." And he ran back down the hall.

I don't remember following him, I just remember the garage, then the driveway and the truck. And the smell. It was blood and perfume, a strange mix of the heavy musky scent of Ambush, and the rich, foreign smell of blood. Mama always carried a little bottle of perfume in her purse, and someone had sprinkled the whole contents over her clothes and hair.

To this day, I can't stand certain musky perfumes. The smell of the truck will come back to me, even years later, without any reason. And then I think of Mama, of what I saw in the front seat.

She could barely lift her head off the steering wheel, but she looked at Daddy with eyes that were begging him, for help or forgiveness, I don't know, but she couldn't talk. "Don't try, honey," Daddy told her. "Don't say a word."

Then she let her head drop. One of her arms was hanging out of the open truck door. He jumped on the running board and tugged on her shoulder, calling her name. It was a horrible cry. Ber-ne-ece. He said her name like it was three words, drawing the "e" out till it sounded like a freight train's wail. Mama didn't answer. Her shoulders were slumped over the wheel of the truck, her head drooped down so low then I could barely see her face. Daddy shook her so hard she started sliding away from the steering wheel.

18

I can still see every movement: the shoulders collapsing even more, the head folding away like a puppet. She wasn't my mother any more. I know I couldn't have touched her. Daddy grabbed her, but she slid away from him, down until she lay jagged on the seat, her arms in one direction, her legs buckling on the floor. Daddy's fingers trembled as he searched for a pulse, pressing her neck, her wrist, and then he put his ear against her bloody chest.

That's when I saw the knife in her chest, driven in so that only the handle protruded from the great pool of red that her white blouse had become. By then her eyes had closed, and a tiny moan was coming from her mouth. I thought of a kitten when its eyes are still shut, that distant, weak sound it makes when it's looking for its mother to nurse.

And then Daddy was practically on top of her, putting his mouth to hers, breathing into her, the soles of his elevator shoes sticking out of the open truck door. It must've been five seconds, but it seemed like an hour. Every detail is there, even the number on the bottom of one of Daddy's shoes, "fifty-seven" inked in like a tattoo by the shoe repairman when he'd put new taps on the heels. The hula girl's green skirt shook to the rhythm of Daddy shaking Mama's shoulders.

"She's the patron saint of red Chevys," Mama always told Charlene and me proudly, but that morning the expressionless rubber face looked like a monster, nodding like an idiot.

I ran back into the kitchen and grabbed the telephone receiver from the wall. All I could think of was to dial zero for the operator.

"My Mama's had an accident," I whispered into the phone. "We need a doctor. Quick."

"The address?" she asked. Her voice was calm, controlled.

19

I remembered it. 1730 Mossy Point Road.

I'm going to be late for school, I thought, still holding on to the phone. And then another thought came colliding with that one. Mama in the truck dissolved everything. School didn't matter. Adulthood and authority didn't matter. Everything had collapsed into quicksand. And I was drowning in it.

I stood there in the kitchen, leaning against the phone, my arms folded across my stomach like I was going to throw up. I would be late to school. Mama was going to die. Maybe she was dead already. Daddy's life would never be the same. Neither would mine and Charlene's.

The kitchen door slammed shut and Mrs. Guest, our next door neighbor, was holding Daddy up, guiding him to the kitchen table. She raised her chin up at me.

"Come help me, hon. Your Daddy's gone and fainted at my door. Looks like he scraped his face." She eased Daddy into a chair and knelt beside him, rubbing her hands up and down the inside of his arms. "Get me a cold wash rag, hon." I dashed to the bathroom and heard the wail of a siren as I held a cloth beneath the faucet. The wail grew until the ambulance was flashing in the driveway. I ran outside, twisting the dripping washcloth. Two men jumped out of the ambulance, their feet crunching the gravel.

"Where's the accident?" one of them asked me. Mrs. Guest wasn't far behind.She was always eager to help people, even when they didn't need it. "Butting in," Mama called it, but she was quick to add that Mrs. Guest was a good woman, even though her husband had left her for a waitress in Gulfport.

"Oh, we didn't need an ambulance," said Mrs. Guest, looking at me. "Did you call for this, honey? Your Daddy just fainted, that's all." One of the men rolled his eyes, and they started to climb back inside the ambulance.

"No," I said, half thinking if I didn't say it, it wouldn't be there, that body in the truck that was Mama. I pointed ahead toward the pick-up, gleaming at the dark cavernous opening of the garage. "My mother." My voice was sticking in my throat, and I had to push the words out.

The men went forward in their white suits. Later, the moon explorers would remind me of those two men, of the way they moved toward that truck with their stretcher, all bulky and awkward. It was their trepidation, like they didn't know exactly what they would find. Maybe it was the stench. You could smell the blood and perfume even down by the ambulance. Something as strange as moon dust in the air.

The kitchen door opened then and Daddy came wobbling out, holding on to the stair rail. Mrs. Guest ran up to him. "Harry, what's happened to Bernice?"

Daddy braced himself against the rail. "Bernice had an accident in the truck." They were words he would say many times that day, as if to convince himself no one had meant to drive a knife into Mama's chest. Then he climbed into the ambulance and crouched while the medics lifted the stretcher into the back. A smear of red was drying across the side of his face, from where he'd tried to hear her heart.

Above the white sheet, Mama's head turned from side to side, her eyes closed. I ran to her and touched her forehead before one of the medics pulled me back. Her face felt cool and smooth and for a moment her eyes flickered, as if in recognition of my fingers against her skin. A red stain was beginning to swell into the whiteness of the cloth.

"Oh my lands." Mrs. Guest clapped her hands to her face when she saw Mama. I backed into the gardenia bush

21

so that the branches surrounded me like a hug. In the center of the leaves nestled green gardenia buds, hidden there as if they held a mystery. Next month, I thought. Then the flowers would unfold, perfuming the yard, taking away that smell. Mama could pick a fresh one every morning to wear in her hair, the way she did when they bloomed each year.

"Get dressed, hon. Hurry now. I'll take you to the hospital." Mrs. Guest was talking to me.

I looked down. I still had on my pink robe and slippers, muddied from the gardenia bed.

The ambulance pulled off, spurting gravel, and the siren wailed again, like Daddy's voice screaming "Berneeece."

"C'mon, sugar." It was Mrs. Guest. She put her arm around me; her powdery perfume floated with her, light as her touch. I didn't need her to guide me inside. I wasn't going to faint. Instead, everything was clear and stark. Through a crack in the sidewalk, a cluster of dandelions had broken through. Those things'll grow anywhere, Mama complained every spring. I stepped over them, careful not to brush them with my muddy slipper, and went into the house.

At the hospital, Daddy collapsed again and they put him on a cot. I called the high school to get Charlene, but the secretary wouldn't believe me until I handed the receiver to Mrs. Guest. The assistant principal told her he'd drive Charlene to the hospital, personally.

Mrs. Guest and I waited in a nook at the end of the hall where they'd put some chairs and magazines like *Field and Stream* and *National Geographic*. I remember counting: the linoleum tiles in the floor, the flowers in the wallpaper. Mrs. Guest sat with her feet planted slightly apart so the dark brown tops of her stockings were visible.

Lying in the seat of the chair beside me was *Highlights*, a kid's magazine. I flipped through it, stopping on a page with a puzzle: "What Is Wrong With This Picture?" Beneath was a drawing of a school playground. A janitor held his mop upside down, a little girl rode her bicycle backwards, and a boy slid up a steep sliding board, defying gravity, his hair waving behind him. In the sky above were both a crescent moon and the sun, but a group of children held umbrellas to fend off an invisible rain.

But the weirdest thing was what some kid had done to the picture. With an orange crayon, the kid had drawn circles around the normal stuff: the teacher reading a book to children gathered at her feet, the flowers blooming in a garden, the baby bird perched in a nest, its beak opened wide to its hovering mother.

Strange kid, I thought. She would've belonged in the picture, herself. Or she belonged in the chair where I sat, feeling like all the rules in my own life had been reversed. A doctor appeared at the door, and stared at Mrs. Guest. "You're the relatives of Bernice Starling?"

She nodded at me. "This here's her daughter." The newspaper slithered to the floor as she got up, pushing her hands hard on the chair arms. "The husband, Harry, he's in a room down there." *The husband*, I thought, like Daddy was a character in a play. Her finger shook when she pointed down the hall.

Don't you dare nod at me like that, I wanted to shout at Mrs. Guest. I'm not part of this.

Charlene was coming down the hall, her yellow dress standing out like a Yield sign at an intersection. Her face was pale white, her eyes round. Beside her, the assistant principal wore a stern look, like he'd caught Charlene in the girls' restroom lighting up one of the Marlboros she smoked and he was suspending her. Yeah, I thought, we must have done something wrong, both of us. At that moment at Biloxi Baptist Hospital, Charlene and I were both suspended, but from everything, even gravity, it seemed. My head felt detached from my neck, a balloon on a string.

The doctor sucked on the temple of his glasses. Richard Powell, M.D., it said on the tag clipped to his pocket. "Come back and see your mother. She's asking for you."

Asking for us! Maybe she wouldn't die. We followed him down the corridor through double doors that said Intensive Care. Daddy stood before one of the curtained stalls. I was glad he was back on his feet. He whispered, "She asked for you girls," and pulled back the curtain for us.

But when we looked at her, lying on a high narrow bed, I couldn't imagine how any words had escaped her body. Tubes ran everywhere, into her nose, her elbow, like a maze in *Highlights. Can you find your way out?*

Charlene took her hand, lying limp outside the sheet. "Mama, Mama," she cried.

"Shh," said Daddy.

Mama turned her eyes toward us, as if only then she realized we were there. Her lips puckered a bit, and for a second I was afraid she would cry, but she lifted her fingers and I knew she was trying to blow us a kiss. Charlene started to reach over to kiss her, but Daddy took her arm. "There's too much equipment there, honey," he whispered. "You could knock something loose."

We blew kisses. "You'll be fine," Charlene squeezed Mama's hand. "We'll be waiting here till you're well."

But in the air there moved something almost imperceptible, so powerful and mysterious and peaceful I could feel the air swelling to accommodate it, like a tide rolling in from a foreign sea. Mama lifted her hand to point at something beyond Daddy's head, and we all turned to look. There were only the green walls, but her eyes looked focused on something far away, as if the walls had faded into translucent curtains, the kind magicians might use to disguise a levitating body.

"What have you done for the human race, Harry?" Her lips barely moved to release the whisper.

"It's all right, sweetheart," said Daddy. "You can talk when you're stronger."

"What's that around your head?" she asked him. Charlene and I looked, but there was nothing. Daddy put a hand to his head. "White," said Mama.

"Aw, I haven't gone gray yet," said Daddy. He tried to laugh. It was a joke between them, but the words lay on the air, flat. A smile flickered over her face, and she closed her eyes, but it seemed as if she were still looking at us, only from somewhere else, beyond the bustling nurses and the dripping drugs and loudspeaker announcements. I was with her, then, behind her eyes for a moment, enough to feel the hurrying nurses and doctors' directions as inconsequential intrusions into a quieter place, into the peace around Mama. She was going to die, I knew then, but she would be all right. Her breath came in shallow inhalations, a fragile thread connecting her to her own body. A nurse hurried over and studied one of the instruments hooked up to her

"What is it?" asked Daddy, taking his eyes off Mama for the first time.

"Blood pressure's falling," she said, and jerked her head toward the doors, signaling Charlene and me to leave.

At the door, I looked back. That peaceful tide was still rolling in, a blue, enveloping wave impervious to gravity, to any of the rules we impose on the world. It was bigger than anything in the room, as if it could swallow us all, but I knew only Mama was inside its embrace.

"She's dying," I told Charlene, checking her face for any sign that she knew, too.

But she was watching her feet, placing her new Easter sandals carefully inside the green squares of linoleum. "She'll be fine," she said, but her voice was dull. "We should buy her a card in the gift shop." We walked in silence back to our chairs and waited while Mrs. Guest made nervous talk, asking about our school, about Mama's singing. But I could hardly listen, still feeling that strange movement, as if Mama and I were both in a bubble rising slowly above language and noise.

After a long while, Dr. Powell came in, and turned to Charlene and me with a pad of paper and pen. The bubble broke when he entered, and my heart beat faster. He sat beside us, asking our names. Charlene kept staring at the floor, as if she couldn't hear, so I told him. "Do you have any relatives in town, Jubilee?" The bags under his eyes sagged like they carried the weight of the world. In that second, I felt sorry for him. "We'll call them for you," he added.

"Where's my daddy?" I asked.

"Resting. He'll be all right in a little while."

Daddy had probably passed out again, so I took over. "This is my sister, Charlene," I said, and her head jerked up, as if she'd been awakened from a prayer. "And we have Aunt Sylvia. Sylvia Tattershall. She's an artist in New York City. She just had a gallery show."

"Bernice and Sylvia," Doctor Powell said softly. "Of course. The Tattershall girls." A smile flitted across his face for a second, taking about fifteen years with it, and then his mouth fixed in a grim line. He rubbed my shoulder. "I'm sorry," he said, his eyes down.

"Sorry for what?" Charlene's voice was angry.

I didn't want to hear the answer. "There's Uncle Clayton," I went on, since he seemed to know the family. "Daddy's a salesman at his furniture store."

"The Starling Furniture Company?" He started to scribble on the note pad.

No, I wanted to say. Uncle Clayton's the one who burns the steaks at the Fourth of July cook-out, the one who gives my mother a hug when she gets mad at us kids, and teases her out of it. Get it right, if you're writing it down, I wanted to say. But those were dangerous facts to think about, facts that pushed me back into the fire or the flood that raged that morning. So I started thinking about something else, about those sofabeds from Taiwan that Uncle Clayton had all the complaints about last winter.

"Did you ever buy a sofabed from my dad?" I asked.

He shook his head, and the sadness in his eyes deepened, as if he were sorry about that, too.

"That's good," I said. "The hinges stuck."

"They did not!" said Charlene.

He smiled again, a crescent on his lips, and he beckoned to Mrs. Guest. "Could I speak with you privately?"

She planted her feet and heaved herself up. She wasn't a heavy woman. It just seemed as if she'd picked up some of that weight in Doctor Powell's eyes. The two of them disappeared down the hall, but I could still hear the low drone of the doctor's voice. The word "expired" rose above the others, and I remembered how Mama said her driver's license needed to be renewed. Then it was Mrs. Guest: "Oh law!" she cried. "Oh my Jesus!"

When she came in a minute later, Mrs. Guest's smile wavered at me and her eyes were watery. She smoothed my hair, then Charlene's, pulling us both over beneath her

27

arms. "He's calling your uncle, sweetie-pies."

"Mama's dead." I pulled back away from her and looked up into her face. It was bland and kind, like a cow's.

"She is not!" Charlene corrected me, but her voice was scared, not bossy.

"What do we know, sugars?" said Mrs. Guest. "What do we ever know down here, anyway?" It made me think angels were watching while we floundered along, unaware of how blind we were. Maybe Mama was watching us now, I thought. The peaceful wave had rolled out, taking Mama with it.

Mrs. Guest kept stroking our heads, wordlessly.

Chapter Three

When we got back from the hospital, parked cars lined the street in front of the house, like a party was going on. My best friend, Deanna, sat on the front steps eating a drumstick of fried chicken. She laid down her *Seventeen* magazine and put her arm around my shoulders while we walked inside. "Your Aunt Martha's crazy as a bat," she whispered.

Uncle Clayton's wife, Aunt Martha, had set up a buffet of cream pies and fried chicken and casseroles on the dining table. It made me sick to look. "Help yourselves, girls," said Aunt Martha, almost gaily, like she was a hostess at some horrible party where the guests wore pale masks and kept repeating the same words, "Isn't it terrible" and "What a tragedy." Deanna took another drumstick.

It was like Aunt Martha thought there was nothing else to do with all the food people kept bringing but throw a party. She stood behind the table, set with Mama's china. Aunt Martha had had her hair done; I could tell by the smell of the hairspray and the curls at her forehead. Despite the gray and black print dress she wore, her eyes looked happy behind her cateye glasses. Mama used to say Aunt Martha loved a party because she hadn't gone to enough of them when she was younger – a real wallflower, Mama said. But maybe that was just when Mama was around, stealing the attention.

"Have some of this green bean casserole," she told Loretta Holliday, ready to dish it out. But Mrs. Holliday set her plate on the table. There was a little ring of red lipstick on her drumstick where she'd barely nibbled.

"Thank you," she said, "but I've got to pay my dues at Levi Litvak's house." She twisted the bangle bracelet on her thin wrist. "I worked for him, you know, down at WLOX." People said Loretta Holliday thought she was a celebrity because she was Levi Litvak's secretary at the TV station.

Aunt Martha's eyebrows shot up, making thin crescent moons over the tops of her glasses. "Why, who on earth would be there?"

"I hear a rabbi from Mobile's come. I brought a cobbler and my ham and cheese casserole. He might have family from up North."

"If he's got family, they're a bunch of communists," said Aunt Martha, but Mrs. Holliday didn't seem to hear. She draped a white sweater over her arm, the kind women always carried for the air conditioning, and headed for the door.

Aunt Martha made me as sick as the sight of that food did. I wanted Mama's sister, Aunt Sylvia, to be there, to hug us and smile like Mama. She was flying in from New York as soon as she could, I'd overheard Daddy telling Uncle Clayton. Daddy was somewhere with Uncle Clayton now, either the hospital or the police station.

The doorbell rang, and before I could get it, Aunt Martha swung open the door. It was Pearl, a black woman who did ironing for Mama. She was wearing a blue dress that I knew she'd made by hand, every stitch. That was before she got a sewing machine, but she was still prouder of the blue dress than any other, every stitch was so even. "By hand!" Mama had said, standing back in awe when Pearl first wore it. "She put every stitch in that dress by hand," she told me, and then turned back to Pearl. "It's beautiful. Let's see how you did the back." And Pearl had turned, showing the line of beaded buttons down the back.

Now Pearl stood on the porch awkwardly, holding a dish wrapped in foil. "Here's a little something," she said, looking just to the side of Aunt Martha, avoiding her eyes.

"What is it?" Deanna eyed the foil, her mouth full of chocolate cake.

"Blackberry pie," said Pearl, and her chin lifted. Mama talked about how good Pearl's pies were.

"Take it round to the back," said Aunt Martha. "There's folks in the kitchen who'll take it."

Pearl headed down the steps. "Wait!" I said, brushing past Aunt Martha. "Come on in." But Pearl kept walking toward the back door, circling Daddy's vegetable garden. I kept pace beside her. "You don't have to go to the back. Here." I tried to take the dish from her, but she held it higher, away from my reach, and smiled down at me.

"Your mama, she was a good woman," said Pearl. "I got used to coming in the front door at this house. Aren't many houses in Biloxi like this one."

I followed Pearl to the back door, where she went in

and set down the dish on a counter. Mrs. Guest took it. "Thank you, Pearl," she said. "Everybody knows what good pecan pies you make."

Pearl smiled. "Bernice liked my blackberry pies best."

Mrs. Guest looked confused and pursed her lips into an awkward smile. "We're going to miss *Mrs. Starling*, aren't we?" She carried the dish straight to the dining room.

"Come on in," I said. "Have a seat."

Pearl tucked her clutch purse more firmly under her arm. "I best not stay," she said.

"Mama would want you to." I got a dish off the kitchen table and brought it to her. "There's a lot of food."

"I'm not hungry, sugar," said Pearl. "And Walter's waiting at the bus stop." She brushed my hair from my eyes, something she'd never done before. Her fingers felt smooth. "You be careful with that Deanna girl. She's trouble."

I looked up at Pearl, startled that she knew so much. "Trouble?" I asked. Mama had already warned me about Deanna.

She nodded. "Stealing. Now I know you wouldn't do. . ."

"Never," I said.

Pearl kept smoothing my hair, petting me. It felt so good I wanted her to sit down and let me put my head in her lap, fall asleep that way. "Bernice raised herself some fine children. Some white folks here, all they know how to do is hate. You be proud of your mama. Proud of yourself, too. Hold your head high."

From the way she said those last words, I thought she'd said them a lot, to her own daughter, maybe. She had a girl about my age. I'd met her one Christmas a couple of years before, when Mama and I had driven to the dusty

31

streets where Biloxi's black people lived. Mama had made a sewing table with drawers underneath to give Pearl, and we trundled down the rutted streets, trying to keep the wood from sliding in the bed of the truck. Dusk was settling in, and in the maze of roads, we got lost looking for Pearl's address. None of the streets were marked, and finally, we pulled up beside an old man walking near a ditch. Mama leaned out the window and called to him. "Could you tell me where Pearl and Walter Robinson live?"

The man looked at his feet and shook his head. "No, ma'am."

"Where is Ring Road?" she asked.

He shrugged. "Don't know."

"Thanks anyway," said Mama.

We bumped on down the road. "We're in the wrong place," I said.

"He doesn't want to say where Pearl lives," said Mama. "They don't know us. All they see is a white person out looking for somebody, and they think the worst. Just imagine what they go through, trying to protect themselves." She stopped in front of a cottage where a woman sat on the front porch. "Excuse me, ma'am," she called. "Do you know where Pearl Robinson lives?" The woman waved her hand in front of her face, as if she could erase us that way.

"I'm trying to deliver a Christmas present to Pearl," Mama said. She pulled a gift from her purse and held it up.

"What's that?" I asked. The sewing table was in the truck bed, under a quilt. Mama smiled at the woman.

The woman's face eased and she pointed down the road where a small, unpainted house stood, its front yard marked with broom strokes in the dirt. "Right there," she said.

"Thank you." Mama backed the truck up to the yard. Pearl had come out, waving. Her daughter was behind her, wearing a blue checked dress I recognized as one Charlene had once worn. I hadn't wanted it.

"Say hello to Mary," Mama nudged me. I got out and said hi, and Mary's lips moved. She was trying to speak, but the resentment in her eyes wouldn't let sound escape.

Inside, we settled around the table in Pearl's living room, and afterward, while Pearl gave Mama a glass of water to drink, Mary looked at me and tipped her head toward a door. I followed her inside a bedroom, and Mary pointed to a framed photograph on what must have been her dresser, a picture with two men in it. The older one was smiling, but the younger man frowned at the camera, a stiff, old-fashioned collar forcing his chin up. "My granddaddy," said Mary. She looked at me with an expectant gaze, but I didn't know what to say. She wasn't shy in her own house, like she was when she came with Pearl to ours. "He died," she added.

"I'm sorry," I said, thinking of my own grandfathers, still growing soybeans and raising a few cows to sell on their farms. The face in the photograph squinted out at me. "He looks too young to die."

"That's right," she said. Something in her eyes wanted me to ask.

"How?"

"White men." She watched me. "KKK."

"What did he do?" And then I wanted to bite back the words, steal them from the air. "He didn't do anything, did he?" I said.

She stared at me. Her light brown eyes sparkled with what could have been either amusement or hatred. Or both. "You don't know nothing," she said.

But there was Pearl, standing in the doorway with the

little gift box Mama had had in her purse. It was perfume that smelled of flowers. She took Mary by the arm. "You say you're sorry. You talk polite to your company, you hear?"

"No, I'm sorry," I said, but what good would sorrow do? "I'm the one who's sorry."

Mary looked at her shoes, white Keds with ink drawings and autographs on the canvas. "Sorry."

Mama stood beside Pearl, who was looking from Mary to me, and Mary reached out and put the photograph face down on her dresser.

"What're you doing?" Pearl raised it up. "Be proud."

"It's private," Mary whispered, but we could hear.

"That's her grandpa," Pearl told Mama. "Walter's dad."

"He's a goodlooking man," said Mama, but Pearl threw her a sharp look.

"Dead now, that's where his good looks got him," she said, and Mama had the same expression on her face that I could feel on my own.

"I'm sorry," she said.

On the way home, Mama looked tired and she even ground the gears a couple of times. Before, all she talked about was what a fine piece of furniture she'd made for Pearl, a solid table for her sewing machine. But she couldn't hide the sadness in her eyes as she drove home.

"What's wrong?" I asked. "Pearl liked the presents."

"They don't trust me." She pointed to the white skin on her arm. "It's this. And it's no wonder, the things that've been done to them."

"You know that picture Mary turned over? That was her grandfather. . ."

"I know," said Mama.

"The Klan killed him. That's what Mary said."

34

The truck swerved for a second, then found the asphalt again. "Oh Pearl," Mama whispered. "It's a wonder she has anything to do with us."

"She knows you're her friend." From the side of my eye, I could see Mama's pursed lips, and how tightly her hands held the steering wheel.

"Think about it. Must have been a lot of white folks driving into their streets, looking for somebody to hurt, for them to be so suspicious of you and me. Must've been a lot of people like the men who killed Walter's daddy."

After that night, something changed in Mama. She'd leave a store when she heard people talking "hateful words." We've got to live in the same world, she said. Once, she left the beauty shop with her hair still in rollers because of the "bad talk." She lost a few vocal students after that. The hairdresser, Onita Tate, said Mama would be teaching "We Shall Overcome" in her voice lessons soon, and everybody laughed. Her daughter, Wanda Tate, started going all the way to Mobile to take her voice lessons.

"What's going on?" Deanna came into the kitchen where I was watching Pearl's figure recede down the steps. A few crumbs of pie crust clung to the corners of her mouth.

"Nothing," I said. "C'mon."

Deanna and I dodged Aunt Martha and went to sit on one of the twin beds in the room I shared with Charlene. She scrambled in her purse and pulled out some Tabu perfume. "Look," she whispered. "I brought you a present. Got it from the drugstore." Now that Easter had come and gone, Deanna could go back to shoplifting from the Rexall's Drugstore at Big Circle Shopping Center. She'd given it up for Lent.

"How do you get the nerve? Aren't you scared you'll get caught?" I asked.

"Grady Pickens was watching out. All he got was a bunch of *Mad Magazines*." She rolled her eyes at the idiocy.

I took the Tabu, but Deanna seemed like a friend who belonged to someone else, a girl I'd been years ago.

The phone rang, but I let it. Aunt Martha would get it, and she seemed to know what to say to people. "We're just in shock," I'd heard her say. Or, "Only the Lord knows what to make of it." And, "It's the girls. That's my main worry."

This time, though, she came to my bedroom. "Pick up, Jubilee. Your Aunt Sylvia's in New Orleans at the airport. She wants to talk to you."

Aunt Sylvia's voice came, "Honey, I'm coming as fast as I can get a taxi. I love you and Charlene to pieces."

It wasn't long before she was there, standing in the living room in her black net stockings and high heels, stooping to hug Charlene and me so tight I couldn't breathe for a second. Oh, it was good, those thin arms around me, her small breasts pressed against my chest, not like Mama's big soft ones, but as close as anybody could get.

"Where's Harry?" Aunt Sylvia asked, putting her hands on both our heads as she rose.

Aunt Martha dried her hands on the apron she was wearing. "Have some ham, Sylvia? Potato salad? Look what Bernice's friends have brought." She held out a tupperware container. "You must be hungry, coming all the way from New York City in one day."

"No." Aunt Sylvia shook her head like she couldn't quite believe the question. "Where's Harry?"

She shrugged. "He's missed all his houseguests, just about. Went off with Clayton somewhere."

Aunt Sylvia dragged her suitcase back to the hall, and then pulled Charlene and me into Mama and Daddy's room, where we sat on either side of her on the double bed. She put an arm around both of us.

"We'll get through this together, girls," she said. Then she saw a bottle of red nail polish, the color Mama always wore, on the night stand, a bag of Q-tips open beside it. Mama had been polishing her nails just the night before.

She picked up the bottle and cradled it in the palm of her hand with a stunned look on her face. She screwed the lid as tight as she could, as if she could hold something inside herself that way. "We'll manage. . ."

Her voice broke and she hurried to the bathroom. The door closed behind her with a soft click. Charlene moved close to me, and put her arm in the same warm spot where Aunt Sylvia's had been. We sat together, unsure of what we could do but listen to Aunt Sylvia cry.

For a couple of days, everybody talked about what a terrible coincidence it was that two tragedies like Mama's murder and Levi Litvak's accident could happen in so short a time. An editorial in the *Biloxi Sun-Herald* said the stars must have been crossed over the town.

After the murder, we stayed with our grandparents. We couldn't even drive into our garage at home. The police had roped it off with yellow tape, and when we went back to pack our suitcases, a string of cars was cruising down Mossy Point Road, with people staring and pointing at the driveway where the truck had been. I thought I could still smell Mama's perfume, as though a pocket of it floated near the garage.

"Smell that?" I whispered to Charlene, while we tried to ignore the people staring.

But Charlene picked a gardenia and took a deep smell.

"They're everywhere," she said, and walked so quickly to the door I couldn't explain that other mysterious smell.

Inside, while Aunt Sylvia helped us dump pajamas and dresses, toothbrushes and make-up, into Daddy's old green Army duffel, we didn't talk. We were too busy trying not to hear the sound of Mama's bare feet coming down the hall, the smell of her perfume, or the feel of her hand pushing our bangs from our faces. Daddy was talking, so fast and soft we paid no attention because we knew that he, too, was trying not to hear Mama's voice. Every time he came into our room, his face looked pale and empty; only his mouth moved with soft staccato sounds. Then he'd leave again, filling his own suitcase. At least Aunt Martha wasn't there anymore.

We got Daddy's car loaded, the blue Chevrolet station wagon, and edged through the snaking traffic to escape to our grandparents' house. Mama's parents lived on a farm about ten miles north, and that's where Daddy headed.

It wasn't right, being on the farm without Mama. I couldn't remember ever going there with just Daddy. Daddy dragged the duffel bag into the room that used to be Mama's when she was growing up, and Charlene and I tried to get ready for bed. Grandma had turned on an old fan that made the room only a little less stuffy. Charlene backed up against it and lifted her nightgown, hogging all the breeze.

A new stain had appeared on the blue wallpaper, the shape of a long drop of water that seemed to shimmer in the flickering gas light, like a permanent shadow in the room where we made shadow puppets on the walls for fun when we were little. I couldn't imagine ever having fun in that room again. The things that had been Mama's, a purple perfume decanter and a miniature Swiss chalet, seemed to have belonged to someone else.

I picked up a silver thimble with an Eiffel tower on it. Mama had bought it in New Orleans, to remind herself she'd get to Paris someday. "This'll be Pearl's," I said.

"What makes you think Pearl wants it?" Charlene asked.

"She sews," I said. "And she probably wants to see Paris someday, like Mama." I slipped the thimble in my purse. Anything Charlene was going to say was stopped by a knock on the door.

"Girls?" It was Grandma Tattershall, wearing a plaid robe Mama had given her last Christmas. She looked tiny, sitting on the double bed Charlene and I shared at her house. In the shadows, we could just make out her features, her eyes gleaming, maybe from tears. "We need to pray, girls." She took our hands. "Lord, help us to forgive the sinner who took the life of the mother of these children. Help us to understand Thy mysterious ways. . ."

I stopped listening and tried to pull my hand away, but Grandma had a stronger grip than I'd thought. Forgive Mama's killer! I wanted to find him and push a knife into his chest. There wasn't room in my heart for forgiveness. But Charlene kept right on holding Grandma Tattershall's hand while I watched them both, their eyes shut tight.

Quietly, like a ghost, Aunt Sylvia appeared at the door, listening to Grandma's prayer, her head bowed more in sadness, I thought, than reverence. When Grandma said amen, Aunt Sylvia said, "Mama, don't you think it's too soon for anyone to think about forgiving?"

Grandma kissed our foreheads, and went straight to Aunt Sylvia on her way out. They stood outlined in the doorway, Aunt Sylvia's tall, thin figure hunched over Grandma. "It's never too soon to forgive, Sylvia," she said, and tipped up Aunt Sylvia's chin with a gnarled finger. I could see their profiles, face to face, the slight humps in their noses looking almost identical, except Grandma's nose was longer. "And it's never too late to forgive, either. You're the only daughter I have now, and I want you to be a good Christian."

Aunt Sylvia pulled away to the side, as if she were guarding herself, the way I imagined her doing when she was a teenager getting scolded for listening to rock 'n roll or wearing too much make-up. "I have a lot of faith in how Jesus would want people to make this world a better place."

"Well, don't forget forgiveness while you're changing the world." Grandma put her hands on Sylvia's cheeks and looked at her, hard, in the light of the doorway. "You're a good girl, Sylvia Tattershall. You're always in my heart, no matter what you do." Grandma kissed her on the forehead, and then walked away with her hand over her eyes, like the light was too bright.

Sylvia stood in the door like a child, arms folded across her chest, as if it hurt. Grandpa's deep voice came from the living room, calling to Grandma. "Maude, Maude." I could smell the spice in his pipe tobacco. Mama had told us stories about her own grandfather, a riverboat gambler, and in my own mind this had become my own Grandpa – reckless, always ready to sail away. But that night, he sounded as if he wanted Grandma as badly as I wanted Mama. Soon, I heard the clicking of crochet hooks, Grandma weaving her way through this sadness while Grandpa let his pipe go out.

I woke in the darkness, hearing Grandma's mantel clock clang four times to strike the hour. At first I wasn't sure where I was. Then I saw Aunt Sylvia, sitting in a straight-back chair she must have pulled up beside our bed after we'd fallen asleep. "Go back to sleep, Jubilee," she whispered, and stroked my cheek the way Mama would've done. The dream I'd been having, about car headlights and duffel bags, eased back into my mind, and I slept until sparrows woke me early the next morning, twittering under the eaves outside.

"What happened, Harry?" Aunt Sylvia was whispering to Daddy. She poured him some coffee in Grandma's kitchen. "Do you have any idea who killed Bernice?" Her eyes had dark rings under them. I wondered if she'd slept at all.

Daddy's jaw was working. "Everybody loved her, except for that trouble at the beauty shop."

"What trouble?" She leaned forward, her voice hushed.

Daddy shrugged. "You know Bernice. She doesn't stand for any hateful talk, and she got riled up once when she was getting her hair done."

"Who was it?" The words were clipped and hard.

"Sylvia, you won't fix anything by confronting folks. Just a bunch of silly ladies who thought Bernice was some kind of agitator. Gossip, that's all."

"Bernice hated it." Aunt Sylvia's eyes snapped.

"They'll be yakking about me, I reckon," he said. "Chief Jones asked me a lot of questions at the station, even when I said I needed to go. Had me fingerprinted."

"They think you did it!"

"Nobody loves Bernice more than I do. Loved." His voice shook. "They impounded the truck. Maybe they'll find evidence."

"Have there been other murders here?" She sat at the table, her hands circling the warm coffee cup, as if they were cold even though it was spring.

"A stabbing at the Negro club, but they found a knife on the man who. . ."and then he saw me standing in the door. He gave me a stiff smile. "There's my sweet pea."

"If anybody thinks you killed Mama, I can prove you didn't." I felt like throwing up, but there was nothing in my stomach. "I'll tell them how you looked when you came to the bathroom door to get me. . ."

He reached out and pulled me close. "Don't you worry. Everybody knows I . . ." He couldn't finish the words.

"You think Onita Tate did it?" I could see her stiff helmet of hair and the bleached fuzz of mustache on her upper lip. When she washed out hairbrushes, her strong arms would rub the bristles together quickly, making a thick lather of suds. It was easy to see a weapon in those hands.

"Who's Onita Tate?" Aunt Sylvia's eyes darted to Daddy.

"Hairdresser." Then Daddy shook his head at me. "Onita didn't like Mama's ideas, but that's no reason to. . ."

"What does 'impound' mean? Did they arrest the truck?"

"They're looking for fingerprints and such."

"Will they ever find out who did it, Daddy?" I asked.

"The world isn't always fair," he said softly.

I thought a lunatic like Norman Bates in *Psycho* had escaped from a mental asylum and killed Mama. For the next few nights, in Mama's old bedroom, I stayed up late with Charlene, whispering until I thought I'd figured it out, even where the lunatic was hiding. Once, we heard the mantel clock strike twice and we weren't sleepy yet. I didn't even cry. I was too busy working the murder over in my mind like a puzzle, as if we'd get Mama back that way.

"The criminal always returns to the scene of the crime," I told Charlene, to get her to stop crying. It was a line I remembered from some Nancy Drew book, but this was much worse than anything Nancy Drew ever solved.

"What if Daddy did it?" she asked, one night after I thought she was asleep. "They took his fingerprints."

A cold knife went through me. "Daddy loved Mama."

"Sometimes that's why people kill."

Daddy's face, white and stunned as he stood in the bathroom door after finding Mama, came back to me. Then I remembered: there had been no blood on his hands, no streaks on the door knob. His hands had been clean until he helped Mama. "No," I said. "Wouldn't there have been blood on his hands? There wasn't any, and I was right there."

"What if he washed them first?" Charlene whispered.

"You didn't see his face. He wasn't thinking about his hands. Why would Daddy kill Mama? He loved her. We'll get the real killer, you'll see. I've got it figured out," I said, but this time Charlene didn't seem to hear.

"You've got a wild imagination," she said.

"Yours is wilder," I told her. "Daddy washing blood off his hands! That's crazy."

She made a spooky sound, "Imagina-a-a-tion." Years ago, we'd watched an old movie of *The Turn of the Screw*, and I'd been terrified of the ghosts. "It's just their imagination," Mama laughed, and pulled me into her lap. But I didn't know what imagination meant, so for a while I thought it was another word for ghosts. Charlene and I would get into our beds at night, and as soon as the lights were out, she would start. "Jubilee? Imagination. Imagina-a-tion."

At Grandma's, I pulled the covers over my head til I fell asleep, though the heat was suffocating. Grandma didn't believe in air conditioning God's world. She'd still run that little fan,though. I could hear Charlene through the

43

quilt. "Imagina-a-tion. . . " After the murder, though, it was my imagination that saved me.

But like Aunt Sylvia, I couldn't imagine forgiveness. Sometimes, I thought Mama would come home, even when Aunt Sylvia went to the house to go through Mama's clothes, picking out the dress to bury her in. She chose a blue silk sheath Mama had worn when she sang her last church solo. Aunt Sylvia picked out the casket, too, and Uncle Clayton checked the insurance, all the things Daddy couldn't do.

A few days after Mama died, Loretta Holliday found a letter in Levi Litvak's desk when she was cleaning out his things. She brought it to the news bureau at the New Orleans ABC affiliate. The letter told the whole world that Levi Litvak had wanted to marry my mother. If he couldn't have his "sugar muffin," it said, nobody could. The *Biloxi Sun-Herald* ran a picture of his typed letter the day before the funeral, with his picture above it. Something was wrong with the little "i" in muffin. It jumped up above the others, like it was trying to keep its head above the water line.

That's how I felt, too, when I saw that awful letter on the front page, like I was trying to keep from drowning. Now the whole town knew. I could still see Levi Litvak's face when he watched Mama sing in our living room only a few months before, and I wanted to pull his eyes right out of his face. Imagining ways to find the killer couldn't save me any more. The police closed the case.

Daddy didn't want to believe the love letter Levi Litvak had written to Mama, so he never did. "That Litvak," he said. "Just another nut in a squirrelly world. Couldn't be famous enough, predicting the weather. Had to make up a story and die so the town would talk about him."

Brother Beeker delivered the eulogy at the Sweet Gum Funeral Home in the country near the farm. Dr. Powell was one of the first ones at the funeral, with that same soft smile that flitted across his face when he'd said, *Of course, the Tattershall girls.* I hoped someday somebody would say that about Charlene and me, with that same smile. *Of course, Charlene and Jubilee.* Maybe I'd be a famous blues singer, like Mama wanted to be, with Charlene singing back-up, and Dr. Powell would see our picture in *Life Magazine* and say just that. *The Starling girls. Of course.* Then he'd buy our latest record, a song I'd have written for Mama.

Up in front, the oak casket was open, its lining of blue satin looking like one of Mama's pin cushions. Aunt Sylvia had refused to let the funeral home do Mama's hair, so she'd done it herself. Her red hair curled over the shoulders of the blue sheath. Two spots of rouge stood out on her face, and that was all I saw before I turned away. Somebody swooped her arm around me, saying, "Isn't she pretty? Look at your Mama, isn't she pretty?"

I pulled away and found Charlene in a seat on the front row beside Aunt Sylvia. She held my hand. Beside me, Daddy sat with one elbow on his knee, his forehead sunk into his hand, as if he were praying and couldn't be bothered. Uncle Clayton draped his arm over the pew behind Daddy, to let him know, in silence, that he was there. That's how brothers do it, I thought, looking at Charlene's hand in mine.

As people settled in, their fans wagging in the heat like accusing fingers, Onita Tate eased in the side door, wearing a green dress. She propped against the door frame, looking from side to side, surveying everybody. The funeral director tried to guide her to a seat, but she shook her head. Charlene handed me a program, and when I looked back, the door was empty. There was no green dress among the black and navy clothing filling the pews.

A familiar-looking dark man with frizzy silver hair strolled down the aisle, all the way to the front. He looked stiff in a white linen suit, but he swung a saxophone by his side. He lifted it to his lips, closed his eyes, and the moan of a tune came out that I hadn't heard since I was a little girl. Just like his face, I couldn't quite place it. Then it came to me: "Time After Time." It was a song Mama used to sing. Daddy must've told him to play it.

I turned to Charlene and whispered what the song was, and saw Aunt Sylvia's profile. She was watching the saxophonist, his body bent back from the waist like a reed blown by the wind. You could see his hipbones against the white linen, that's how thin he was.

Aunt Sylvia's ex-husband. Claude. Of course. His hair had gone from black to silver in five years. The first and last time I'd seen him, Aunt Sylvia was sitting in his lap at Grandma Tattershall's dining table. He was feeding her chocolate wedding cake with strawberry hearts on it at the reception my grandparents gave them after they'd eloped. Then Claude had pulled out his saxophone and, while Mama sang, together they had performed "Time After Time."

From the way their sounds had moved together that night, they had done that song many times, on stages at small New Orleans clubs, years before. It was a love song, about how lucky people were to have someone love them. Mama had looked from Sylvia to Claude, then to Daddy, her eyes lit with delight because she'd introduced Sylvia to Claude. It was the same teasing glitter that I remembered when she sang Charlene and me to sleep with racy songs. She had loved Daddy; that was all I wanted to know.

46

After the last note, Claude lowered the saxophone, but the music didn't stop so much as drift away. He slipped into the pew beside Sylvia and held her hand, glancing at her briefly before he lifted his chin and looked straight ahead, like he knew just where he was going. After the funeral, I never saw Claude again, but that day, he was a member of the family. When the organist played "What A Friend We Have in Jesus," a picture came into my head: Mama, waltzing around the kitchen and singing that song when I was little, after I said I'd kill her. My heart thumped with guilt.

At home later, Loretta Holliday waltzed up to Charlene and me, sitting with Deanna on the piano bench. Her hair stood in frizzled strands about her face, and a wild look blazed in her eyes, like someone who had escaped a burning building. There were a few ash-gray hairs I'd never noticed among the brown. Tears had streamed down her face, taking her mascara with them in black rivulets. "I don't know what I'm going to do without your Mama. My voice'll go to pieces. You know, I waited that morning till near eleven for Bernice to come. I missed my hair appointment, waiting . . ." She patted the bed of flattened curls on top of her head. "And just look at it today. Isn't it an awful mess?"

Charlene nodded at her with that hateful look I'd seen her give the gym teacher when we'd both been at Tallulah Junior High. "Sure is," she said, and thumbed through a music book, leaving me to be the polite one.

"Are there any clues?" Deanna asked. "You can't have a murder with no clues."

But I was staring at Mrs. Holliday, at the emerald eyeliner that turned her eyes into green slits, glittering like broken glass. Her husband, Joe, had packed up and left her a few days before. Rumor was he'd moved to Alabama.

He was always leaving them. I couldn't help but think how she and her daughter, Kathy, wouldn't have those green and yellow bruises on their faces anymore, like they'd been struck by a flock of wild parakeets, leaving dust from the random beating of their wings. For the first time, she seemed pretty, under all that pancake makeup.

From behind, Mrs. Guest's arm descended heavily on my shoulders. I knew who it was by the smell of her talcum powder. "Oh law, what do we know anyway," she said. "What on earth do we know down here?"

"Personally, I don't know a thing," said Mrs. Holliday. She patted her hair again and walked off, wobbling a little on her high heels.

But Mrs. Guest didn't seem to hear. She kept saying, "What on earth do we know down here?" as if the words were an incantation, or a prayer to a god she wasn't sure was listening.

Chapter Four

Not long after the funeral, the telephone rang when Charlene and I got home from school, while Daddy was working at the furniture store. I picked it up and someone was breathing so softly I could barely hear it. "Who do you want to talk to?" I asked, but there was no answer, just the slow rhythm of breath. Charlene saw the confusion on my face and grabbed the receiver, thinking it was some boy.

"Talk or hang up." She listened for a beat, then slammed down the receiver. "Don't let any boy treat you that way, Jubilee," she said. "It's not respectful."

48

But I didn't mind. It was a comforting breath. So, when the phone would ring after school and Charlene was watching TV or doing her homework, I would pick up and sit still to listen to the quiet breathing. Slowly, my own would begin to match it, and it seemed as if we existed in a secret world, halfway between dream and speech. We were breathing the same rhythm in a strange duet, as if there were a shadow of myself on the far end of the telephone wires that ran through the familiar streets of Biloxi into an unknown place. I'd found a twin who knew things I could not say, who even knew my dreams, maybe. But just as mysteriously as they started, the calls stopped after a few weeks. I missed them.

Daddy got letters from thrill-seekers offering to buy the truck, the "murder vehicle," some said. Often, they wanted to know if the seats had blood stains. Daddy wadded them up. "Sickos. What's the world come to?"

One afternoon in late May, Charlene and I were eating tuna fish sandwiches in the living room, watching *As The World Turns* on TV. Part of me felt like I was keeping up with the show for Mama, for when she came back.

Daddy hurried in, waving an envelope. "Look at this, girls," he said. "All the way from California, and it's got a legitimate check inside. Man from Los Angeles wants to buy the truck for ten thousand dollars. Says if it's a 1948 pick-up in good shape, he'll add it to his collection."

"Does he say anything about blood?" Charlene asked, through a mouthful of white bread.

"Not a word," said Daddy. "He's legit."

"Mama loved the truck," I pleaded. I swallowed the tuna as fast as I could. "You're not going to sell it, are you?"

"Ten thousand dollars? Come on. Think of the clothes and records we could buy," said Charlene. "We could go see Aunt Sylvia in New York." She kicked me under the coffee table.

Daddy looked happier than I'd seen him since before Mama died. "This check'll be for your permanent record."

"What permanent record?" Charlene looked scared and put down her sandwich.

"Your college educations. You know how much your Mama wanted you to go to college. You girls can teach awhile before you get married, prove you can support yourselves. There's a lot of self-respect comes from that." He paused. "That's what your mama always said."

So that was why Mama gave voice lessons to people who couldn't carry a tune. "I wouldn't dream of going to college on blood money," I said. "I'll get a trumpet scholarship."

Daddy's face went pale. "Blood money?"

"That's what it is," I said, though Charlene kicked me again. "That truck was as precious to Mama as anything, and we'd be losing her twice if we sold it. The truck is how I'll always remember Mama. We might as well just burn her pictures if we sell it. Don't do it, Daddy. Please."

Charlene looked at me hard, then reached out and squeezed Daddy's hand. "Don't do it." I could've kissed her.

Daddy went to the kitchen and propped the check on the windowsill above the sink. "You girls think about it," he called, but the next morning the check was in the garbage, torn into pieces.

"The truck belongs to you," Daddy said at breakfast, looking from Charlene to me.

"I couldn't sit behind that wheel." Charlene kept stirring her egg into her grits, not looking at us.

I spoke fast, before Daddy changed his mind. "I'm a good driver, like Mama. I'll take care of it."

"You shouldn't even be driving, Jubilee. You're not fifteen yet." It was an argument Daddy and Mama used to have a lot, before Mama would take me on the back roads and show me how to shift so smoothly the hula dancer would barely bow. Daddy always lost those quarrels. "Clayton says you were driving a tractor when you were eleven, Harry. Who are you to talk?" Mama would rattle the keys at him.

I was eyeing those same keys, lying on the windowsill above the sink. "Mama taught me. How could I have had a better teacher?" I frowned at Daddy. "You've seen me drive. You know how good I am."

That's how the truck became mine, and I went to work on it. I propped the doors open for days, to air out the smell of blood and perfume. I even burned two vanilla votive candles on the dashboard, making puddles of wax right next to the little hula dancer that I had to scrape off. The grill had gotten dusty, so I took a chamois cloth and eased it between the chrome strips and then over the rounded hood, thinking of Mama's soft breasts.

On the side, I always thought it said "Thirstmaster" in silvery script and I polished each letter, wondering for the first time what it meant. I closed my eyes and pretended the letters were Braille, imagining what it would be like to be one of those blind kids in Mobile, singing in a choral group. That was when it came to me: the thirst that ran through Mama's life, the way the truck was probably the only thing that could satisfy it. And, for a while, Levi Litvak.

When I opened my eyes, the letters gleamed in the sun, and I realized the word was "Thriftmaster." Nothing to do with thirst at all. Then I thought of Daddy, how he'd frown when Mama bought new sweater sets for Charlene and me, the sale tags still attached, or records she'd teach us to dance to, while the living room floor quivered under our feet so hard the needle would jump. I liked "Thirstmaster" better.

I brought an old toothbrush and some Clorox to scrub at the blood stains, but all they did was fade to pink, and a little hole appeared in the fabric, where I rubbed too hard. "You'll damage the truck," I told myself, and I could almost hear Mama agreeing. And was it right to fade out the blood that was Mama's? So I brought out some nice bath towels instead, and tucked the ends into the crack between the seat and the back, to hold them in place like slipcovers. Mama would always be there, a kind of secret between us.

The blood and musky odor in the truck finally began to fade after I burned more vanilla candles in it. The familiar smell of grease filled the garage again, along with a faint, flowery smell I couldn't place. I was sliding under the truck to check out a clunking noise one afternoon when I saw a bright red cloth behind Mama's carpentry tools by the door. Every spare rag was useful to the truck, so I picked it up. It was a long chiffon scarf, red with orange poppies, soiled from the concrete floor. The flowery smell grew stronger as I put it to my nose. It wasn't Mama's perfume, too sweet. And I knew the scarf wasn't Charlene's.

While Daddy was making soup for dinner, I showed it to him and Charlene. "Where in the garage was it?" asked Daddy. "Right by the door?" Holding it by the hem, he dropped it into a paper bag from the Piggly Wiggly.

"What does he think?" Charlene wrinkled her nose when he left the kitchen. "It's a bomb?"

He was calling the police. "No sir, never seen it before," he said. "Might be evidence." A minute later, he slammed the receiver down and came back in, a smile pasted on his face as he sat down.

"Evidence?" I asked.

He frowned. "You shouldn't eavesdrop. The police don't think so. Case closed, they say."

"Deanna," said Charlene. "She probably put it there. She said it couldn't be a murder without clues."

"She may have problems," I said. "But she wouldn't do that."

"It's a crime, if she did," said Daddy.

Charlene made a gesture of pocketing the salt shaker. "She's *your* friend," she said.

The bag with the scarf disappeared, and I thought Daddy had thrown it out until I saw it up on a shelf in the garage, the bag secured with gray duct tape.

I still practiced my trumpet in the garage, imagining I was playing to Mama. Miles Davis was my favorite, and Mama's woodworking and gardening tools vibrated against each other when I'd do "Old Devil Moon." It was like her applause.

Mrs. Guest saw me with the votive candles, and told Brother Beeker that I'd made a "sacri-religious shrine out of a motor vehicle." He stopped by the house one Saturday afternoon, just as Charlene was bleaching my hair a lighter brown. We had to stop so I could explain how a vanilla candle absorbs odors, even the smell of blood. The kitchen screen had a hole in it, and a fly kept buzzing at Brother Beeker's sweet hair pomade. He ducked away from it, and held our hands at the kitchen table to pray for the family. He finally left, with the fly nestled in a thick swirl of hair.

At least he's good fly paper, I thought, but Charlene rushed me to the sink to wash out the peroxide before the words were out. By then, my hair was as white as Grandma Starling's. Until the brown roots started show-ing, people said I'd gone prematurely gray with grief.

In the glove compartment, I found a file of Mama's notes, written in her precise, block letters, on when she'd changed the oil, re-lined the brakes, and bought new spark plugs for the six cylinders. She loved that truck, all right, all those Sunday afternoons she'd spend in the garage, checking the transmission fluid or the air in the tires, preening it like it was a wild bird that might fly, something she had to keep tamed, a thirst to be quenched.

For weeks, I had the same dream. Mama would be walking in the vegetable garden when her chest would begin to bleed, until it looked like red poppies blooming on her blouse. She was oblivious to it, like it was as natural as a menstrual stain. The blood dripped down her arms and legs, and she began to stagger, leaking the red liquid as if her heart had broken for all Biloxi to see. I'd be tapping on a window in the living room, trying to warn her, but she couldn't hear. Always, she'd climb into the truck to escape her fate. By then, she'd be solid red, looking like a bride or a nun sacrificed to the inevitable ceremony that lay before her, the black of a habit or the white of a wedding gown gone to crimson. She would start the motor, and there was nothing I could do but watch. When the engine roared, her blood became flammable, and the truck began to crackle with fire, a sound like the snapping of brittle bones. The truck would disappear down the road, Mama's upright body a darker pillar of red borne inside the orange flames. Then, somehow, it was me who was driving, the flames engulfing all but my face.

When I drove around Biloxi in the truck, the dream would snap into my mind and I'd shiver, feeling as if I were driving an inferno through the streets. But it was a secret fire, a sacred fire.

I went to Tallulah Junior High every morning in the truck until school let out for the summer, though people

54

stared and pointed. Though I was too young to get a driver's license, nobody had the nerve to stop me, not even the police. The truck made me immune, made me feel immortal. It was like Mama's gift from heaven. Sometimes I'd spin the wheel and it seemed like Mama's fingers were guiding it.

When I was cruising down the highways outside Biloxi, testing the limits of how close to New Orleans I could get before I'd be late getting home to the hot dogs Daddy fixed for supper, I knew why Mama prized it so much. It was her ticket out, her reminder that she still had her freedom, an escape from her singing lessons at the Methodist Church, or from the kitchen. Maybe even from us, her kids and husband.

When I offered Charlene a ride, she admitted she was scared of it. "How can you stand driving it?" she asked. "Those towels on the seat don't make any difference." I was a dumb little kid who thought I was grown up, she told me, but her eyes told me I was fearsome to her.

For one thing, I'd started going to Saint Sebastian's, the Catholic church where Deanna's family belonged. Charlene told me she prayed for me to come back to the Baptist church, but I bobby-pinned a lace handkerchief on my head and went off to Mass. The last time I'd gone to my Baptist Sunday School class, one of the girls, Ruthie Joy Stevens, had led the class in prayer. She asked God to help the fundraising drive for wall-to-wall carpeting in the sanctuary. Then she said, "And help Jubilee, God." For a second, I thought she was trying to comfort me, but she added, "We ask Thee to help her calm down, to stop bleaching her hair and skipping school. Help her to obey the laws of our fine state."

I couldn't believe my ears. I looked up, and the whole class had raised their heads to stare at me. Ruthie Joy's blonde head was bowed, and she went on, her fingers clasped in her lap, the toes of her black leather pumps pointing together, like two shiny convertibles about to collide.

"Lead, guide, and direct Jubilee Starling not to burn candles in her truck, making a sacri-religious shrine on the dashboard. Help her not to drive without a license, and to know Thy ways, and not to wear glitter in her nail polish. Guide her to use her trumpet to knock down the walls of Jericho, not to build up the sinful walls of jazz-i-co. Help her to finally get over her mother's death after these most tragical weeks, and. . ."

I slammed the door behind me before I could hear the rest. Build up the walls of jazz-i-co? Who on earth helped Ruthie Joy with that speech? That's what it was, a speech, not a prayer, like one of Brother Beeker's sermons.

Ruthie Joy's mother said she'd be Miss America one day, she had such poise. She'd been one of Mama's voice students, but Mama never thought she had talent. I reminded myself of that when I left the church and never went back.

There were other reasons I left the Baptists. Brother Beeker said we were all responsible for a small tornado that ripped through a trailer park up in McComb and killed a baby. We were evil, he said. We listened to snakes in the grass, chewing hard on every apple of knowledge that dropped our way. "Every time you bite down, the juice just spurts from your mouths!" he yelled, rising up on the tiptoes of his shiny black shoes, his finger pointing to the chandelier. "Poison! That's what it is. God's shakin' his finger at you, and you, and you." He jabbed his finger at one of the deacons, then Grady Pickens, and finally at Tommy McCarty's grandmother. Grady looked proud, but the other two bowed their heads. Tommy's grandmother picked at a thread on her purse. "He's showing you what Judgment Day'll be like. You thought that tornado was something, didn't you, cars crushed like unto tin cans, trailers blown like a baby tossing his blocks into the air, that baby having himself one of the Devil's own temper tantrums? Well, you're going to see a whole lot more on Judgment Day." Why didn't he say "we"? He sounded like he was sitting by God's side.

I couldn't believe I had any responsibility for a tornado, or a baby dying in one. I'd studied how hot air could be dangerous under certain conditions. I learned a lot about hot air from Brother Beeker's own sermons, even while Charlene sat beside me, inhaling his words like they were God's own.

On Sunday nights, we'd stand in a line for "Sword Drills," when the class would rip through their Bibles to see who'd be first to find the verse called out by the teacher. "Draw swords," she said, and you'd pull out your Bible and hold it in the palm of your left hand, your right hand laid gently on top. But as soon as the verse was called, there was nothing gentle about it. My Bible might have looked bad, its edges curling up and torn, but I won a lot of gold stars on my sword drill card. It drove Charlene crazy, that her renegade sister might know more about the Bible than she did. You won enough of those stars, and you got a hot fudge sundae or a chocolate malted, your choice, from the church kitchen. But it was my downfall, all that knowledge, like Eve with the apple. That winter before Mama died, I gained five pounds in a month on all that ice cream. Mama said I'd have to start cheating on the sword drills, so I wouldn't win those free desserts.

"It goes right to your fanny, Jubilee," she'd tell me. "Your fanny and here." She pinched some flesh beneath my chin. "We'll have to roll you down the church steps if you keep remembering all those verses, sweetie. Good thing you've already been baptized. You'd flood the church if they dunked you now." Mama was never strong on tact, but I lost the weight after I quit going to First Baptist.

The main reason I stopped going, though, was the way the invitational hymn called people down to have their souls saved. I didn't want to think we had choices. It made it seem that maybe Mama didn't have to die after all. Then the injustice would hit me so hard I could barely hear the choir sing. The worst part was that Mama's alto wasn't there, soaring over even the sopranos.

I liked the way everything seemed preordained and fated at Saint Sebastian's, even the incense and robes and school uniforms. Free will, all the crazy rages and joys we have on this planet, began to seem like nothing more than the smoke from a votive candle that knows the inevitable direction of its burning wick. It was a comfort, feeling that nothing could be avoided, that all we had to do in life was hold on tight until the ride ended.

Father McGallagher never said God had sent a tornado to blame us for our wicked ways. His Latin was beautiful, so exotic and strange that I started studying it harder in school. It sounded as mysterious as incense, and I would think that was where Mama must be, somewhere in the smoke of incense and the lull of Latin invocations.

I felt closer to God when I drove, with the accelerator pushed to the floor, and Mama's patron saint nodding her approval on the dashboard, telling me I might understand the mysteries of the universe if I could learn enough Latin. Then I might make it to sainthood, myself. It was just me and the road and Mama's truck, a trinity made into a single being by movement and speed.

After Mass, I explored back roads, speeding along

highway 90 that stretched from Biloxi to Pascagoula, past scrubby pines that lined the way like pathetic footmen bowing as I blew past at sixty miles an hour. I told myself stories about how Mama had felt sorry for Levi Litvak, hunted by the Klan the way he was, and then how she'd made him furious when she told him that it didn't matter what he said, she loved Daddy and her girls. He'd gone crazy with love for her, I told myself. Maybe for the same reason I loved her. It didn't matter to Mama what anybody said, what gossip was spread.

The latest rumor in town was that Levi Litvak didn't die in the Thunderbird crash, after all. Somebody else drove the car, people said. Levi got away with murder, and ran to Puerto Rico, smoking big cigars.

On a Sunday afternoon in late July, I decided to skip the evening mass and find the cypress tree where Levi Litvak's T-bird had crashed, see for myself how badly damaged it was. Maybe there was a clue about whether he survived. It was out in the swampy lands near New Orleans, so I headed west, watching the sun edge toward the brown horizon of the Gulf. I wished I had a map, one with arrows, a treasure map I could unfold and see where Levi Litvak had gone on that April morning, careening his convertible down back roads, his hair waving crazily in the wind until he crashed. Did he hit that tree on purpose, knowing there was no way he could survive either a murder trial or a life without Mama? How could someone else have been driving his car? But one cypress-lined road looked just like the next, so I turned back when the sky grew dusky and all those mossy shadows seemed scary.

I was getting close to Long Beach when I spotted a woman in a red dress hitchhiking. Company, I thought. And it was awfully hot for anybody to be hitchhiking. I'd seen a white family once, hitchhiking by the side of the road, with paper bags and boxes tied with rope. They had two little kids with deep rings beneath their eyes, sitting on one battered suitcase. The father had his thumb out. I remembered the look in his eyes, the same weary hopelessness that the rest of his family had, and the way Daddy had said we just didn't have room for them when I asked. "Where would we put them all, hon?" he said. Mama reached to the back seat and patted my knee. "I love you, Jubilee," she'd said.

So this time, I pulled the truck over. After I stopped, I recognized her red dress from morning mass, in Saint Sebastian's third pew. It was Loretta Holliday. From the sandy berm, she waved with a handkerchief, but when she saw me at the wheel, her face puckered up, like she was going to cry.

"Mrs. Holliday?" I asked, leaning across to open the door for her. She hesitated before she climbed in, scraping the mud from her high heels on the edge of my running board. A clump of clay hung there. I resented that. I kept the truck polished, the inside spotless, the way Mama had.

"Take me back to town." She smoothed the towel on the seat, but it was wrinkled and one of the bloodstains peeked out. She sat on the edge of the towel, like she wanted to touch as little of the truck as possible. I saw her glance for a second at the bloodstain. Then she fixed her gaze on the horizon, gray with rain clouds, and remembered her manners. "I appreciate your help."

"Did your car break down?" I started the truck, and peered into the scrubby pines along the highway, thinking her car might have rolled down the slippery pine needles into the woods. I felt sorry for her. Now and then, Joe Holliday would come back to town, and disappear again after leaving those awful bruises on Loretta and Kathy. Loretta didn't seem ashamed of the bruises when she'd go to work at WLOX, even though she sat right in the lobby at the front desk. She'd put extra make-up on her and Kathy, but she'd tell anybody how crazy Joe was, how she wished he'd stay gone. She told Onita Tate that she'd bought herself a little pistol, might kill Joe one night, or at least scare the pants off him. When Loretta showed Mrs. Tate the gun, people began talking about how Loretta might belong in Whitfield, the state mental asylum up near Jackson. But I could understand how she might buy a gun, thinking about Joe Holliday's fists.

"No. My ole car's got another fifty thousand miles in her," she said. She took a pack of cigarettes from her purse and scratched a match against the package. Beneath a round hole in the sleeve of her dress, I could see pink flesh.

"Mrs. Holliday," I said. "Did you know you have a cigarette burn in your dress?" What I was trying to say was, don't you dare put a burn in this truck.

She put down the matches and lifted her arm to look at the hole. "You want to know what happened to my dress?" She didn't wait for an answer, just smoothed out her skirt to show me two more ragged, round holes near the hem. "Joe, he got mad at me one night and put my clothes in the yard. Great big pile, everything but what was in the dirty clothes basket. Lucky he didn't think of those. If Joe Holliday doesn't understand something, he's liable to shoot it."

"What's to understand about a dress?" I asked.

"It's red, right? It's sexy, isn't it?" She pulled at her skirt to show me how tight it was, then waved the lit match through the air to extinguish it, as if she were fanning away my words along with the flame. "Joe grabbed his pistol out of the kitchen drawer, and — kablam! kablam! — fired a whole round of bullets into my best clothes. Got holes in my underwear, too. Slips, panties, bras. I tell you, that's as close to shooting a person as you can get."

I considered it. "I guess so."

"Girl, I didn't even think about stopping him. Not when he gets like that. Think God will forgive me for wearing my holey clothes to church?" She laughed, and took a tug on the cigarette, making the stub burn redder.

"Maybe that makes them holier," I said.

Mrs. Holliday eyed me above her cigarette. "You really believe that, don't you, honey? That's right sweet of you. Holy dresses, yessir. My best dress, and I just couldn't patch it up. Look at me! Loretta Sweeney from Ocean Springs, with holes in her best clothes. My mother used to tell me I was going to be Miss Mississippi, that's how pretty she thought I was. That's what mamas are for, isn't it?" Then she blushed. "I'm sorry about Bernice, hon."

"You're still pretty." It was true, except for her teeth. The front ones overlapped and protruded slightly, but she had nice eyes. "Mrs. Tate does a good job on your hair."

She looked at me sharply, like she didn't believe me. "Onita Tate respected Bernice, no matter what folks say."

"What do people say?" I asked, and wondered if I really wanted to know.

"Onita came to the funeral to pay her dues, you know, even though they disagreed about things."

"I saw her," I said. "She never sat down."

"She'd had surgery. Kind that makes it hard to sit without one of those pillows with a hole in the middle. Doughnuts, they call them. She's a prideful woman, and I don't blame her for not carrying it with her."

"What kind of surgery?" Now that I was Catholic like Mrs. Holliday, surely I could ask a question like that. All kinds of mysterious things ran through my mind.

She laughed. "Kind of surgery you don't ever want to

need." She lit another cigarette, squinting as she inhaled. "Reckon it's going to rain dead mules.Mighty gray up there," she said, peering through the glass. She tapped the divider that split the windshield into two frames. "Looks old-fashioned. The new ones have a solid piece of glass," she told me. As if I didn't know. "You ought to get yourself a cute little sports car. An MG."

What kind of money did she think Daddy made? "This truck runs great," I said and pointed to the hula dancer on the dashboard. "So smooth she barely moves."

Loretta frowned. She looked like she was starting to say something, but she stopped. There was nothing but the sound of her blowing cigarette smoke right at the windshield. Some people will aim a lungful at the ceiling or out the window, to be nice, but not Mrs. Holliday. Instead of puckering her lips to blow out the smoke, she made a curved slit of her mouth, so the haze billowed out in all directions. It was like a crack in an inferno blazing inside her.

"I sure do like the Catholic church," I said. The smoke reminded me of her veiled face on Sundays. "It's the smell, and the stained glass. And that statue, you know the one of the guy with all the arrows in him? He stares at the ceiling with his sad eyes, like he can stand the pain that way."

"Saint Sebastian," she nodded. "Yeah, I know him." She sounded like she knew him personally. "Got tortured a long time ago so they made him a saint." She ground out her cigarette on the bottom of her shoe and tossed it out the window. "Now he stands around with sticks in him."

"So that's Saint Sebastian." I coughed, trying not to be embarrassed. "He's got the church named after him, he oughtta be there. You been going there long?"

"Hard to say. I don't go when Joe's in town. Makes

him mad."

"It makes him mad when you go to church?" I'd never heard of that.

"Roman Catholics, you know," she said. "Joe thinks we're too close to the Jews."

I thought about it for a second, but it didn't make any sense. "But we have Christmas." In the Hollidays' front window, a shabby little tree always flickered with tinsel at Christmas. Ugliest tree in town, Onita Tate always said.

"'Course we do, honey. Joe doesn't like the pope, Catholics, or Jews. We're not like Joe, that's why he doesn't like us."

"What church does Mr. Holliday go to?" I couldn't imagine him in a coat and tie.

She laughed. "Church of the Need-to-Be-Redeemed. I've seen Joe in a church once, when his mama died. He knew I was Catholic when he married me, but," she shrugged, "what with Kathy on the way, Joe's daddy just about whupped him into marrying me. Gave him a bloody nose. Damn near broke it. Joe had scabs all over his face when he asked me to marry him. He wasn't a pretty boy that day. Looked at me all dog-eyed and sad. 'Okay, Loretta, I'll marry you.' It was enough to make me feel sorry for him." Her voice was softer. "He was fightin' back tears."

"Did you marry him because you felt sorry for him?"

"Why honey, what choice did I have? Real romantic, huh?" She laughed again, like she thought she was talking to a grown-up who'd laugh along with her. I didn't, so she lit another cigarette, and looked at me like something had just occurred to her. "You're too young to think about these things, aren't you? Don't go getting pregnant someday and having to marry a boy like Joe Holliday, just because he made your knees go wobbly when you were

64

sixteen." She looked at the thin plain band on her finger and twisted it, like if she turned it long enough, she'd find a diamond there.

How could she stand marrying a man she didn't love? A sick feeling rose in my chest, like she had told me more than she should have. Mrs. Holliday studied me. "Course, I don't guess you have a boyfriend yet, do you? Try not to wear those glasses all the time, darlin."

"I just wear them to drive," I said, feeling hurt. They were cat-eye frames, with blue glitter on the upturned edges. I was proud of them. "At movies. Things like that."

"A nice pink lipstick would be pretty on you. Lipstick makes your eyes look bright. You could use a little."

I didn't want to hear Mrs. Holliday give me one of Charlene's lectures on how I could look better. Charlene would come up and twist my hair into shape and say, "You know how your hair would look *good*?" The message was that I didn't look very good the way I was.

I changed the subject. "What do you think about Medgar Evers getting killed?" I was trying to make grown-up talk. Everybody was talking about how outside agitators from the North were coming down and riling up everybody. In June, somebody had shot and killed Medgar Evers up in Jackson, in his own driveway. I felt sorry for his children, who ran out and saw their dad lying there, dying. People said all the violence made us look bad.

She jumped like I'd stuck a pin in her. "What?" She took a long puff and squinted at me, the longest look she'd given me. "Why's everybody asking *me*?"

I said, "It's all anybody talks about." Ever since some black people and white northerners had gone to the Biloxi beach in what the newspapers called a "Wade-In," everybody worried about what the communists would do next.

She stared ahead. "What're they saying?"

"Well, you know." I was stumped. How could Mrs. Holliday have missed it? "How the communists are making Mississippi look bad. Some people say it's only a bad joke, that Medgar Evers wasn't even shot, much less killed. It's just the national press, they say."

"Yeah, it's a bad joke, all right. I tell you what, Joe Holliday knows some bad jokes. He asked me if I'd been getting any chiggers this summer, and I says no. Joe says, good, 'cause we got to call them chegroes now." She rubbed her temple like she had a headache.

My skin felt prickly, thinking of how somebody like Grady Pickens would laugh. "Mama always said jokes are one of the meanest ways of keeping people down."

She laughed. "Your mama, she'd say something intellectual like that." She crossed her legs and looked absentmindedly out the window. "Course, Levi liked that about her."

The words came so softly I wasn't sure I'd heard right. "Levi?" I asked.

"Did I say that out loud?" Her eyes darted about, and she smoothed her skirt. "Lord knows, all that talk about civil rights workers has me to where I don't know if I'm talking or thinking." She laughed, a little snort. "You ever get that way? Talking and thinking, it's all mixed up?"

Was that what it meant to be crazy? "Sometimes," I said, to be polite. "I talk to Mama when I drive. I told her about Medgar Evers getting killed and all."

Loretta stubbed out another cigarette on the sole of her shoe and threw it out the window.

Medgar Evers and freedom riders were all the grownups talked about, and usually you could start up a conversation fast about it. Charlene said Brother Beeker had preached a sermon on the civil rights workers and all the distrust they kicked up like July dust down here. Faith in each other, that was what Brother Beeker said we needed. I was glad I hadn't been there to sit still for it. Charlene told me one of the deacons, Mr. Wishburn, had come into her Sunday School class to give an educational talk about Martin Luther. Mr. Wishburn had had three fingers blown off in a fireworks explosion when he was a teenager, and it was always awkward to shake his claw-like hand on the way out after the sermon. He still seemed mad about losing those fingers. He told Charlene's class how Baptists were different from Methodists, different even from Protestants, since Baptists never protested. He said the word "protest" as if it were a bad word, something sinners and Methodists would do.

But he kept saying "Martin Luther King" instead of Martin Luther, until he was red-faced and spluttering, trying to correct himself. He finally slapped the lectern and shouted, "Martin *Luther*!" to stop himself. Charlene told me the Sunday School teacher had started to applaud, gently, to keep Mr. Wishburn from going on, though everybody knew you weren't supposed to clap in church.

Charlene said she didn't learn a thing, except that sometimes clapping in church might be a necessary evil.

"What do you know about Martin Luther?" I asked Mrs. Holliday, thinking I could tell Charlene about him.

"You mean Martin Luther King? Look, we don't know a thing more than anybody else. Stop talking about this stuff." For the thirty miles to Biloxi, the only sounds were matches striking and the occasional crinkle of a cigarette package.

When I pulled into the Hollidays' driveway, crunching shells and sand under the wheels, she sighed. "Joe's back. Been out with his buddies again." I stopped in front of her house. "Just drive on in." She pointed to a ramshackle garage where the broken oyster shells ended, and I could smell her perspiration when she raised her arm to gesture. "Give it a tap and it'll fall over." She laughed, but there was no happiness in the sound. She sat there, staring at the square box of a house, its shutters and front door peeling green paint. "I'll have to change the locks again, but it doesn't do a bit of good. He gets in."

The door had a line of black marks right at knee level. Someone's boot had landed there, Joe Holliday's work boots, no doubt. She turned to me with a sad look, like she'd forgotten I was only thirteen and wouldn't know what to say. I hesitated, trying to think of something. "How come he never takes you on his vacations?"

"Hon, if I ever get to take a vacation, I'll fly myself to London, England, not ride in some truck to Mobile, Alabama." She got a faraway look. "Maybe Italy, see the pope himself. I'd sure tell about Joe Holliday."

"Tell what?" I asked.

She waved her hand. "Oh, to pray for him, all that." She thought a minute. "I'd tell him how scared Joe is."

"Of what?" I couldn't imagine him scared of anything.

"Colored folks. 'They're gonna rise up,' Joe tells me. 'And ain't no stopping 'em from slitting our throats like hogs.' Yeah, he's scared of what'll happen if the coloreds ever think they can get away with killing us. He's been scared for a long time, but let that be a little secret between you and me. Wish he was scared of *me*." She went on, thinking about escaping him. "I got cousins in San Jose, California. I'm saving to visit them someday." She looked at me sharply, fear glinting in her eyes. "Don't you tell Joe. 'Course he couldn't find my savings even if he turned the house upside down. And that's just what he'd do. He'd set that money on fire before he'd let me use it."

I tried to imagine stopping Joe Holliday at the Pack-A-Sack, telling him, 'Your wife told me she's saving money for a vacation. Alone.' "Don't worry," I told Mrs. Holliday.

She patted my hand. "Thank you, darlin'. Joe's been in McComb, I expect. Hunting. What's a lady like me supposed to do? Pluck dead ducks? Joe Holliday, hah. Only holiday he ever gave me was his name." She looked at me. "That's a joke. Lame as some of those damn birds he brings home for me to clean." She opened the door. "Well, thanks."

"Bye," I said, but it came out in a whisper. What if Joe Holliday heard his wife complaining about him?

She walked to the front door, looking around as if Joe could be hiding in the thick shrubs. The stench of decaying conchs from the Gulf hung in the air, thick as moss. Joe Holliday's bait, the same smell that wafted from him if I got too near, in the convenience store, his tackle box in one hand, cigarette money in the other. I half expected to see a monster rise up. I backed up as fast as I could down the long driveway, hoping I wasn't spraying her with sand.

That house had always given me the creeps. Every Halloween, Joe Holliday put up the scariest decorations – witches cackling from speakers in the bushes, a skeleton glowing in the front window, and ghosts that hovered in the lower branches of the pine trees alongside the driveway. We'd make that long walk down the Holliday drive on dares, or as excuses to hold a boy's hand, but we'd run as soon as we saw those ghosts.

"Why'd you give Loretta Holliday a ride?" Charlene asked when I told her. She turned down the sound of Elvis blaring out "Devil in Disguise." It was Charlene's favorite song, and she played it all the time, singing the lyrics. When it came to the part when Elvis sang for heaven to help him, because of the devil in his girlfriend's eyes, I always thought about Levi Litvak and Mama, but Charlene didn't notice the connection. She was too busy thinking about Art Johnson, a boy with blue eyes and a red Impala he drove around the Dairy Queen, where kids went on Friday night to socialize. Elvis's voice was Charlene's own special pick-up truck, transporting her where no one else could, places like Art Johnson's arms. That was how we both got through the summer, pretending we were someplace else.

But she was mad enough now to stop singing. "Loretta Holliday's as crazy as that husband of hers. They're talking about sending her to Whitfield. She bought herself a gun, you know. They say she carries it in her bosom. Right in the middle of her bra." She shivered. "Just think what would happen if it went off."

"It was going to rain dead mules," I said. "Wouldn't you pick up a lady you knew, if she was hitchhiking?"

"Cats and dogs. That's what it rains. Who's seen dead mules coming from the sky? Holliday's a stray cat, herself."

"You been seeing cats and dogs coming down, Charlene? Who're you calling crazy?" I figured Loretta Holliday was nuts, but that was no reason to call her a stray cat.

She blushed, one of the few times I'd ever seen her do that. "Why are you defending Kathy Holliday's mother? She sure isn't a lady. That woman was never anything but trash," Charlene's voice was sharp. "Even if she is one of God's own. He made both the wicked and the good, didn't he? When she was in high school, she beat up a girl just for giving her boyfriend a ride home. She pulled out a wad of the kid's hair, then glued it like a scalp on her locker."

"Where'd you hear that?" I asked.

"Aunt Sylvia heard it from Mama," she said, a triumphant note in her voice, as if Truth itself had spoken. "Mama went to Tallulah High with her. Or didn't you *know*?"

"Why would somebody need to sit on a pillow with a hole in it, after they've had surgery?" I asked.

She looked at me like I was a Martian. "Why are you always talking crazy? Hemorrhoids, probably. Who had 'em?"

"It's why Mrs. Tate didn't stay at Mama's funeral."

"Figures." With that, she adjusted the knob on the record player, and Elvis's voice soared through the room again. She closed her eyes and leaned against her pillow, a smile on her mouth. Elvis was singing the part about walking like an angel, and Charlene was probably thinking about Art Johnson and his red Impala.

There was no doubt Mrs. Holliday was strange, but if she was truly crazy, it was because of that husband of hers.

That night, the red scarf was in my dreams, floating on the Gulf breeze like a strange bird, uncertain if it should land. Every time I tried to pull it from the air, another would appear, until the night sky over the beach was filled with orange and red, billowing like fire and smoke.

Chapter Five

In October, when the coastal breeze had lost its summer warmth, Grady Pickens's father knocked on the kitchen door. He was inviting us to go up to Jackson to the Mississippi State Fair. He gave Daddy the Shriner handshake. At least that's what Charlene and I called it when they'd shake hands and grab each other's shoulder with their left hands while they pumped away with their right. Daddy had known Henry Pickens since they were boys, and they'd joined the Shriners the same year, 1948.

He would drive, Mr. Pickens told Daddy, and there was plenty of room in his new Buick for Charlene and me, and a friend of Grady's named Tommy McCarty, who lived in the neighborhood. Mostly, Mr. Pickens came to show off his new car to Daddy, and sell him a bottle of whiskey he'd bought in New Orleans for re-sale in Biloxi: bootlegging, most people called it, but Grady said his dad was an entrepreneur. "Entrapanure." He said it as if it rhymed with manure. Kids made jokes that Grady's dad was a shit trapper.

No one joked about that new Buick, though. "It's got air-conditioning and seatbelts," Mr. Pickens told Daddy, and they rode around the block so Daddy could see how smoothly it drove. Sometime on that drive, Daddy agreed to let us go to the fair. He came home and kissed me with whiskey on his breath and a bulge in his back pocket, a flask. "Henry Pickens is a fine man," Daddy said, putting the flask in an upper kitchen cabinet. "A good Shriner. He doesn't drink the whiskey he buys, just sips it to be sure it's decent. I know you girls hear the bootlegging talk, but Henry Pickens pleases his customers. That's what America's all about."

Like us, Grady didn't have a mother. She had left his dad when Grady was six, so Mr. Pickens wanted to do something special for us motherless kids, I guess. Grady wanted to be with Charlene, and I was the tag-along kid sister with only Tommy McCarty for company. Tommy never said much, but he could deliver a newspaper right to your front door, first time, every time. When he talked, that was what he talked about, so I was prepared to hear a lot about how you fold the *Biloxi Sun-Herald* to give it the best momentum. But I'd heard about the big fair in Jackson for years, and never been, so I was glad to be going.

Charlene wished Art Johnson, not Grady, had asked her. "Just think," she said, a moony look in her eyes. "Then we'd get to drive in that red Impala."

"He might be cute, but he's too old for you," I said.

"I don't like him just because he's cute. He's nice. He looks at me in the gym."

"Oh, you think he likes you or something?" I tried to sound as sarcastic as Charlene could.

"Maybe. But you wouldn't know what that feels like, would you?" Charlene was good at ending conversations.

Mr. Pickens turned us loose at the State Fairgrounds east of downtown. "I got business in Rankin County," he said, and told us he'd pick us up in two hours. "Have fun." He handed Grady a wad of dollar bills. But we hadn't known it was what they called "Negro night" at the fair until we got to the turnstiles. The man taking tickets gave us a funny look. "You outside agitators? Freedom riders or something?" He laughed with a mouth of jagged teeth, brown from chewing tobacco, and tore our tickets in half.

Everywhere you looked, people had dark skin. They stared at us and pointed, laughing. I'd never seen black people look so relaxed and free, and my shoulders tensed when I realized they were looking at us. It was like passing through a mirror, the most exotic place I'd ever been. Out of the mass of faces, I thought I saw Pearl. She looked younger and prettier, out with her friends, without the iron hissing up at her face. Her husband had won a teddy bear for her, and she held him loosely by the arm. I waved, relieved to see someone I knew.

"Hey Pearl!" I wanted her to brush the hair from my face with her fingers, and tell me to hold my head high.

"What are you doing?" Charlene whispered, eyeing the people who were staring. "Shut up."

"It's Pearl," I said, still smiling.

"Are you nuts? That's a teenager."

In an instant, the laughing girl before my eyes was no longer Pearl. What had I been thinking? I felt dizzy, as if I were in another land, a place where people's faces could float away like balloons and come back, changed. The voices and laughter began to sound like the indecipherable noise from a foreign country. I wasn't even sure how long we'd been there. Time seemed out of focus, like the blurred faces laughing around us. A slight wind sent dry oak leaves scuttling down the asphalt Midway like brown bands of refugees, hurrying past our feet. I felt like I was watching the world from a great distance, the way I had when Mama died in Intensive Care, but this time there was nothing peaceful about it.

"Yeah, they all look alike, don't they?" said Grady. *Broom-makers*, I could still hear Grady in the auditorium.

"Shut up." Charlene glared at him. "She does look like Pearl." She glanced at me, but I didn't feel better. The girl I'd thought was Pearl had started to smile at me, but her friends laughed and said something that made her grin. I felt like I'd lost a friend. What if it *had* been Pearl? Would she have even smiled at me? People pushed in line ahead of us and made us wait longer to get cotton candy. I knew then what it must be like to have black skin and walk down Biloxi's Main Street, full of white people who either ignored you or made fun of you. So this is what it's like to be a Negro, I thought, huddling closer to Charlene.

"Let's go," I said, but Charlene pointed at an enormous stretch of white cloth across a makeshift clothesline.

"Somebody's underwear," she said. "Heavens. Who would wear that?"

Grady hooted. "The fat lady! C'mon!"

Pictures of strange creatures had been painted on the canvas tent that read "Oddities and Freaks of Nature." There was the fat lady, her dress looking like a tent itself, with two tiny feet painted beneath. Beside her was the bearded lady, with black tufts of hair descending from her chin. But there were other creatures whose costumes I couldn't imagine how the fair made. The "Fish Girl" had eyes on either side of her head, and flippers instead of hands and feet. "Torso Man" was half a man on a table, his arms dangling. He wasn't missing just legs, there was nothing at all from the waist down. How did he hide his legs? Above another picture, the letters read "Dog-Faced Boy!" It looked like a boy wearing a mask. This would be funny, I thought. I'd get a good idea for a new Halloween costume.

The line of spectators coiled inside, between two ropes, and as we wound closer, I could see the strange creatures sitting, as advertised, in stalls. A small table rose from the sawdust, and on it perched a man wearing a striped shirt. He didn't need pants. He had the shirt tucked under where his stomach ended. The cotton candy began to rise in my throat. The people here were horribly deformed. I stared at the man who was only a torso, at the thick calluses on his knuckles. That was how he walked, I thought, with a sickening lurch to my stomach. It wasn't magic.

One girl pulled at her boyfriend. "Let's get out of here." Other teenagers laughed. I looked back at the torso man. His eyes were dots of dark hatred, piercing from his face at me, at the horror he must have seen in my face as I looked at his knuckles. His eyes didn't want to be there, trapped in that body. I opened my mouth to apologize, but nothing came out. Beside him the Fish Girl sat on a wooden bench, with enormous eyes so far apart she surely couldn't see straight. Instead of hands, she had fleshy flaps without fingers. The tent had become a house of mirrors where the reflections were horribly distorted.

Charlene stood before the fat lady, a mountain of flesh with a sack of popcorn. "Want some, honey?" She extended an arm trembling with loose fat and held out the popcorn to a little boy sucking his thumb. "Why, you're skinny as a pole." The boy stepped back and sucked harder. "There's nothing wrong with being a freak, honey," she said. "I'm just like you, 'cept for all this." She lifted her upper arm and wagged the skin that hung down. People laughed, but I felt sick. A sweaty, medicinal odor, like Mercurochrome, was mixed with the sweetness of cotton candy. I dropped the pink cloud of sugar into the sawdust, but a little boy with bright eyes like a magpie's snatched it as it fell.

Charlene whispered. "Let's get out. This is *real*."

We pushed our way out, and then Grady appeared. "Hey, did you see that dog-faced boy? Man, he wasn't even wearing a mask!" He whistled. "Do you get born like that, or what?"

"We're all flawed," said Charlene, so low I could barely hear her. Was she thinking of Mama?

"What?" Grady leaned down to hear.

"There's something wrong with all of us," she said. In that moment I loved Charlene more than ever.

"Nothing wrong with Tommy and me," said Grady.

Tommy pursed his lips and frowned, looking confused. "Everybody's a sinner, aren't they?" he asked. "That's what we forgive each other for."

"Yeah." I looked at Tommy's face. Why was he so earnest, all of a sudden?

"Hell, you've gone Catholic, girl. What do you

know?" Grady looked at Charlene like he thought she'd laugh at me.

"A lot more than you do, Grady Pickens," said Charlene.

"You girls don't know how to have a good time." He swaggered to the next tent, with Tommy following. On a stage in front, women pranced in high heels, wearing low-cut blouses and skirts they flicked around like Marilyn Monroe in *Some Like It Hot*. Long feathers framed their heads like peacocks preening at the New Orleans zoo. "Club Lido" flashed above the tent. "All bare!" said the sign.

"They're not wearing panties," I whispered to Charlene.

She looked at me like I was crazy. "What?"

One of the women flung out her arms and spun so fast all you saw was a blur of naked flesh under her skirt. "Told you so," I said. When she stopped, she winked at Grady, her long lashes brushing her cheeks. She bent over to blow him a kiss, her breasts swinging under taffeta that barely contained them.

"I know you don't get born like *that*!" Grady's eyes bulged almost as much as their bosoms. "Hey, let's go."

The tattooed man at the booth glanced at a guard and shook his head. "Too young, boys. Next year."

"What are you kids doing here?" The security guard wore the biggest belt buckle I'd ever seen, visible even under the fold of his belly. Above his ears, his white scalp showed through his crew cut. A blue cap hid the rest. "Don't you know it's Nigra night?"

"My dad left us," said Grady, his voice trembling. I'd never heard him sound scared. "We didn't know. . ."

"You better call your dad to come get you." The guard's face relaxed a little.

"We don't live here," said Charlene. "We're from Biloxi, and Mr. Pickens is here on business."

"Pickens from Biloxi?" The guard gave his belt a heave, but the buckle didn't budge. "Henry Pickens?"

"Yes, sir," said Grady. "I can't call. . ."

"Well, you kids be careful." He ambled away.

"Your dad's famous," said Tommy.

Grady puffed up. "Let's try the Tilt-A-Whirl, my treat." Without even speaking to each other, we got behind the last person in line, our minds still too numb to think of anything but the fat lady and the torso-man. Only Grady still had his cotton candy.

Charlene threw up on the Tilt-A-Whirl, and Grady hovered at her elbow when we staggered off. "Get away," she said, and wiped her mouth on her sleeve. He looked hurt for a minute, then went over to one of the cheap jewelry booths dotting the Midway, and found a silver heart on a chain.

"Charlene," I said, while she slurped from a drinking fountain. "He's buying a heart."

"Oh God," she moaned. "Don't let that be for me."

At the booth, a gray-haired woman leaned on the counter with an engraving tool that buzzed into the heart. She blew on it, polished it with her apron, and handed it proudly to Grady. The look on her face surprised me. It was the first time I'd seen anybody at the fair look proud of their work.

Grady strutted up and dangled the chain in Charlene's face. It said "G.P." and, beneath, "C.S." He reached to put it around her neck, but Charlene took it. "Thanks, Grady," she said, with a weak smile.

"You're giving a girl a necklace?" asked Tommy. "Why?" He looked betrayed, but Grady ignored him.

"Thought it'd make you feel better," he told Charlene,

78

She dropped it into her purse. "You're not gonna wear it?"

"I might lose it here," she said, and he nodded at what he thought was her wisdom.

As Grady was getting his weight guessed, a loud speaker blared out. "Grady Pickens, to the entrance. Grady. . . "

Grady thought he'd won something. He'd signed up for a drawing, but he couldn't remember what it was. "I'll share it," he told us. "Promise."

But it was his father waiting at the gate, furious. Mr. Pickens' face was bright red, and he grabbed Grady. "Why did they let you kids in? Don't you have any sense? Can't you see who's here?"

"It was our only chance for the fair. . ." Grady began, a whine in his voice I'd never heard before.

"Where would we have gone?" asked Charlene. She lifted her chin at Grady's dad. "You left us here." That quieted him. Grady looked at her softly, admiring how she'd stopped his dad, the man whose bootlegging was famous all over the state, the man the police wouldn't even stop. We slept on the long drive home, curled against the plush upholstery of the new Buick. Tommy McCarty twitched once, and woke me, muttering in his sleep about the Fish Girl and forgiveness, and I knew there might be more to him than aiming newspapers.

When Halloween came around, a new moon left the sky black, twinkling with stars. If there had been a witch sailing on her broom, no one would've known. Every year before, I was a beatnik, wearing black fishnet stockings that Aunt Sylvia had once given Mama for Christmas. I'd wave a long silver cigarette holder in my hand, one Daddy bought as a joke for Mama in New Orleans. Charlene had a witch hat she'd made out of papier-mâché, with silver glitter glued on it in the shape of stars. It was too good a hat to use just once, so on most Halloweens she was a witch.

But this year, we felt too old to join the little kids. We were sitting on the sofa watching *Seventy-Seven Sunset Strip* on TV when Deanna knocked at the door. She carried a paper bag with "Piggly Wiggly" on it, like most kids carried for their candy. She wore a black turtleneck and stretch pants, with the neck pulled up over her mouth and nose.

"What am I?" Her voice was muffled and I could barely hear her.

Grady Pickens stood with her, kicking the bottom step with his tennis shoe. He had flesh-colored pimple cream caked on his skin in big mounds, like a clay volcano at the elementary school science fair, and wore a rubber animal nose.

I tore my eyes away from him. "You haven't been over here in ages," I told Deanna.

She shrugged and adjusted the turtleneck. "I've been busy. What do you think I am?"

A terrible friend, I wanted to say, but I knew I'd lose her forever that way. "A beatnik?" What a copy-cat.

"Get me your cigarette holder." She was glazed-eyed and breathless, like she'd get before she went shoplifting.

So that was why she had come over. "I don't know where it is," I lied. "Be a bank robber, that would work."

"What am I?" Grady pulled on the animal nose.

"I don't want to know," said Charlene, her lip curled.

"A volcano at the science fair?" I asked, but he ignored me.

"The dog-faced boy!" he said, laughing so hard the pimple cream cracked.

"That's sick, Grady," I said. Sometimes, I still saw the

80

hatred in the torso man's eyes.

"You should trick-or-treat as the fat lady, big butt."

"Jubilee can't help her rear end," Charlene hissed.

"Sorry," Grady kicked his toe against the step again.

"Why are you trick-or-treating?" I asked Deanna. "You said we were too old now." Her sack looked full. I reached for the caramels Daddy had bought and handed her one.

"Thanks," Deanna said, mushing it against her braces to soften it. "But I'm not after candy. We're going to get Mr. Holliday. Come on." She opened her sack and showed me the eggs and toilet paper inside.

"Why didn't you ask one of your new friends?" She sat with other girls at lunch now.

"They're having a party, and I wasn't invited. Some friends. But we've got to get Mr. Holliday, pay him back."

"After last year?" Charlene huddled in the door. "I wouldn't go near that place. It's devil's work."

"It's revenge," whispered Deanna, her eyes big above the stretched turtleneck.

"I won't let anybody hurt you," Grady told Charlene. "Not this time."

The year before, the Hollidays' house had been dark except for candles in the windows. Slowly, we had made out a skeleton and the tips of what looked like white sheets in the trees. The usual Holliday ghosts, we told ourselves, and pushed on. Then, as we kids crunched down the drive, a corpse with a rope knotted around its neck descended from the magnolia tree and dangled in our faces. Its feet were low enough to rake Charlene's witch hat, and she screamed. Its pants billowed in the air, and we could see it was only a man's clothing, stuffed with lumpy scraps. It blew in the balmy coast breeze like it didn't have a care in the world. But Mr. Holliday had painted the workgloves that hung from the sleeves black. The head was covered with a hood. A mock lynching.

The bushes rustled at the side of the house and we ran like ghosts were after us. We stood at the end of the long driveway, panting from the escape. Charlene had fallen and scraped her elbow on the broken shells that paved the drive.

"You hurt?" Grady had asked Charlene, but she ignored him.

"You think they even bothered to buy candy?" I asked.

"If they're giving out anything at that house, it's bullets," said Charlene, brushing sand from her elbow. "That's what Mr. Holliday gave out last year."

Mr. Holliday thought it was a treat to drop in a few bullets with the Tootsie Rolls and Lifesavers kids got from other houses.

Grady nodded. "I knew a boy who found BBs in his bag. Mr. Holliday put 'em in with the candy. The kid tried to eat one. Almost broke a filling out, my mom said."

"Grady, you don't have a mom," said Deanna. It was just the sort of thing she'd say. I wondered why Grady put up with her. She was always making him go shoplifting with her and then saying mean things about him.

Grady blushed, a crimson that rose to his crewcut. "Aunt Liz. She's like a mom, even if she lives in Florida."

For the first time, I had wanted to stick up for Grady. "My Aunt Sylvia would be like that, if our mom died."

A shiver ran down my arms at that memory. I knew what Aunt Sylvia would say about our going to Mr. Holliday's house on Halloween, with BBs and mock lynchings.

"We don't have costumes," Charlene told Deanna. "How can we go trick-or-treating?"

Deanna laughed. "There's no treat. It's all tricks." We didn't need costumes, she said, since we were just going to Joe Holliday's house. And if all he had were bullets, they had eggs for sure. "C'mon," she said to Charlene. Even though Deanna was still mostly my friend, I was glad she invited Charlene. We were both lonely.

"Okay," said Charlene, without even asking me.

We eased our way down the Holliday's dark drive. I could still hear Loretta Holliday saying, "Joe's back," and see that line of black marks on the front door. But now there was cackling somewhere, like a witch.

"Record's scratched," said Grady, and we laughed, like we'd known all along it was just a record. It felt good to laugh. Deanna clutched the sack full of eggs, and Grady had taken the toilet paper to hide under his jacket. It didn't feel like much ammunition against Joe Holliday.

You had to look up at the sky to see your way down their driveway, it was so dark. Against the sky rose the silhouette of the pine trees lining the drive, but I couldn't see any white sheets out there. Maybe Mr. Holliday was out of town.

But – whump! Charlene screamed. A dummy in a suit and tie dropped from a tree with a noose around his neck. We started to run, but Deanna grabbed me. All that shoplifting must have given her nerves of steel. "Wait," she whispered. "It's Levi Litvak. Look." The head lolled to one side, as if appealing for mercy. I glanced at the pompadour toupee glued to the top and the yellow socks on the dangling ankles. On the back of the head was pinned a little round cap.

"No." My voice croaked like a biology frog before dissection. Deanna reached into her sack, and I heard the steady *whump whump* of the eggs she was throwing. It was a sickening sound, and Loretta and Kathy would have to clean up the mess. I hoped they were hitting the ground instead of that battered little house, but I didn't turn to see.

A shout came from the bushes, and a stocky figure rose from the shadows. "Hey! What're you doing?" he yelled. A red glow that must have been a cigarette wagged with the words. Then his face emerged, the same face I'd see at the Pack-A-Sack with a cigarette scrunched in those thin lips and the eyes squinting as he stood at the counter buying beer. He always wore a sleeveless camouflage hunting vest, open down the front, so you could see a tattooed claw reaching up from the neck of his shirt.

The brown and gray patterns on his camouflage vest were right in front of me. A stubble of beard darkened the lower half of Mr. Holliday's face, and his eyes were as cold and flat as turquoise beads. He had never noticed me before. He'd even stepped on my toe once when he left the Pack-A-Sack and kept on going without saying a word.

He saw me then, though. "You kids get back here!" he yelled, as the red glow fell to the ground.

We ran with the sound of his boots pounding briefly after us. We were all out of breath when we got to the street. "That dummy was Levi Litvak," said Deanna. "I swear."

"Nah," Grady said. "Why would he hang somebody who's already dead?"

"Maybe he's not dead, like people say," said Deanna. "He got away and he's living in. . ."

"You're scaring Charlene." He tried to put his arm around her, but she shrugged away.

"We're not scared." I could see what might be tears in Charlene's eyes. I asked Deanna, "Did you hit the house?"

"Yeah," she grinned. "He'll never know it was us."

How much of me had he seen in that dim light? His eyes seemed like they could see in the dark, and I wished

I'd worn a mask.

Charlene said she hadn't looked at the dummy. "The only dummy there was Joe Holliday." We laughed till our sides hurt, like it was the funniest thing we'd ever heard. That was how scared we were.

The face of that dummy stayed with me for weeks, until something else replaced it: Jack Ruby's gun, and Lee Harvey Oswald doubling over. The day we heard the news about Kennedy's death, someone stepped on a frog in the hall outside the boy's restroom, a smear of green translucent belly and blood and gaping mouth. Somebody had smashed it under the heel of his shoe. You could see the imprint, and how deliberate it had been.

Aunt Sylvia called that night and all I could think about was the frog, how awful kids could be. Someone cheered when the news about the President came over the PA system, and afterward my science teacher went right on talking about how the digestive system connects the body. "How could he keep talking about that?" I asked Aunt Sylvia. "And why would anybody smush a poor frog?"

Her voice was raw. "I don't know. There's good in the world, don't forget, even after a year like this one."

"Mama liked Kennedy," I said. "Did you know?" Mama didn't tell just anyone, but she'd have told Aunt Sylvia. I remembered how, the year before, when James Meredith integrated Ole Miss, the students had yelled at the federal troops, "Go to hell, JFK," and how mad Mama had been when we watched it on the news. "Look how hateful their faces are," she said. I wondered how those students felt now that he was really dead. Maybe they were celebrating with beer at their fraternity houses.

"Of course she loved Kennedy. He was a good leader for us." Then Aunt Sylvia's voice rose, a false note, and she changed the subject. "Do you girls like the Beatles?"

I'd seen their faces on a record album, *Meet the Beatles*, at the five and dime store at Big Circle Shopping Center. Charlene and I were pooling our allowances to buy it. Their faces were half in darkness, half in light, like half-moons, the way I felt most of the time. But that wasn't why I liked them. It was the music, the way it took you to places you'd never been. Even Elvis hadn't done it this way for me. Elvis sang like he could see right through your clothes. The guys in the Beatles sang like they were happy, like they had a secret you could learn only by moving to the rhythm, dancing for the sheer joy of being one with the music.

"Sure," I said. "We're saving up to buy their record. Have you heard 'I Want to Hold Your Hand'? I get chills."

"Well, you remember that feeling. It's joy. Don't forget it." She breathed a sigh into the phone, but then her voice sounded brighter. "Tell you what. You and Charlene start looking for that album in the mail. I'll mark it fragile. You spend your money on something else."

Sure enough, a few days later, a square flat package arrived. It was a cool day for November, and Charlene and I took it inside to rip it open. There, staring at us, were the four faces of John, Paul, Ringo, and George. Charlene traced the angles of George's solemn face. "He's adorable." She stood over the floor furnace, her skirt billowing like a hot air balloon. "He looks so intelligent."

But it was Paul that I studied. "I like this guy." I tapped his nose. "He's got great eyes."

"That's Paul McCartney. Don't you know anything?" said Charlene. She started to rip the cellophane, then stopped, staring at the label. "It's in stereo," she said slowly.

"So what?" I asked. "We can still hear it, can't we?"

"We need mono." She looked sad and a little pissed. "Doesn't Aunt Sylvia know Daddy hasn't bought us a stereo? What does she think we are, rich?" She stared at the little box-like record player we kept on the dresser.

A note had fallen out. "Enjoy," it said in Aunt Sylvia's angular scrawl. "Remember the 'joy' in that word."

"Don't be mad at her. She's being nice to us," I said. "We'll exchange it at Big Circle. Look, the plastic's okay."

We got two dollars back from the exchange to mono, and picked out new Cutex lipsticks with the money. Charlene bought one that smelled like Daddy's Halloween caramels.

From then on, the Beatles' music filled the house. I played trumpet softly to "This Boy," and added jazz riffs on "I Saw Her Standing There," though Charlene complained. It seemed to change the colors of the walls, to raise the ceiling of that small house a little higher. Mama would have approved.

PART TWO

MISSISSIPPI 1967 - 1968

Chapter Six

On the day Daddy re-married, the sky over Biloxi was the color of cardboard, gray like the inside of the shoe box that my powder blue, dyed-to-match pumps came in.

Charlene and I should have known he would marry again, but it was a shock when he did. He was too lonely to stay single. We'd heard him talking to Henry Pickens. Daddy's voice was soft, but you could always hear Mr. Pickens' voice. "You're talking about the virile needs of a man," he told Daddy in the living room. "That's legitimate business. A man can't deny his needs."

"Gross," said Charlene, and put the Beatles's album, "Revolver," on our new stereo console and cranked it up so loud that Daddy and Mr. Pickens went outside to talk.

Almost four years to the day after Mama died, Daddy married Marilyn Dixon in a ceremony with the Justice of the Peace and what Daddy called the immediate family, which included Henry Pickens, grinning and hugging the bride. Aunt Sylvia couldn't come, something about a gallery opening, but I had a feeling she didn't want to be there.

The ceremony was simple, but Marilyn wore a gown with a train that almost filled the Justice's office. The color was called "candlelight," since the wedding was her second. The rest of us stood with our heels against the wall, trying not to step on the satin. Marilyn was only twenty-six, and her father had the same gray in his sideburns that Daddy did. When the J.P. pronounced them "man and wife," and Daddy kissed Marilyn, Charlene turned her head and refused to watch. Marilyn's father looked down at his shoes.

After we threw rice at them on the courthouse steps, they drove to Pensacola while Charlene and I stayed with our grandparents. Aunt Sylvia flew down to join us at Grandma's house during Daddy's honeymoon. Grandma and I took the truck to New Orleans to pick her up. There was no room for Charlene, unless someone sat in the truckbed coming back, and she wasn't about to ride in the back. "Looking like a redneck," she said. Grandma drummed her fingers along the dashboard like she was playing the piano. "Laissez les bons temps rouler," she said, and turned to me with her bright little blue eyes and sunken smile. "That's Cajun talk. Let the good times roll." She tapped her lace-up oxfords to imaginary music, ignoring how it made her brown stockings pool in wrinkles around her ankles. "I've missed Sylvia," she said. For the first time, part of Mama sparked in Grandma. Or maybe I'd just never seen it before, it had been so buried beneath the finger-shaking and lectures.

At the airport, a silver jet wheeled down the runway and men rolled a staircase up to it when it stopped. After a few men in suits descended, a figure came sweeping down the steps wearing a green and purple sari, with a scarf wrapped around the top of her head like a small turban, the ends tumbling down over one shoulder. Black wraparound sunglasses covered her eyes and cheeks. She looked like an Andy Warhol fantasy. Grandma and I

89

watched from behind the glass in the terminal.

"Where's Sylvia?" Grandma asked, squinting at the emptied plane.

"That's her," I whispered, afraid to point out the creature walking across the runway toward the terminal with the normal passengers. I almost hadn't recognized her, myself. Where the turban ended, her hair stood out from her head in long, frizzled curls. It might've been the hair of one of Michelangelo's angels, streaked purple. She walked with her shoulders thrust back, chin high, bouncing on her toes like a dancer about to leap into a grand jeté. That was how I knew her. The black fishnet stockings, long, straight hair, and tight beatnik skirts were gone.

"Looks like they got the voltage on her shock treatment too high," said a man beside us, wearing a baseball cap and windbreaker with "Campus Crusade" on the back.

"Is that what Christ would say?" I asked, and he turned away. Fortunately, Grandma was hard of hearing. But it was true, it looked as if she'd stuck her finger in a socket. When Aunt Sylvia moved her head, surveying the group of onlookers, her hair looked like a bush with a few flames glowing in it, blown by an unseen wind. It was spectacular.

A smile broke out on her face and we pushed toward each other through the onlookers. She was as thin as ever, and I felt like I could crush her with a hug. European-style, she kissed both my cheeks, and her perfume wafted gently to my nose, like an incense from when I'd last gone to mass months ago.

"Sylvia?" Grandma's voice cracked, and Sylvia pulled off the sunglasses. Her eyes sparkled with tears, and she bent to put her arms gently around Grandma's curved back. Grandma put both hands on either side of Sylvia's face and beamed. "You're always beautiful, just like Bernice

90

was," she said, and Aunt Sylvia's face relaxed. No lectures.

On the way home, Aunt Sylvia crowded into the front seat between Grandma and me, her hair brushing my face, and she had to lean into Grandma to make room for me to shift. Every time she did, Grandma patted her knee.

Grandma tried to make the week-end special by baking a pound cake, but it was awful. The last time we'd stayed on the farm, Mama had just died, and now the wedding felt like another death. Charlene was so upset she could hardly talk. When she did, she said things no one wanted to hear.

"Just think of what they're *doing*. A honeymoon, for pete's sake," she said. "Gross. She's too young for Daddy."

"That's private, Charlene. Don't think about it," said Aunt Sylvia. "Your dad's finally happy. Try to be glad."

Charlene moaned and put a pillow over her head.

"People need some time alone after they get married, that's all," said Aunt Sylvia. "It doesn't mean your dad's leaving you. You're seventeen, old enough to know that, honey." She tugged at the pillow. "You'll suffocate."

"I wish he'd leave us." Charlene emerged, her nose and right cheek pink from being pressed against the pillow. "Then we could live with you in New York."

Aunt Sylvia patted Charlene's cheek. "I'd like that, but Harry couldn't stand being away from his girls."

"Sure he could," said Charlene. "Look how much time he spent with Marilyn. And that was before they got married. He'll forget all about us now." Ever since Daddy had met Marilyn, Charlene hadn't been happy.

"Why don't you wait a couple of weeks, till the anniversary of Mama's death?" Charlene had asked, when he told us his wedding plans.

Daddy looked like somebody had slapped him. We were sitting in the kitchen around a chocolate cake he'd bought at the bakery. He probably knew we'd need cheering up, but it would take more than chocolate for Charlene. She sneered, and the brightness in Daddy's eyes faded.

"It's been four years, darlin'." He reached for her hand, his own trembling. "I know it won't be easy. . ."

Charlene pulled away. "I'm not calling anybody else Mama," she said, and stalked off.

"She wants you to call her Marilyn," Daddy called, just before the bathroom door slammed.

But I was happy for him. He was so lonely we could hear him sighing in his bedroom when the lights were out at night. Charlene would call, "Goodnight, Daddy. I love you," in a false, cheerful voice, forcing him to strangle out, "Love you, too, darlin'." I hated her for that little ritual at night. Couldn't she see he needed to be left alone?

After he found Marilyn, his spirits lifted. Sometimes, we even heard him whistling. Marilyn was a grocery clerk at the Piggly Wiggly, and they'd talk every time Daddy shopped. She slipped him coupons and wrote recipes for the groceries he was buying, making people wait. The manager almost fired her after they complained, so Daddy started meeting her after work. For recipes, he said. But soon he was taking her for drinks at the Green Lizard Lounge. By then, alcohol was legal in nearly every county, and Grady Pickens' dad was selling used cars in Gulfport. "I'll be a little late tonight, girls," he'd say, adjusting the pads in his shoes before shoe-horning them on. "Here's a number if you need me," and he'd scribble down the phone number at the Lounge.

"How can he do that?" Charlene hissed. "Mama used

to sing there, for pete's sake." When he took Marilyn to the Shriners' dance on New Years' Eve, we knew life was certainly going to change.

He was whistling when he looped his tie into a knot, and then rubbed his palms together to warm the pomade for his hair. "You look great," I said, and he kissed my cheek. Charlene turned before he could reach her.

"Wait'll Marilyn sees Daddy on his little bicycle at the circus," said Charlene. "She'll ditch him in a minute." Every March, the Gulf Coast Shriners held a circus, and Daddy was a clown. When we were little, we loved it, watching the sawdust fly under the wheels of the minia-ture bicycle Daddy could drive faster than anyone, his knees pumping like pistons. We were proud of him then. Now, it was unthinkable that anyone would want to marry a man who paraded around in a wig and red nose, even if it was once a year. Surely Marilyn would leave him then. But when the circus came, she cheered harder than any-one, jumping up and clapping her hands. Once she even threw her fist into the air the way cheerleaders did at pep rallies, while Charlene and I watched from a spot by the Coke machine.

"Turned on by a clown," said Charlene, her lip curled. "Disgusting."

Afterwards Marilyn bought the satin wedding gown with the longest train I'd ever seen.

When she was seventeen, Marilyn had married a guy named Jimmy Taylor who worked at Drummond's Five and Dime Store. He was killed in Vietnam. All I remem-bered about him was his blonde hair and his boredom, like he didn't want to be stocking the shelves with toilet paper or toothpaste. He never smiled — Charlene and I both remembered that. Though Marilyn was twenty-six now, sometimes she seemed younger than Charlene and me. We were taller by two inches, and Daddy could put his arm around her without reaching up. Maybe that was what he saw in her. She sure didn't have Mama's style.

The first time I saw her without her Piggly Wiggly apron, she was wearing Capri pants and sling-back pumps, though no one wore Capris anymore. Her hair looked like a light brown cap, stiff with hairspray. When Daddy took us all to dinner at Abby's Little Diner near the Back Bay for oyster po' boys, all she talked about was 'Nam, and how we should "bomb the gooks." It was supposed to be a time for us to get to know each other, but she didn't ask Charlene and me a single question, not even the boring ones, like how school was going, or did we have a boyfriend yet.

"They ought to run those draft dodgers out of the country." She slid across the formica table on both elbows, like it was something confidential. "You know who could do it? Joe Holliday, that's who." Mr. Holliday had taken to hanging out at the downtown Post Office in his camouflage fatigues with a banner, "Don't Negotiate. Annihilate."

"He hates everybody." I started to tell her about the Halloween bullets, but Charlene interrupted.

"Anybody who likes Joe Holliday is a freak," she said, jabbing an oyster with her fork.

"I don't like the man, honey, but this country's in trouble." She stirred her coffee with a scratched spoon.

Daddy kept saying, "It'll be okay, don't you worry," like he didn't hear us at all. He hardly said much anymore, but at least he was happy .He was too busy trying to cheer up Marilyn now. Once, when Marilyn was crying about Jimmy, I heard Daddy say, "He's in Heaven. He wouldn't want you to live your life alone, pretty little sugar muffin like you."

Sugar muffin! I stopped listening when I heard those

words. What did Daddy know about Mama and Levi Litvak? Did he still dream about Mama? Then I wondered if Marilyn was his way of getting back at Mama, proving that he could have a sugar muffin, too, though he still put fresh flowers on her grave every week. Marilyn didn't know about that.

The news that Daddy and Marilyn were engaged stirred up gossip again about Mama and Levi Litvak. People dug their claws into how Mama and Levi Litvak died and kept making up new stories, trying to nail down the truth, like they were sealing a coffin so it could finally be buried.

There were still rumors that Levi Litvak hadn't burned up in the crash. He'd gotten away with murder, they said. "Why, look at those three civil rights workers, making us out to be a bunch of fools," Charlene's Sunday school teacher told Deanna's mom in the beauty shop. "Anybody with any sense knows those bodies in that swamp weren't theirs. They're up North, laughing their heads off while our law-abiding officers are accused of something that happened back in 1964. So who knows whose ashes might've been in Levi Litvak's car?" Though Deanna didn't call much any more, she had to tell me that Mama's murderer might be alive.

Levi Litvak was working on a cruise ship in the Bahamas, some folks said. The elementary school principal spotted him on TV, doing stunts for Matt Dillon on *Gunsmoke*. Miss Tate, the hairdresser, said he'd made a fortune at a blackjack table in Reno. There was a mighty big cover-up, she told women while she twisted rollers into their hair. Could've been the same hired thugs who did Kennedy in. Mrs. Guest said she'd seen Levi Litvak giving the news on a station in Houston when she visited her sister there. He'd gained weight and grown a mustache, but he had the exact same voice, she said. The story of the man who killed Mama became a legend in Biloxi.

So Mama herself became famous, even as far away as New Orleans. She'd always wanted fame, to have the recognition that went with it. But not that way, as the victim in a murder people gossiped about all over the Gulf Coast. I decided Levi Litvak must've really loved Mama, to do what he did. Either that, or she'd driven him totally nuts. Mama did have a kind of power over people. It drove Daddy to wear elevator lifts in his shoes to this very day. Even after all those stories about Mama, Daddy carried his head high.

Mrs. Tate said Daddy was a hero for putting flowers on the grave of a runaway wife. She told Daddy she was thankful he and Marilyn had found each other. Poor Jimmy Taylor, dead in Vietnam, they said, but how nice Marilyn found a good man. That was what Mrs. Drummond, whose husband owned the five and dime store, told Mrs. Guest. The gossip didn't stop, though every time Grandma Tattershall went to town, she told people to mind their own business.

When Daddy married, my friends avoided me again, as if they'd get sucked into misery if they got close. Charlene joined Youth for Christ, where the kids were willing to forgive her for having a mother who was murdered. After the first meeting, she came home glowing with excitement. "One of the kids didn't even know about it!" she said.

"Didn't know what?" I knew what she meant. I just wanted to make her say it.

"She didn't know Mama was murdered, dummy," she said, but she was too happy to stop smiling.

"I'm not the one who's a dummy. That's pathetic," I told her. "You think you can erase the past? Erase Mama?"

She stopped smiling. "Sometimes I hate Mama. Messing around with Levi Litvak, ruining our lives."

"She loved us." I sank down on the bed and stared at her, like my sister was someone I'd never seen before.

"Daddy wasn't good enough for her, that's why she did it," said Charlene. "Who'd marry Daddy? Marilyn, she's good enough." She stood at the mirror, pushing at her hair with the tips of her fingers.

"You hate both Mama and Daddy? What about me?"

"I love you, and you know it." She spat the words out like nails. Those were the last words she spoke to me for a month, but then one night, at bedtime, she came up with a sack of pink rollers and offered to set my hair. "You know how your hair would look *good*? With curls around your face."

Ever since she'd joined Youth for Christ, Charlene set her hair on pink curlers at night. But I stuck to the Beatles look, ironing my bangs so they'd lie straight.

"What's wrong with it now?" I asked, glad she was talking at last.

"I won't dignify that with an answer," she said.

"Do you dignify *anything*?" I muttered, but she was too busy turning my head to the mirror to even hear.

"Look," she pointed at my reflection. "It's hanging in strings like a hippie."

"I like it," I said, and tossed the long ends, trying to prove how shiny and pretty it could be, but she wasn't looking.

She said, "Hopeless," and wrapped a strand of her own hair around the curler, securing it with a pink plastic toothpick. "You don't even have friends anymore," she said, surveying herself in the mirror.

It was true. Deanna never called, unless it was gossip about Levi Litvak. When Biloxi sank its teeth into something, it chewed for a long time.

"You don't even have a boyfriend. But worse things have happened to better people, I guess," she continued. She'd finished her hair and could now devote her full attention to my life. "Look." She pulled out a boy's high school ring and put it on her left ring finger.

"Whose is that?" She hadn't been talking about Art Johnson, not since he got sent to Parris Island.

"Ernie Crenshaw gave it to me at Youth for Christ."

So that's why she was being friendly. "Who's he?" The phone rang a lot for Charlene lately, that was all I knew.

"You wouldn't know," she said importantly. "He's a senior at Libertyburg High." Libertyburg was a little town near the Green Lizard Lounge. She took a red rubber band, one of those that came around the newspaper, and strapped the ring to her finger by crossing the band beneath. "That's how you do it. Some girls melt wax under the stone to make it fit, but I wouldn't want to defile his ring."

"Daddy won't like it," I said. "He'll say it's too close to being engaged."

"He won't notice." She put a hair net over the curlers.

"I can still see those curlers, you know," I said. "That ring's even harder to hide."

"Don't worry," said Charlene. She plumped her pillow and smoothed the case gently, as if it might be Ernie.

"What's Ernie like?" I was too curious to ignore her.

She smiled and sat on her bed. "Gorgeous. Dark hair and brown eyes, and this great smile. I may be in love."

After that, it was still hard to talk to her. When she wasn't with Ernie, she was on the phone, or floating around the house in a trance. They went out every week-end, both Friday and Saturday nights. Once, she came home and told me about it, in the darkness of our bedroom while our transistor radio crackled with far-away stations.

"A cop caught us tonight." She slipped on her gown.

"How fast were you going?" I asked.

She laughed and dotted some pimple cream on her chin. "We were parking, silly. You know, by the baseball field. Then there's this light shining in the car."

"What did you do?" I searched her face, but she turned out the light.

"Covered up. He went away. All pleasure isn't sin, you know." It sounded like something she'd learned from Ernie, a guy who would pick up girls at Youth for Christ.

Covered up? The cracked plastic seats of Ernie's Plymouth must get cold against bare skin. An image of Charlene and Ernie exploring each other, with just the steamy windows between them and a cop's flashlight, came into my mind, but I pushed it out. "Don't let him take advantage of you," I said, feeling like Marilyn.

Instead her voice was hushed. "His body, it's wonderful, Jubilee."

I wished the army hadn't drafted Art Johnson. There wouldn't have been room for Ernie then. Mama wouldn't have liked her talking that way, and I tried to tell her so.

"You're just jealous," she said.

One night she came into our bedroom late and turned on the light to wake me. "Watch," she said. "It's important." I held one hand to shield my eyes against the light while she walked across the room in her mini-skirt, then back. Her pantyhose looked twisted. "Am I walking different?"

"No." All I wanted was to go back to sleep.

"Good." She put on her nightgown and flipped the light out, but then a thought came into my mind and kept me awake. Girls whispered that you'd walk different when you weren't a virgin anymore. Boys would notice, they said.

At breakfast, I whispered, "Why did you wake me up to watch you walk?"

She stared at her cereal. "I got a blister on my heel."

"A blister?" Marilyn put down the spatula and went to get a Band-Aid for her. She wanted to do little things like that. I was beginning to like her, but Charlene would still barely talk to her.

She slid the Band-Aid into her purse when Marilyn came back. "I'll put it on later," she said.

After that, Charlene didn't tell me much about Ernie.

Sometimes the past came roaring back, like a monster in a nightmare, when all you can do is run in place. Before lunch at school, I was passing the teachers' lounge, when I heard the chemistry teacher, Mr. Langstrom, tell someone that Daddy had married a good woman, even if Marilyn was almost young enough to be his daughter. A hot little number, he said, and I stopped to listen. "But that Bernice, she was something else. Racy in high school, wasn't she? Remember when she said she was singing in some New Orleans club? Don't you know a gal as good lookin' as Bernice Tattershall had a sugar daddy over there in the French Quarter?"

Another man chortled, but it was high, a giggle. "At the prom, she ate light bulbs before she sang. Remember that? Nibbled at the glass a little, like this." I could imagine his teeth moving, but I didn't know who was talking. "Said it made her singin' voice better."

"I hear she ate those light bulbs only if they were turned on." It was Langstrom this time. They laughed together, with that chortling sound again, then it died away, and the other voice spoke.

"'Course, it's a shame what happened."

"Don't pay attention to them. They're jerks." A boy

was standing at my elbow. Robbie Godbold. He was the smartest boy in algebra class. He once wore his hair so long the assistant principal sent him home to get it cut. It was touching his collar, and that was the test at Tallulah High. The only person who paid much attention to Robbie was the algebra teacher. She called him "Robert," and used his tests as examples for how to do the equations. The football players hated him for that. That, and his tie-dyed tee shirts. The shirts clung to his skinny chest, showing his ribs and shoulder blades. The football players called him "the only hippie in Mississippi," and one of them tried to pick a fight with him once. Robbie talked his way out of it.

"They're stupid." He pointed to the Teachers' Lounge.

I pushed past him to the cafeteria. The smell of boiled plastic trays and American cheese filled my nose, and even after I ran outside and threw up on the grass, I couldn't stop smelling that boiled plastic.

"Don't listen to them." It was Robbie Godbold again. He held a tissue, trying to wipe the vomit from my mouth.

"I'm sick, that's all." I turned to walk to the truck, but he followed.

"Are you well enough to drive?" Behind his glasses, his eyes studied me like I was an equation he couldn't solve.

"Why do you care?" I asked, but I felt mean when I saw the look on his face.

He was gripping his notebooks so tight the pages wrinkled. "I like you." He smiled a little and shrugged. "You're good at math."

"I know," I said.

"Maybe we can study together sometime." He paused while I tried to think of something to say. "Sure you're okay?"

"I'm fine." I climbed in the truck and moved off, the wind cool against my face. I headed for the coastal highway and drove for a long time. That night, I told Charlene how Mr. Langstrom had said Mama was racy and ate light bulbs.

"Jubilee!" She was beaming. "He means those race records Mama had. Everybody admired Mama. Are you sure he said light bulbs? Maybe he meant some kind of food, like turnips are a bulb, you know. They call it a rhizome. We've been studying it in biology. That's what he meant." She pulled a tee-shirt over her curlers and studied herself in the mirror. "I look like Mama, a little."

"You said you hated her," I said, and her face fell for a moment.

"Will you forgive me for those words?" she asked.

"Why'd you say it?"

Her mouth clamped down as she rummaged through a drawer for a lipstick. "You know I didn't mean it. I'm glad I look like Mama. You look like Daddy; what they call a 'handsome woman'." Her eyes darted at me. "That's what they say about Jane Wyman, you know. And she's not so bad."

In my mind, I could hear the "race records" Mama had collected, the ones I rescued from the garage where Marilyn stored them in boxes on a shelf, beside the decaying Piggly Wiggly bag with the poppy scarf inside. No one had ever bothered to throw the scarf out. I'd taken the bag, too, along with the old recordings of the deep, throaty voices that told gritty tales of life gone bad, songs Mama taught herself to play on the piano while she sang. She had tried to teach me the words, but now I could barely remember them.

My face felt hot. I had to tell her the truth. "That's not what he meant, Charlene. Racy, that's nothing to do with race records." I told her that Mr. Langstrom meant that Mama had gone bad herself. It was embarrassing to know more than my big sister.

"That's not true," she said, so I got the dictionary, but pointing to the definition didn't feel like a triumph.

"That creep," Charlene said. "We'll put sugar in his gas tank. He drives that banged-up green Ford."

I closed the dictionary. "He's not worth it." But I felt like the little lost sheep Mama used to sing about, the one that kept trying to forget. I turned out the light. After a while I heard Charlene crying in the dark.

"Bastard Langstrom!" she whispered, and I got up from my bed and snuggled beside her. I buried my face in the bony spot between her shoulder blades, feeling her shake with tears, and then my own tears came. We fell asleep that way, nestled together like spoons, like kids. I was the little sister again, my arms wrapped around her middle from behind, as if she could face things I couldn't.

The next day, I decided to talk to the school counselor, Mr. Woods, about what Mr. Langstrom said. I'd get that idiot fired, I thought. It was the sort of thing Mama would've done. That's what I told myself when I screwed up my courage to knock on Mr. Woods' door before gym started. It was open a crack, and I could see him looking at some papers. I tapped the wood. He nodded at the chair in front of his desk. "Come on in," he said. He sounded impatient, but I sat down. "What can I do for you?" he asked, still shuffling some papers.

"Something awful happened yesterday," I said, trying to think of what Mama would say to defend Charlene and me. "I heard Mr. Langstrom say our mother was racy in high school. It's mean to talk that way about someone who's dead," I told Mr. Woods. "It's mean and and. . ." I tried to think of the words Mama would've used, "and

103

downright unprofessional."

He locked both hands behind his bald head and stared at me while I talked. I tugged at my mini-skirt, wishing I hadn't worn it. He might send me home. Little hairs edged out of his nostrils and fluttered as he breathed.

I told him about the lost sheep Mama used to sing about, and how could that be racy? When I sang some of the lyrics to show him how innocent they were, he interrupted.

"We know you have a good voice, Jubilee. You don't have to prove it." He surveyed me. "You and your mother are a lot alike. You ought to know better than to eavesdrop outside the teachers' lounge. We've got enough problems at Tallulah without you kids loitering in the halls." The phone rang, and he picked up. "Can't right now. Be with you soon as I'm through with this girl." He laughed, a chortle, like a man's giggle, and a shiver ran down my spine. It was the same laugh I'd heard from the teachers' lounge. He hung up and turned to me. "School policy doesn't allow loitering." He picked at a hangnail, and his eyes and mouth suddenly looked droopy, like they were melting. "When did you stop masturbating?" His eyes flicked up at me, and his voice sounded different, like it, too, had melted.

My mind spun so fast I could hardly think. "You need a new light bulb, Mr. Woods. It's dim in here." His bushy eyebrows shot up, and I glanced at the wall clock. "Gym class," I said, and walked out, feeling his eyes on my back. How many other girls had he looked at that way, like a dog salivating? They all deserved to be fired. From then on, I'd take any course I could to graduate early. I was already in advanced English and math, but I'd even double up on gym, if it meant escaping Tallulah.

I walked straight out of that school, right past the gym

where the girls were leaving the locker rooms in their blue shorts and white shirts. Deanna picked up a volley ball and served it straight into the net, on purpose. It bounced against the bleachers with a bang, and the last thing I saw was Kathy Holliday running to get it. On the boys' side of the curtain that divided the gym, Coach Woods was giving a couple of boys "licks," hitting them with a paddle if they wouldn't say they wanted George Wallace to be President. It was radical to like Nixon, but I was secretly for McCarthy. Robbie Godbold had a McCarthy bumper sticker on his locker, but someone ripped it off until there was just a band of glue left, and the word "Commie" scrawled in red marker.

I heard the whack of the paddle, and hoped Robbie wasn't on the other end of it. But all I could do was save myself.

The sky was dark with clouds, but the cheerleaders practiced anyway, looking like wooden puppets with desperate faces. "Give me a 'T,'" they cried, and jumped with arms outstretched. "Give me an 'A.' They planted their feet apart, trying to look like the letter. "Give me an 'L.'"

I wouldn't give Tallulah High anything.

Chapter Seven

I didn't stop walking until the furthest parking lot, where I swung into the pick-up truck. At home, I lay on the couch, telling Marilyn I was sick, which wasn't far from the truth. She brought me a bottle of Coca-Cola with a straw and a hot water bottle for the cramps she thought I had. She asked which of the two channels I wanted on the TV. It was like she wished she had a little kid, a baby, to care for.

I half-dozed in front of *As the World Turns*, hearing Jeff tell Penny that their song would always be "Younger Than Springtime." Like Robbie and me, I thought, wondering what it would be like to study with him, what his hand would feel like if I reached over and held it. Our song could be "A Summer Place." What would Robbie do if I told him that Mr. Woods had asked me about masturbating? Would he beat him up or get mad at me for telling him? Either seemed possible.

As the closing music came on for *As the World Turns*, a siren began, escalating till I thought a fire truck was heading straight for our house. The April sky had gone from gray to green, the color of the celadon vase Marilyn had put on the mantel, a gift from her first wedding.

Marilyn ran in and grabbed me. "Tornado! I saw it." She pulled me out to the truck, the roar growing like a train in the night, only faster. For the first time, Marilyn got inside Mama's pick-up. She tried to crank the motor, but it wouldn't start. She was barefoot, and she had to point her toes to stretch to the accelerator. Nothing happened, just a whining sound you could barely hear for the roaring.

The long gray finger twisted out of the sky, heading toward the house. "Pump the clutch!" I screamed.

"Hell!" Marilyn cried and threw the keys on the seat. She pulled me back inside our house and together we squatted in the hall, Marilyn's arms tight around my shoulders, her head bent over mine like a bird with its baby. Despite the screaming wind, I felt love more than fear. Marilyn's cotton shirt reeked with sweat, she was so scared, but she never let go of me.

Wind rattled the whole house, and a hard rain began

pelting the roof. Something outside clanged, but there in Marilyn's arms, it was like Mama was back and I was swimming underwater, someone's arms holding me safe. I knew what Charlene meant when she described how Brother Beeker had held her while God washed her sins away in the baptistery.

Then, as quickly as it happened, there was dead quiet. We got up and before I could feel embarrassed, Marilyn ran to the TV, where a weatherman had replaced the soap opera. He said a tornado watch was on. "Stay tuned," he said, and I couldn't help but think Levi Litvak would've known more, where it was going, who it would kill. He would've known about the gray finger already raking the earth.

"A watch!" Marilyn cried. "What on earth does he know? Hell, I watched and *saw*!"

We raced outside. Trees lay in splinters everywhere, so thick you couldn't see the street. It was like a playground where kids had dumped a giant can of tinker toys. Mrs. Guest came toward us, her apron flapping. "That was close." She blinked slowly. "That thing went over like a freight train. I hope this is the worst." She picked up an azalea bush that was whipped to the ground, its blossoms pink and muddy.

As if she were in slow motion, Marilyn started picking up the branches in the yard, so I helped, neither of us saying a word as we piled them by the fence. Some were stripped of bark, so white they looked like broken bones. The sour smell of her shirt wafted over as we worked together silently, and I could still feel the warmth of her arms around me when we'd crouched in the hall. In those strange moments, I loved her so much I had to keep blinking the dampness from my eyes.

Mrs. Guest picked her way through the mess and

107

peered up the street. "Why, here comes Harry," she said, and waved.

Daddy was running, as well as he could, through the terrible rubble. "Everybody okay?" He looked at us and saw the tears in my eyes. He didn't know it was because I'd felt so loved, almost like Mama was back. "You okay, darlin'?" He wrapped his arms around me and one of the tears rolled down my cheek into my mouth.

Daddy drew Marilyn into his arms, too. "I was on my way home for lunch, and I swear that twister picked up the station wagon, and then the wheels would bounce back on the road. That's how hard that wind was. Now the roads are blocked. I parked at the bus stop and walked."

"Oh Harry!" Marilyn threw her arms around him and kissed him. It was the first time I'd ever seen her really care about Daddy. She was usually too busy talking about her own problems to think about him. "How bad was it?"

"Let's see who needs help."

We made our way down the street, climbing over full-grown trees, and Daddy kept saying, "It came close. It sure came close," and then he stopped. At the corner, the next street looked like the worst things in Revelation had come to pass. Charlene would say God had raged over us and judged us wicked. Some more than others. Tommy McCarty's yellow frame house stood upside down, right on the same spot where it had been built a couple of years before. The roof was crushed, and the foundation faced the sky, concrete cinder blocks sticking up like jagged teeth against the gray clouds. A power line lay zigzagged across the yard, a black snake waiting to strike.

Daddy's face went white. "You girls go back on home. Folks are going to need some serious help out here."

We picked a path back home, and silently Marilyn and I started picking up more limbs. Underneath the green branches, all over the front yard, plastic flowers began to appear, scattered like a sudden garden of yellow and red daisies.

"Look!" Charlene cried. I heard her voice before I knew she was there, her shoes planted in the mud. "It's a bouquet from God, a sign that everything is okay." She closed her eyes, and I knew she was praying.

"What the hell?" Marilyn reached down for a red daisy. Daddy told her he didn't like her to curse in front of Charlene and me, but today she couldn't help herself. "Made in China," she read the tag on the plastic daisy. "You mean that thing blew all the way from China?"

In the mud we found toy matchbox cars and broken dinner plates. I picked up a shard. "The price tag is here. Drummond's Five and Dime." A knot tightened in my chest.

"Everything okay here?" Robbie Godbold was coming across our lawn, pulling branches out of his way as he walked.

But before I could answer, Marilyn made a cry, a noise from deep in her throat and she dropped the plastic flower as if the red were a blood stain. "Sweet heaven. It's the shopping center. That tornado must've blown right through it. Oh lord have mercy."

In the distance, sirens wailed again, but this time an ambulance raced past, then a fire truck and police cars, until a parade of them backed up, flashing in front of the house. A great pine tree completely blocked the road. People ran through the lawns and muddy street toward the tree. Daddy was pushing with all his might on the trunk, and Robbie stood next to him and put his shoulder to the tree, his head bent while he strained. The pungent smell of pine filled the air, like a Christmas wreath. The ambulance drivers got out and pushed, too. Marilyn and I started to climb over the trunk to get down to Big Circle Shopping Center and help out there, but Daddy yelled, "Get back in! Look out for those power lines."

"What are we supposed to do?" Marilyn shouted over the sirens. "It's just like Vietnam." There was panic in her voice, and then she was talking to herself. "This must be what Jimmy went through, and here I am, right smack in the middle. Tornadoes coming out of the sky like bombs, aiming right for us." Her eyes were big in her pale face, and I could see the little girl she had once been.

"What can we do?" I shouted, as much to shake Marilyn out of her reverie as to ask Daddy for advice.

"Pray," Daddy yelled. Then someone came with a chain saw, sending pine chips flying.

So we did pray. We sat at the kitchen table, feeling awkward except for Charlene. Charlene reached for Marilyn's hand, and then mine, so I grabbed Marilyn's too. Her hand was wet and cold. I said a prayer for the people at Big Circle Shopping Center, people who might've been buying those plastic daisies in Drummond's. I prayed for whoever was in Tommy McCarty's upside-down house. The ambulance siren screeched, then began to recede, and we knew it had gotten through.

"Help the boys in Vietnam," was all Marilyn said, so Charlene prayed about Revelation, the Four Horsemen and all that. She prayed so long my mind wandered to the terrible sights I'd seen. Was anyone dead under Tommy McCarty's house, feet sticking out from that crushed roof like the Wicked Witch in *The Wizard of Oz*? It was the kind of day when anything might happen, the kind you hope happens only once in your life. And I'd already had one of those, back in 1963. Even though we prayed, I kept thinking that God had already made up His mind.

When we went out again, Robbie was gone, and I realized how much I wanted him to be there. The tree lay in pieces across the road. The flung mud and plastic flowers all over the front yard looked like the Devil's own temper tantrum. I poked at the debris.

A rubber doll was wedged under an oak branch, her head half-buried in the mud. She'd lost all her clothes in the wind, but I recognized her as the kind Drummond's sold. There had been a bin of them, in pink and blue pajamas, in a back aisle. I lifted her out, wiping mud from her glass eyes. "You're fine," I whispered. There were doll clothes packed away in the top of my closet that would fit her.

Marilyn came up and flicked some mud off the doll's ear. "I'll get a big garbage bag for all this."

"I'm keeping her." I tucked her under my sweatshirt.

Marilyn snorted. "You're too old for dolls."

Mama would never have said that. "I'll sew a pretty dress for her, after all she's been through." That's what Mama would've said; I could hear her voice. I set the doll on the steps just as Charlene emerged and surveyed the muddy mess with awe. "'The angel took the censer, filled it with fire from the altar, and hurled it on the earth. . .'"

"Help me pick these flowers up!" I yelled.

"God left a memorial for those He took," said Charlene, gazing at the mad array of colors.

"It's a plastic garden, that's what it is. Garish. You think Mama would've wanted trash in the yard?"

"If it came from God. Of course she would've," said Charlene, and I felt like we'd had two different mothers. "Is that a doll?" Charlene peered at my sweatshirt where a rubber leg stuck out. "Don't you throw that away. Mama would've made new clothes for her. But you don't throw anything anyway, do you? Why do you still want that scarf?"

She meant the paper bag with the red and orange

111

poppy scarf in my closet. "Maybe evidence," I said.

Charlene kept finding matchbox cars in the mud, and stacked them by the garage. "It's a sculpture," she said. "A memorial for the lost kids. The tornado is God's lesson about the mess we make of our lives." She arranged the toy cars in patterns of blue, red and yellow, and I had to admit it was pretty.

"What were you doing at home?" Charlene asked later, watching me rinse the doll in the bathroom sink. The rubber was cleaning up well. Maybe she'd be my own patron saint. "Man, you missed it. We had to go in the hall and crouch, covering our heads. You should've seen ole Langstrom, like he'd pee in his pants. I watched him the whole time. I wasn't scared."

It was a satisfying thought, but not enough to make me wish I'd been at Tallulah High.

The news that night told us sixteen people had died, most of them in Drummond's Five and Dime Store, which was demolished. At dinner, I thought about the record rack, and for a second I wished some good albums had blown our way.

"At least we didn't get any arms or legs in our front yard," said Marilyn. "It was like war, they get limbs blown all over the place." She stared at her tuna casserole.

"Hush," said Daddy. "It was bad enough." He was so tired his cheeks sagged, and I wondered what he'd seen down at the Big Circle Shopping Center. "At least nobody was in the McCarty house. Would've been a miracle to survive that."

Marilyn's eyes glinted with tears. "If Jimmy hadn't gone to Vietnam, he'd have been working at Big Circle, stocking the shelves at Drummond's. Maybe there were traps set for him in his life, no matter what he did."

"Nobody's got traps set for them," said Daddy. He was

so tired he just handed Marilyn his napkin for her tears.

"But it makes it better, don't you see?" she cried out and slammed the table. "If he was going to die anyway, Vietnam just got him first. It makes me feel better this way. Don't you understand?" She started crying hard, and Daddy pulled himself up to put his arm around her.

"You're right." His voice was hoarse. "Jimmy must've had traps set for him. The tornado would've gotten him if the Viet Cong hadn't." Daddy sounded the way he would when he used to tell us fairy tales at bedtime.

Marilyn lifted her wet face. "And who knows what would've gotten him if the tornado didn't?"

"But we made it," said Daddy. "There aren't any traps for us." His eyes were dull, as if he were trying to persuade himself.

That night, Robbie Godbold called to tell me about the shopping center. He started to say how he'd helped pull some people out, but his voice quivered and he said he had to go.

"You got a boyfriend?" Charlene asked when I came back to our bedroom. "He's not cute, but he seemed okay. I saw him cleaning up after the tornado."

The tornado was a good excuse not to go to school the next day. Let Mr. Woods worry that I was taken by the Lord, I decided. Let him suffer, thinking that his evil words were the last I'd ever heard. Let him think my limbs were scattered like a soldier's across the lawns of Biloxi. When the phone rang, it was Robbie, calling from the school pay phone. When he found out I wasn't sick, he asked me to go to McDonald's after school. Everybody was talking about the McDonald's that had come to town, but I hadn't been yet.

As soon as I saw his Chevrolet up close, I liked him even more. A troll doll stood where the hood ornament

113

would have been, and when we hit the road, its hair blew like an undulating rainbow. He turned on the radio, and it was Aretha Franklin singing "Respect," and Robbie sang with her, drumming his fingers on the wheel. He wasn't bad, and soon our voices trailed out the car windows together, a single stream of sound. He kept glancing at me when I'd do riffs with the lyrics, and the gleam in his eyes grew.

"You're great. And you play trumpet, too," he said, and took my hand. His weren't soft, like I'd imagined.

"Why are your hands rough?" I asked. Turned out he helped his dad fix cars on the week-ends, and that reminded me of Mama, made my heart move toward him a little more. "Do you like it when Mrs. Hodges calls you Robert?" I asked.

"Why not?" he shrugged.

"But kids make fun of it."

"They do?" He thought for a minute, then squeezed my hand. "Who cares? You can't let a few jerks get you down."

"Mind if I call you Rob?" I asked. It was neither what the rednecks or the algebra teacher called him.

He thought a second, then nodded. "I like it."

Rob started calling every night and Charlene got mad at me for tying up the telephone. "Ernie's trying to call," she said, as if I should know that her calls were more important than mine. It was true Rob wasn't as cute as Ernie Crenshaw – he was skinny with a patch of acne on his cheek – but I still had some rights to the telephone.

I'd always told Charlene I didn't mind how people treated me, if they were rude or nice, but with Rob being nice to me, I started singing around the house again, like Mama used to do. I'd belt out Christmas carols, show tunes, Baptist hymns, rock 'n roll, and blues. Rob said I sounded like Janis Joplin. Even Charlene said it almost made things normal, having somebody singing in the house again, not just my awful trumpet blasting off her ears.

Rob and I spent a lot of time together, walking on the beach and talking about Mama sometimes. Charlene said Ernie prayed that Mama's murder would stop following Charlene and me everywhere, even when we'd try to read or watch TV, and it seemed to have worked for her. All she thought about now was Ernie.

But, like I told Rob, I couldn't watch the TV weather report without thinking of Levi Litvak. Instead of weather charts, I saw Levi Litvak's dark hair pushed into a pompadour, and sideburns sprouting on his cheeks like a thin hedge along his face. Mama used to get nervous when we'd all watch the weather. She'd buff her nails or sip iced tea, but she'd never take her eyes off the screen. Daddy teased her that she was jittery about the weather because it was the one thing she couldn't control. Daddy didn't understand. It was the weatherman she couldn't control.

I'd tell Rob these stories, and he would hug me so tight until all I could think about were his kisses, and how warm his arms felt around me. "Try to forget it, Jubilee," he said. "You've got me now."

In the Piggly Wiggly, I heard Loretta Holliday telling Evelyn McCarty, Tommy's mother, that Levi Litvak wasn't burned up in the crash. They were in the check-out line. It was safe to gossip about Mama in the grocery store now that Marilyn wasn't working the cash register anymore. They'd been talking about how Mrs. McCarty's insurance was slow paying to have her house rebuilt, but Mrs. Holliday shifted the conversation to the murder, how Levi Litvak survived.

"Oh Loretta," said Mrs. McCarty. "You're not still

talking that nonsense, are you?" Maybe that tornado had knocked some sense into at least one person in Biloxi.

Mrs. Holliday edged her basket closer to Mrs. McCarty and bumped her plump rear end. "Levi Litvak is right here on the Gulf Coast, of all the nerve! He never even left."

Mrs. McCarty moved away from Loretta Holliday's basket, but Loretta kept pushing it forward. "Oh, Levi has a few scars from that accident," she said. "Wreck like that, who wouldn't? He's not as handsome as he used to be. But he's pumping gas over in Pelahatchie, big as you please. If anybody could resurrect himself, Levi could. 'Course, he's wearing his hair shaved, so he looks bald." She ran her red nails around the back of her neck. "Only a fringe of wavy hair at the edges, bleached yellow like a woman's. That gorgeous curly brown hair, all gone."

Mrs. McCarty laughed. "Loretta, he was burned up four years ago, hon. Listen, I knew some folks didn't care much for Bernice, liking the coloreds the way she did. But Levi Litvak killed her out of love gone bad, not hate. You tell me, how could he put his ashes back together again?"

I bent my head over the shampoo counter, trying to hear. Mrs. Holliday dropped her voice to a whisper, but it was loud, like an actress onstage. "Weren't his ashes, that's how. And you know what? He's keeping Bernice out on Deer Island. Took her right out of the hospital in the dead of night, in his own two arms, and stole her away from Harry, just like he always wanted. Poor woman's stranded."

Mrs. McCarty shook her head. "Stuff and nonsense, Loretta! I went to Bernice Starling's funeral. If that wasn't her in that casket, who was it?"

"Wax." Loretta leaned close to her face, her green eyes gleaming like a cat's. "You know what they can do with

116

wax nowadays, don't you? Have you ever been to Madame Tussauds' in New Orleans? Why, just last week, Kathy and I went, and I thought, if they can do that with Queen Elizabeth, just think what Levi could've done to make that look like Bernice. He was an artist with his hands, you know. I saw some sculptures he did at the TV station, things with wire and metal. A murderer's gone free, I tell you, and unless I tell it, nobody's going to know it. 'Course, he might come after me next, but when I think of Bernice out on that island, living all by herself, why, it gives me the shivers."

Evelyn McCarty glanced at Loretta out of the corner of her eye, then rolled her basket on to the cashier. "God bless you, Loretta Holliday." Her voice had gotten soft and quiet; she pushed forward and left. Mrs. Holliday kept on smiling, her red lips a jagged crack in her face.

That night, I lay in the bathtub for a long time, soaking in warm water until my toes wrinkled up. Daddy's old razor lay on the soap dish, the one Charlene and I used to shave our legs. I scraped it against my leg, starting with my ankle, and was halfway up to my knee before I noticed blood edging into the water. The redness billowed into the tub like something alive, like a jellyfish in the Gulf, pushing itself through the water with the grace of its translucent umbrella. The cut on my ankle didn't even hurt and when the bleeding stopped, I thought maybe it had been like that for Mama when she was stabbed, painless and even a little beautiful, with the liquid warm against her chest, her heart freed from its cage.

I pushed the dull blade against my calf, but nothing happened. Was that how numb I'd become, I wondered, feeling nothing, even when I bled? I pushed harder and a thin stream of blood rose in the water like smoke and I watched, satisfied at the sting, until it dissipated into pink and merged with the gray soapy water.

Chapter Eight

Mrs. Holliday was a chaperone when several Gulf
Coast schools took a field trip up to the Delta to tour
Parchman Farm, the Mississippi State Penitentiary.

For hours, the buses rolled in a caravan through scrubby piney forests, then through lush kudzu-covered hill
country. Ernie's bus from Libertyburg High was in front of
ours, and he sat in the back, turning to wave at Charlene
every now and then. Beneath the seat in front of me, someone had left a *Look Magazine*, and I picked it up. On the
cover, guys with long hair made peace signs at the photog-
rapher while girls glowing with body paint danced under
a brilliant California sun. Something magical was happening out there. Those kids looked beautiful, as if they
understood something about life, and how free you could
be. Charlene looked over my shoulder. "Look at that guy
with the face paint," she said.

"You can hear the music, when you look at that picture," I said. "Jefferson Airplane, you know? Don't you
wish we were there? It's Berkeley."

But she'd caught Ernie's attention again and blew him
a kiss. "What?" she asked, but I didn't answer.

Finally, we made it past Jackson, heading toward the
Delta, where James Chaney, Andrew Goodman, and
Michael Schwerner, the three civil rights workers, had
been murdered near Philadelphia, Mississippi three years
before. This was the kind of place where the Neshoba
County sheriff and his deputy could sit in a courthouse
with their cowboy boots propped on the table, chewing

tobacco and grinning, while they were being arraigned for murder. It was the kind of place where the sheriff was still free.

Flat cotton fields stretched for miles on either side of the road. Parchman Farm sprawled in the middle of a big cotton field. I wasn't sure why it was important that we kids tour a prison, but it gave everybody a chance to giggle when Mr. Miller, the social studies teacher, talked about the "penal institution" we were going to visit. He'd push his glasses up on his nose and frown, like he didn't have a clue.

Mrs. Holliday huddled close to Mr. Miller when they took us around the barracks. She warned the girls not to get too close to the inmates, and certainly not to ask them what they'd done to get sent to Parchman. We might hear stories we had no business hearing, she warned. "There's stories here about rapists, bank robbers, even those who have murdered little. . ."

Mr. Miller caught her arm and shook his head, so she quieted down, a funny little smile on her lips.

When we walked outside, she pointed to the long whip that was looped on a hook on the side of a building, coiled there like a sleeping rattlesnake.

"Black Annie," she told us, fingering the tip of the whip, as if there might be blood dried there. She whirled around and whispered to Mr. Miller, "Twenty lashes from her, that would cure Joe Holliday. Cure any man's crime. No, make it fifty lashes." She planted her spectator pumps and cracked an imaginary whip in the air.

Mr. Miller flinched, his thin shoulders hunching under his plaid sports jacket, as though crimes we couldn't imagine lay hidden in his heart, waiting to be cured.

"Hah!" said Mrs. Holliday, flailing her whip against the air once more. "But would it cure a woman's crime?"

119

Was she talking about Mama? I grabbed Rob's hand and hurried by, pretending I hadn't heard or seen anything.

The warden himself took us to see the electric chair. "Anyone care to try it out? Have a seat," he said, smiling. He waved his arm at the contraption, like he was just exercising good old Southern hospitality.

Ernie Crenshaw grinned and sat down in it, with those great wooden slabs for arms, and the dark leather straps hanging down. It sat up on a wooden platform like a throne. Charlene grabbed his hand and pulled him back. The warden laughed, and so did some of the kids, like it was a scary ride at the state fair in Jackson. Or part of the freak show. Grady Pickens laughed so hard he bent over double, holding his stomach. It was just because he still liked Charlene, I thought. I remembered how hard he'd laughed because he was scared of Joe Holliday's Halloween decorations. Now he was laughing because he was jealous.

"You know it can't be turned on," I whispered, looking around for a plug. But Charlene looked like she might cry.

"That's where Levi Litvak should've sat," she told me. "Why did we have to come to Parchman and not him? Who wants to see a bunch of convicts?"

I nodded. "Yeah, I bet kids in Berkeley get to hear Allen Ginsburg read poetry on *their* field trips."

"Who?" asked Charlene, but she wasn't listening. She was staring at the electric chair.

I stared at it, too: the monstrous thick belts everywhere, the hideously stained seat, as if grown men had left their urine there. Levi Litvak could have fried in that seat till his hair sizzled and his eyes smoked like Uncle Clayton's burned steaks.

"That's where Cecil Price should sit," said Rob, meaning the deputy sheriff who was in jail for killing the civil rights workers. "This place is creepy."

My skin prickled, and I shivered. But in the spring of 1968, it was already so hot that Charlene said that it seemed like God wanted everybody in Mississippi to fry, like we were all guilty of something we didn't even know about.

Led by one of the prison authorities, a slight man in a white shirt, we filed through a room where women in striped dresses sat at sewing machines, zipping out seams straighter than Mama ever could. None of them looked up at us. They kept their heads bowed and one black woman moved her lips gently, as if she were praying over the cloth.

The guide waved and led us to the next stop, a gray corrugated tin structure that must have been blazing hot in the summer. The noise was so loud inside we heard a buzzing even before we got to the doors. Men in black and white stripes stood at long tables covered with sheets of metal. Perspiration streamed down their faces, made dark circles under their arms. A burly man with tattoos on his hands stamped out rectangular pieces of the metal, and at the end of the room, someone else stacked car license tags in boxes. Over each number was a big white magnolia, with "Mississippi: The Magnolia State," at the bottom. The guy who loaded them up wiped off the sweat from each plate with a gray rag.

"What do you think they did?" Charlene yelled, over the noise. "Think they murdered somebody?"

I put a finger to my lips. Maybe they hadn't done anything but been in the wrong place when a white person was mad about how his day had gone.

It was a relief to step out of that noise and into air that was cool by comparison. At the end of the day, the prison band played so we could dance. "Parchman celebrities," Loretta Holliday tugged at Mr. Miller's sleeve and whispered in his ear, though he pulled away from her. "Just look at them. Black as night." She pointed to the bass guitarist and the drummer.

They did songs like "Mountain of Love" and "Ring of Fire" and "I'm So Lonesome I Could Cry," things that made me think about Mama's music, so I didn't feel like dancing. Nobody else was dancing, either. The music was a long way from the Beatles.

Kathy Holliday started laughing at the three guitarists and the drummer in their striped pants and shirts. She giggled until a wave of hysteria went over some kids huddled in the far corner, but the band sang harder. A white guy with terrible acne sang, his tendons straining against his neck, like they were trying to escape the prison of his skin. He didn't look much older than we were. A sound like howling or shrieking came from their scarred guitars, the kind of music Mama loved, Big Bill Broonzy and Robert Johnson. We were deep in blues country, with its nooses and moonshine whiskey and the Klan silently moving through cotton fields. *Teardrops sliding down the mountainside, many times I been there, many times I cried. . .*

It made me want to cry, too, and Rob put his arm around me. He could tell when I was sad, that was one of the things I liked about him. I leaned my head against his shoulder, but Mr. Miller wagged a finger at me to sit up straight.

"We might as well be in jail, too," Rob said, and he wove his fingers through mine.

Ernie tugged at Charlene's hand to pull her out on the dance floor, an empty spot in the cafeteria where rows of scratched formica tables had been pushed away. It was probably just to show up the kids who were laughing at the

122

band, and it made me wonder how much he cared about Charlene's feelings. "C'mon," he kept telling her, his other hand flat against the small of her back, pushing. "Let's show 'em." It was just like Ernie, wanting to dance to that sad music, to make some holier-than-thou point.

Charlene tried, but Ernie danced almost as badly as Rob did. It was a slow bop, and he tried hard to find the rhythm. Then he gave up on the bop and started doing the twist, looking like some machine gone crazy, its parts moving in different directions. Charlene finally stopped shuffling her feet. It was Elvis's "Jailhouse Rock," but no one could make it come to life in that place. All those men in stripes, and Levi Litvak not among them, though I couldn't help searching for a brown pompadour, rising above a face that might've gone gray from prison.

Rob was looking at me, his blue eyes piercing. "You're still looking for Levi Litvak, aren't you? You'll drive yourself crazy. Try to get over it."

"It's not like having the chicken pox and you get over with a few little scars," I said. "I'll always be different because of what happened to my mother." Every time I thought Levi Litvak was finally gone, he reappeared in a dream, a carpenter hammering nails into a wooden coffin, or a cop who would stop me in the truck to give me a speeding ticket, blue lights flashing until I could see the face above the badge. He'd push back his blue cap and there was Levi Litvak, the cleft chin and brown eyes squinting, as if I were the one who'd done something wrong.

"I'm trying to help you," said Rob, but the music swept his words away.

The guy with the acne kept straining with a desperate ache in his voice, as if he could make his girlfriend hear, wherever she was. *Mountain of love, mountain of love, you should be ashamed. . .* He wasn't singing to us. His eyes were fixed somewhere far away. I felt better. He surely didn't know Kathy Holliday was laughing at him the way she probably wished she could laugh at her dad.

After that day, I knew I needed to go as far away as I could, like Mama had probably wanted to. While Charlene was skipping classes to be with Ernie, I doubled up on advanced courses at Tallulah High, and even went to summer school so I could graduate early. Rob didn't like it, and one Sunday afternoon, we came as close as we'd ever come to having a fight.

"You won't get to graduate with me, Jubilee," he said. We were sitting at the kitchen table, drinking Cokes Marilyn had poured. "Just think, we can go to Mississippi Southern together. We'll get out of Biloxi, just wait." The only problem was, Mississippi Southern was in Hattiesburg, up north about an hour and a half away.

"Yeah, sure," I said. "The kids at Southern come *here* to have fun, that's how boring Hattiesburg is."

His eyes drooped. "How about State? They have a great math program. We could go to Jackson for fun."

"If I can get in, I'm going to Berkeley. That's where the whole world is changing."

"My parents would never pay for me to go out there," he said. "C'mon."

"If I can't go there, I'm not going to college. It's the only place I want to be."

"Not even with me?" His voice dropped.

I didn't have a chance to answer. Charlene came in, carrying the Sunday comics. She dropped them on the table and invited herself to have a seat. She was waiting for Ernie to come. "You're so weird, Jubilee. That's where all the anti-war protesters are," she said. "What would you do way out there in California?" She'd been eavesdropping. Typical.

"That's why I want to go, to find out," I said.

"I'm the only one in this family who's *not* weird." Charlene put the comics in front of her face.

"It's hard to get into Berkeley," said Rob. "You should at least apply to State, for back-up."

A wave of anger rose from my stomach to my face. "'For back-up'?" I imitated him. "You think you're so smart."

"You're smart, too." His voice was quiet. "I just want to be sure you get to college."

"Well, you're saying all the wrong things," I told him.

Charlene stared at *Peanuts*, where Charlie Brown sat in front of Lucy's psychiatrist's booth.

Rob was silent for a while. "I guess I could come out to visit," he said slowly. He was watching my face, and I tried not to look at his eyes. There was too much to look forward to in California, and I couldn't let Rob hold me back. "Maybe at Christmas."

I nodded. "Sure, if your parents will pay for a plane ticket." There was sarcasm in my voice. I didn't know it was there till I heard it.

Rob's jaw was working the way it did once when football players called him a faggot and he kept on walking across the school parking lot. He was brave, I said, but even as I had taken his hand, something in me wanted him to fight back, to at least call them rednecks. "Maybe they will," he said. "Do you want me to come, or not?"

Charlene gathered up the comics and left.

"'Bout time," I said to her retreating back.

"Well? Would you want me to come?" asked Rob.

"Sure," I said, but I already knew there was no place

125

for Rob in the world where I wanted to be. Maybe there was no place for even Charlene and Daddy. Who knew? Maybe there would be no place for me there, either. And if there wasn't, then I might not belong in the world at all. I'd live the rest of my life inside my head.

For my application, my statement of purpose was a long poem I wrote about growing up in Mississippi, about how my trumpet could blow away the blues, how the music could blow ghosts away. I worked on it for weeks, trying to make it sound like the notes that echoed off the garage walls. I even painted some of the lines in day-glo on our bedroom walls and ceiling, so I could read them in the middle of the night when I couldn't sleep.

Charlene got mad about it. "Are you and Rob in some kind of a cult?" she asked. "All those letters give me the creeps. God didn't make words to glow in the dark."

"It helps me concentrate," I told her. "When I wake up at night, I think about my poem. It's hard work."

"You think it's really great stuff, don't you?" Her eyes narrowed like she was focusing a pair of binoculars to scrutinize me. "Well, I guess we all have to find a way to feel good about ourselves, don't we? Even if it's trying to be a hippie poet."

"Is that why you hang out with Ernie, to feel good about yourself?" I tried to curl my lip the way she did.

She looked shocked, staring at me wide-eyed, the binoculars gone. "That's a terrible thing to say to your own sister. I'd help you through anything and you know it. So would Rob, and you don't even appreciate how he's trying to help you get into Mississippi State."

"Why did you say my poem is just a way of feeling good about myself, then?" I asked. "How does that help me?"

"You're too sensitive," she said, and stormed out of

the room, banging the door behind her.

"What's going on?" called Daddy from the living room, where he and Marilyn were watching a western called *Palladin* on television. The hero would flash his card: "Have Gun, Will Travel." I liked the show until I realized he was always on someone else's mission. "Have poem, will travel," I thought, and it would be no one's journey but my own.

Neither of us answered Daddy. I turned out the lights in our bedroom. The words stared down at me in green through the shadows. Maybe they would work their magic at Berkeley's admissions office.

When the letter finally came with the University of California at Berkeley seal at the return address, my hands started shaking. The rest of my life lay inside. I ripped it open and had to sit down. The poem must've been what got me in, because they gave me a scholarship, too. When I could believe the words, I showed the letter to Charlene.

"Look." My hand was still shaking when I stuck it between Charlene's face and the magazine she was reading.

She read it twice, then took it from my hands and ran her fingertips over the raised gold insignia of the University of California. Her face was glowing when she looked up.

"I prayed for this, Jubilee," she said. "I know I've said some mean things, but I want you to be happy." Her face shone with tears and triumph, whether in pride for me or for her successful prayers, I couldn't tell. I hugged her and a sob came out of my throat, a sound I didn't expect.

Charlene was happy, but she would be left all alone in that house. She had Ernie, though. So why was I crying?

Aunt Sylvia persuaded Daddy to let me go. She came

down for a visit to get to know Marilyn, and they all started talking about Berkeley as they sat around the kitchen table drinking coffee.

"What?" Daddy said. "A teenager running off to California all by herself? To live in a dormitory with who knows what kinds of dope addicts? Why, all she's ever known is Biloxi."

"Jubilee and I've been independent for a long time," said Charlene.

Marilyn scraped an emory board across her fingernails, back and forth, like everybody knows you're not supposed to do. "And sex maniacs," she added, not even looking up.

"What?" We stared at her.

From the look on Charlene's face, she was wondering what Marilyn might know about what she and Ernie Crenshaw had been doing in the back seat of his car. Marilyn liked Ernie, mostly because he admired the soldiers in Vietnam so much that he wanted to join the Army.

"What do you mean, sex maniacs?" Charlene asked, her face flushed.

Marilyn looked confused. "Dormitories full of dope addicts and sex. That's what Harry said. Listen to your father, Charlene." She looked at me. "You too, Jubilee. Berkeley's a strange place. Anything could happen."

Aunt Sylvia let out a snort: the first time I'd heard her make a noise like that. "It's one of the best universities in the country. . ."

The timer on the stove began to shriek, and Marilyn jumped up to turn on the television for *The Price Is Right*. It was her favorite show because she was so good at it from studying the catalogs she kept stacked in the bathroom. She forgot everything when the game shows were on. Talk about drugs, Charlene said; just look at Marilyn sitting in a trance before the TV.

"But those hippies running around out there," Daddy told Aunt Sylvia. "Look what's happening in your own city, up there at Columbia University, students going wild, having sit-ins. What on earth would Bernice have said, God rest her soul?" He lowered her voice, so Marilyn couldn't hear. He rubbed his stomach, like his ulcers were acting up again. For the first time I could see how much he'd aged. His cheeks caved inward and gray hair sprouted just above his ears. But his eyes had aged the most. They were like gray caves hollowed into his head, forlorn places where a hermit might live. And then I saw it clearly, how marrying Marilyn had been a life raft that couldn't hold his weight. He was sinking again, the way he did right after Mama died. Marilyn would get jealous even when I'd sing Mama's old blues songs at talent shows. Maybe she had reason to be. Daddy's eyes would get misty and soft, like he wasn't even seeing me perform, but remembering Mama. Then, sure as rain, Marilyn would pick a big fight with him. So if he mentioned Mama, he kept his voice quiet.

Sylvia was quick. "Bernice would say 'go for it,' that's what," she snapped, a glint in her eyes. Then she smiled at my father's fears. "Don't you worry your handsome little head, Harry," she teased, tousling his hair so that a curl flopped down his forehead. She wiped the pomade from her fingers on a paper towel, laughing. "Jubilee's a good kid. And smart, too. How else would she have gotten that scholarship? Bernice would've been so proud. Don't take that away." Then she looked over at Charlene. "Of course, we're all proud of Charlene, too. You have two wonderful, smart girls."

While Aunt Sylvia was there, Walter Cronkite broke into a TV show to announce that Martin Luther King had

129

been killed. At first we sat stunned, unable to believe it. It made me want to leave the South even more. When the *Biloxi Sun-Herald* ran an editorial suggesting that King was shot so he could become a martyr for civil rights, Aunt Sylvia wrote a letter to them about what she called Southern Nazis.

The night after they printed the letter, Daddy was sitting out in the backyard drinking a bourbon and water, trying to avoid the irate phone calls we'd been getting. Somebody kept calling and breathing heavily, but most people wanted to tell Sylvia that all the outside agitators like her could go back where they came from. One woman said whoever pulled the trigger on Martin Luther King was a hero. Some of the callers remembered that Aunt Sylvia had married Claude. A slut, one guy called her.

Daddy poured himself a stiff drink and slammed the back door behind him. It was the worst he'd seen of Biloxi, he said, his face pale. Aunt Sylvia and I were arguing with Marilyn about what Martin Luther King stood for, when Charlene spoke up. She played with the salt shaker, not looking up. "Just think, tiny babies trying to grow up in a world like this. How would you raise it?"

I guessed she thought that if she had to live with Marilyn, she had to be more philosophical about things. After all, I was the one leaving home in a few months, so I could afford to mouth off to Marilyn. Look how much better the junior high basketball team was doing since the school integrated, I was saying, when the screen door slammed and Daddy came inside.

"Damn these mosquitoes!" he said. "They're everywhere." Marilyn got up to squeeze at his arm, and we heard her whisper, "You got an agitator in the family, hon."

"Shut up." The words shot from Daddy's throat, and

he headed over to the cabinet above the sink to reach for the bourbon. I'd never heard Daddy tell anybody to shut up before, and Marilyn looked like she'd been slapped. Charlene and I stared at each other. Marilyn left in a huff and soon the bedroom door slammed. Daddy poured himself another drink. As soon as he took a sip, the phone rang again. This time he answered. "What is it?" he asked. Then his mouth knotted and he hung up. In a voice so low I could barely hear, he told Aunt Sylvia someone was threatening to kill her. He picked up the phone again and dialed the police, but all they did was tell us not to leave the house.

Aunt Sylvia packed her clothes and some sketches she'd done and left for a Holiday Inn in New Orleans, saying she'd never come back. "This isn't my home anymore," she said.

"You won't come back even for us?" asked Charlene.

Aunt Sylvia stopped long enough to hug us. "Of course I'll come back for you." She reached for a strand of her long hair and twisted it, the way she did when she was worried. "And you visit me whenever you want."

She didn't give up the campaign for me to go to Berkeley. She called from New York and told Daddy things like, "People are people, you know. They're not so different out in California." But when I got on the phone, she told me, "It'll be different out there, honey. Wait and see." I told Charlene she could come, too, out where people wouldn't point at you or call you names, but Charlene said she didn't think there was such a place, not on earth, anyway.

Sometimes I prayed to Mama, telling her I was going to Berkeley, that I was going to find clubs there to sing in if I could. Or a band where I could play my trumpet like Miles Davis. It would make her happy, I knew.

Chapter Nine

Late on an August afternoon, I walked into our bedroom with my arms full of things I'd bought for my dorm room at Berkeley – sheets and towels, even a small pot for coffee, though I didn't drink it yet. Charlene was dressing to go to a Youth of Christ meeting. "You'll be late," I told her. She was struggling to pull her panty hose over her stomach. She tried to suck it in, but she couldn't.

"Charlene! Look at that belly! You're fat," I blurted out before I even thought about it, and then I knew.

In the mornings it was all she could do to keep her breakfast down. The scrambled eggs and grits Marilyn always cooked had made her gag that morning, and she'd run to the bathroom. "I'm okay," she called, but we heard her vomiting.

I sat on the bed and stared at the bulge beneath her jumper. She plucked the fabric out with her fingertips, trying to make more room for her stomach. "What'll we do?" I whispered. "Does Daddy know?"

She reached behind her neck to fix the clasp on a sterling silver heart Ernie had given her for Valentine's Day. I thought of the cheap engraved heart Grady Pickens gave her at the state fair so long ago, and wished suddenly we were still those girls, pushing away boys we didn't like.

"Think Daddy'll ever notice?" she asked, patting her belly. "He doesn't care about anything but you and Marilyn. That's all I hear about, Berkeley and Vietnam. It's like I'm the only one who lives here in Biloxi anymore."

"He loves you and me. You know that." I thought about all the nights Daddy and I had sat at the kitchen table, talking about my scholarship and application. Where had Charlene been? Out with Ernie. Or watching television, alone. I got up to hug her, but she put up her arms to fend me off. "What does Ernie say?" I asked.

"Not much," she said. She picked up her hairbrush and picked at some curls around her face.

"What are we going to do?" I asked.

"It's my life, not yours."

"When is the baby due?" A real baby! I could hardly believe the words.

She shrugged. "Maybe five months. Around Christmas, probably."

"You've got to see a doctor, don't you? Terrible things can happen if you don't." A girl in Gulfport had given birth to a baby in her own bed a couple of years ago, and nobody had even known she was pregnant. Her mother had gone to wake her up for school and found her, asleep, with a baby in her arms. "You can't have the baby at home."

"Ernie doesn't want me to go to a doctor," she said.

"Are you going to get married?" The bulge in her stomach looked enormous now.

She adjusted Ernie's class ring. "'Mrs. Ernie Crenshaw' for the rest of my life? I don't think so."

"Why not? You love him, don't you?" The thought of having Ernie in the family made my toes curl, but it was the only thing that could save us.

She kept biting her lip and turned her left hand, so that the red jewel in Ernie's class ring flashed in the light. "You know what? I don't even like Ernie anymore. Remember Art Johnson?"

"Of course," I said. "Is he the father?"

She threw me a black look. "Are you joking? He was back in town for a few days. He was at Parris Island, you know. Got drafted. He looks good even with his head shaved. I saw him at the Dairy Queen. He bought me a Coke and we just talked. He's so different from Ernie, he's so. . ."

"Smart?" I asked, and she didn't look offended.

"Yeah. Parris Island sounds like hell. He had a big brace around his whole middle, a bad back. The Army didn't want him like that, so he's going to State. He's going to write me, he said."

"Listen, I get tired of Rob sometimes, too, but I still like being with him. You're not going to like somebody all the time, every second, even Art Johnson."

"Yeah, well, Ernie's an idiot. He says I'm not really pregnant. That's why he doesn't want me seeing a doctor; he's afraid it's true. He'd have to tell his Mommy and Daddy. Coward." A soft look replaced the anger in her eyes. "I told Art Johnson I thought I was pregnant, and you know what he did?"

"You told him? What for? Now the whole town'll know." My own sister, telling a stranger before she told me.

"He was nice, he held my hand. And he won't tell anybody." She tilted her head back and stroked mascara on her lashes, her mouth open slightly.

"But what about the baby?" My head spun, and my throat tightened.

"A lot of people would give a baby a good home." She capped the mascara and spritzed hairspray around her head, but the reflection of her face in the mirror was like a mask.

"Adoption?" I'd never get to see my niece or nephew.

Carefully, she styled each strand of hair as if it took all

her concentration. Watching herself in the mirror, she said, "Do you know about 'ensoulment'?"

The store where Daddy bought his elevator shoes came to mind, the way they'd raised the price for the thick soles he ordered, but that wasn't what she meant. "No," I said.

"It's when Catholics say the soul enters a baby before it's born. They say babies don't have a soul till just before they're born. Right now, it's just tissue and . . ."

"Abortion?" Another wave of nausea made my stomach lurch. "You can't make it all right by using the Church. They don't like abortion." I felt like crying.

She gave me a hard look. "Your life is so easy. Here you are, off to Berkeley, and look at me." She pointed the brush at her belly. "What can I do? I've thought about every possible plan. That's what I lie in bed doing, while you're writing day-glo poetry."

"Abortion is Ernie's idea, isn't it?"

"The baby doesn't even exist to him. But I read some old Catholic manuals at the library, and it sounded like souls come down and enter the womb later. And there's a doctor in New Orleans who. . ."

"Oh Charlene." I didn't know if I wanted to hit her or hug her. "Don't. I'll love your baby just like it's my own. All I know is that you and me, we've always had soul, and Mama had soul, and we couldn't do anything like take a soul from a baby." A terrible thought came to me. "What on earth are we going to tell Grandma?"

She turned away from me. "Just don't worry about it." She gave her hair a final shot of spray, then pointed the brush at me in the mirror. "I can take care of myself."

Charlene was only eighteen. What could she know about taking care of babies? And abortions could kill you.

"I'm calling Aunt Sylvia," I said.

"Go ahead." For the first time, she smiled, a secretive sliver on her lips. "But she knows."

"You told her? And you didn't tell me?" She'd shut me out again, just like with Ernie, and for a moment, I hated her. "I wish Mama was here. She'd know what to do," I said.

"Mama must've been p.g. with me when she got married," said Charlene.

Dates flashed through my head. September, 1949 had been their anniversary, and Charlene was born the following August. "They had you right away, that's all. Why do you always put the worst possible face on things?"

"Ever seen their marriage license?"

"Have you?"

She shrugged. "No. But how do we know they really got married in September? Mama's stomach is poochy in their wedding pictures. And why else would she marry somebody like Daddy? It was all my fault she ruined her life."

Charlene's words sank into my mind like stones. It was true. In the pictures, Mama was wearing a blue dress, full-skirted with a low neck. Beneath the gathers of her skirt, Mama's stomach was round, not flat the way I remembered it. "She loved Daddy, that's the only reason she married him. Daddy's great."

Her lips tightened. "I'm glad you and Marilyn think so." She fiddled with her bottle of Windsong perfume.

I put my arm on her shoulder and this time she didn't push me away. "Listen, I've never told you this. I heard Mama talking to Levi Litvak, right before she died. She was telling him she loved Daddy, and that she loved us. She didn't want Levi Litvak, Charlene. She wanted us."

Hope glinted in her eyes, a steely kind of hope. "Why didn't you ever tell me?"

136

"I thought it would upset you. It was us that she loved. Levi Litvak, he was just passing through."

Ernie's car horn beeped outside. She gave me a faint smile, picked up her Bible, and left.

I drove the pick-up truck to the pay phone where Drummond's had been re-built, and called Aunt Sylvia collect. I didn't even bother to say hello, the words tumbled out of my mouth. "Charlene's pregnant. Please come do something."

"Has she told your dad?" asked Aunt Sylvia.

"No, she's mad at Daddy. But her stomach's sticking out like crazy. You should see her."

"She'll tell your dad when she's ready," she said.

"Charlene's waiting for Dad to notice. And she doesn't even want to marry Ernie." My voice shook.

"I know," she said. "She doesn't have to."

An old woman came up behind me and fumbled in her purse for a nickel. I lowered my voice. "She doesn't even like Ernie now. She wants to give the baby up."

"Maybe that's best," she said, and I could hardly believe my ears. "She has her life ahead of her, like you do at Berkeley." She paused. "I may adopt the baby myself."

Aunt Sylvia with a baby? Mama always said Aunt Sylvia would rather change the world instead of diapers. "But you're not married," I said. "How can you have a baby? What would Grandma say?"

The old woman coughed and rattled her change in the cup of her hand. Every time I turned my back to her, she moved around to listen.

Aunt Sylvia laughed softly, and it felt good to hear it, even if she was laughing at me. "You don't have to be married, honey. And I'm a grown-up; Mama doesn't have anything to do with it. She might be happy for us. Anyway, nothing's definite now. Charlene has to get used to the idea. Give her a hug, let her know that you love. . ."

"I tried, and she pushed me away," I whispered, turning so the woman behind me wouldn't see the tears that were rising. "It's my baby, too! Our family! She's talking about abortion."

The old woman edged nearer, studying me with beady eyes suddenly curious, bright as a bird's. She looked like she'd spied a juicy worm and wanted to chew it.

"Oh honey," said Aunt Sylvia, and her voice sounded like Mama's, sweet and southern. "It's the family's baby, and we'll take care of it. We'll take care of Charlene, too. Try not to worry."

"Aunt Sylvia?"

"What?"

The words were caught in my throat, but I forced them out, cupping my hand around the receiver so the old woman couldn't hear. "Did Mama and Daddy have to get married?"

My pulse pounded in the silence, but Aunt Sylvia finally answered. "Why are you asking me a question like that? No, of course they didn't have to. People get married because they love each other."

"You know what I mean. Was it Charlene?"

"Charlene had nothing to do with it," said Aunt Sylvia. "Your parents loved each other more than any couple I've ever seen."

"I better go, Aunt Sylvia." I wiped my nose on my sleeve. The old woman brushed up so close I smelled the mothballs in the sweater she carried over one arm, even though it was hot.

"I love you, honey," she said. "I'll call tonight. You've got California ahead of you in a few weeks; your whole life, don't lose sight of that."

"You're one of those Starling girls, aren't you?" asked

the woman when I hung up. Her eyes shone in triumph, her head cocked. A pigeon, I thought. I shook my head and hurried to the truck, pulling the keys from my purse as fast as I could.

"That's the murder truck, isn't it?" I could still hear her words as I cranked the engine and sped away.

All day, I thought of nothing but Aunt Sylvia's call that night, what I would say. Rob kept calling to ask what was wrong, but I didn't want to see him.

When the phone rang during supper, I leapt to get it. "Aunt Sylvia?" I said.

Marilyn sighed. "That girl thinks everybody who calls this house is going to be Sylvia. Can't get Berkeley off her mind." She dipped her pork chop into a mustard sauce.

"Hi honey," came Aunt Sylvia's voice over the line. "How are you feeling?"

"Okay." It was a lie, and Aunt Sylvia knew it. I turned my back to the kitchen table, but I could feel Charlene's eyes boring into me. The phone wire curled and uncurled around my fingers.

"Where's Charlene?" asked Aunt Sylvia.

"Right here," I said. "You want to talk?"

"Please," she said.

Charlene had already risen, pushing her chair back far so she wouldn't brush her belly on the table. How had I not noticed? She went back to the bedroom, and I listened for a couple of seconds while she picked up on the princess phone. "Aunt Sylvia," she said, and there were tears in her voice. Then her voice hardened. "Hang up, Jubilee," she said.

I sat down and picked up my fork, but I couldn't eat.

"What's that about?" asked Daddy. "You girls plotting a trip to New York?"

139

"Too much money," said Marilyn, and she went on about how we had to save just to buy groceries.

I ducked my head when my chin started to tremble, but tears slipped out of my eyes. "What's wrong, Jubilee?" Daddy interrupted Marilyn and put his napkin on the table. "What's the matter?" He reached across to wipe the tears from my eyes with his thumb.

"It's Charlene," I said. "But she has to tell you." I'd said too much, and I knew it.

Charlene stood in the doorway, her hands on either side of the bulge under her jumper. "It's a baby," she said, and at first Daddy didn't get it.

"What?" He'd just taken a bite of mashed potatoes.

"Oh my stars," said Marilyn. "I should've known, all that throwing up in the morning. Ernie Crenshaw, isn't it?"

Daddy swallowed and then his jaw went slack. He looked at Charlene, then Marilyn, then at me. Then he pounded his fist on the table so hard the silverware jumped. "Ernie Crenshaw! Where is that bastard? I'll beat the tar. . ."

I'd never heard Daddy use language like that. Charlene rushed to him and put her arms around his neck. He pulled her into his lap and cradled her like a baby while she cried.

Marilyn scraped back her chair and started clearing the dishes, staring blankly at the plates as she dumped the leftovers into the garbage. Usually, she'd save even the smallest scrap of meatloaf, but that night, it seemed like nothing was worth saving. Such was the mess we'd all made of our lives. And wouldn't I make an even bigger mess by going to Berkeley? I sat at the end of the table, unable to stand, unable to even look at Daddy and Charlene.

Charlene's sobs dissolved into hiccups. Marilyn handed her a box of Kleenex and rubbed her back.

Daddy said, "Hon, I have an errand. You okay?"

Charlene's face went from collapsed to incredulous. "You're not going to Libertyberg, are you?"

"That's what your Daddy's for." He patted her hair.

"Oh, Daddy," she said, burying her head in her folded arms. But there were no tears this time. Maybe she was happy that at least one man in her life would stand up for her.

After we heard him back out of the driveway in the station wagon, Charlene reached for her purse. "C'mon, Jubilee."

"Where are we going?"

"You're going to drive me to Ernie's. What if Daddy tries to shoot him?"

"Daddy?" The only time I'd seen Daddy with a gun was one November after he nicked a deer that got away. He hadn't gone hunting since. "More likely, Mr. Crenshaw will be firing a few rounds at Daddy."

"All the more reason to go," she said.

"Bye, Marilyn," we called, though the water was running behind the bathroom door to hide the sound of her crying.

Charlene didn't know the way as well as I expected her to, and we were late getting to Ernie's house. It was a little ranch house, the kind that tried to look upscale, with bricks on the bottom and white shingles on top. A bank of faded azaleas lined the driveway, dying. Mr. Crenshaw had planted an American flag on the porch, for Labor Day, I guessed. "Does he always have that flag there?"

"Don't know," she said. She was watching Daddy on the porch, where he was talking to Ernie's dad. Daddy kept poking his finger at Mr. Crenshaw's chest, and Mr. Crenshaw started talking so loud I could make out most of the words.

". . .not Ernie's," he said. "No offense, Mr. Starling, but I don't know your daughter, and I don't think my boy knows her well, either."

Daddy pulled back his fist, but slammed it into his hand instead of Mr. Crenshaw's face. I opened the truck door. "What the hell are you doing?" hissed Charlene.

"Defending you. You wanted me to come, didn't you?" I made my way across their neatly cut crab grass. "Aren't you Ernie's dad?" I called.

Daddy's mouth dropped open, then he clamped it shut and glared at me. "What do you mean, coming here? This is business!" He squinted. "Is that Charlene out there? You girls go home. I'll be there soon."

But I was already on the porch. "Do you have any idea how much time Ernie spends at our house, Mr. Crenshaw? Or how long he's dated Charlene?" For the first time, I saw Mr. Crenshaw's frantic eyes, darting anywhere but my face.

"Ernie goes to everybody's houses for Youth for Christ," he said, and I almost pitied him. His voice shook with the same tremor that made his eyes seem to tremble. "He's a good boy, our only child. He wouldn't lie to his mother and me."

Daddy clenched his fists. "You're saying my daughter's a liar? This is life, and you and me are going to be grandfathers. If you want to teach your son to be a man, then show him how."

Mr. Crenshaw's face darkened, and he pumped himself up to his full height. "I'm a bigger man than you are."

That's when Daddy drew his fist back for the second time, putting his weight on his back leg. Before I knew it, I reached out to stop him. His eyes were red from tears and rage, and the muscles in his arm were strong under my hand. It scared me, like he'd unleashed some power in himself that I'd never known. "C'mon, Daddy. Let's go."

That was enough. Daddy's arm relaxed, but he jabbed a finger at Mr. Crenshaw. "You talk some sense into that boy of yours. First, you better get some in your own head."

We walked to the truck, and Daddy reached in to kiss Charlene, still waiting in the seat. "You want to drive back with me, sweetheart? Jubilee, you follow real close."

As I trailed them, I could see their heads, nodding sometimes, and I wondered what they were saying. What would happen to the baby, now that Ernie said it wasn't his?

We drove into the shadowy driveway, the place where I sometimes still saw Mama, her body slumped. Marilyn was in the kitchen, sitting at the table with her hands running over the green formica, as if she might read the future there. We all sat down, and looked expectantly at Daddy.

His lips were so tight he could hardly talk, and he wrapped his arms around Charlene. "Ernie's not worth it, honey," he told her. "That whole family's trash."

"What happened?" asked Marilyn. Fear began to overtake the fatigue in her voice.

"Wouldn't take responsibility," said Daddy. "They raised a sorry excuse for a boy." Charlene and I looked at each other. That, we knew, was an understatement.

"Did you hit him?" Marilyn's voice had a breathless quality, and her eyes glinted in the dim light. I knew how she felt. I wished Daddy had hit him, too. Scared old Mr. Crenshaw, lying for that lousy son of his, so he could go off to Ole Miss or Southern and get a college education without a crying baby to get in his way.

The next night, a police officer came and delivered a paper saying that Daddy couldn't come within fifty yards of Ernie's father. Having a policeman at the door reminded me of when Mama died, and this time I wanted to listen. Daddy was talking. "I might have lost my temper, but I wasn't going to hurt him, no matter what he said about that ignorant, fool-headed boy of his," Daddy said. "No sir, there's no way I'll go to the Crenshaw house again, papers or no papers. I wouldn't dirty myself by standing in their doorway." When the policeman left, Daddy wadded the papers and stuffed them into the garbage. "A grown man, crying to the police like a little baby! Trash, that's all they are."

Charlene broke up with Ernie over the phone. I couldn't hear much of what she said, but I did hear her tell him, "can't handle the truth." She mailed his ring back to Libertyburg, along with the heart necklace. But when the next Youth for Christ meeting came around, she dressed in one of the loose jumpers she'd been wearing. Rob had just come over to watch *Laugh In*.

"You're kidding," I said. "You're not really going, are you? Ernie'll be there. They'll make fun of you."

"If they're for real, they won't," said Rob, and I shot him a dirty look.

"God loves me," Charlene said, turning sideways to eye her belly in the mirror over the mantel. "Besides, if they accepted me after Mama died, they'll accept me now."

I started to tell her how that was different, how they could feel smug about themselves for forgiving her for having a mother who was murdered, but that this was her own sin. She put the strap of her new purse over her shoulder and picked up Daddy's car keys. "Bye," she smiled, and wagged her fingers at Rob and me in a little wave. That was when I knew she was going to test them. She didn't really expect that everything would be just fine.

Marilyn, Daddy, Rob, and I sat in the living room watching TV but we were too nervous about Charlene to pay attention. Marilyn made popcorn, but Rob was the only one who could eat. I finally took the tupperware container away from him. "You're getting on my nerves, all that crunching," I said, sliding the popcorn out of his reach.

He nodded like he understood, and laughed out loud at something Goldie Hawn did. "There's nothing you can do," he said when he saw my eyes. "Relax."

It wasn't long before the car door slammed in the driveway, and Daddy turned off the TV and opened the front door. It was Charlene, but at least she wasn't crying. Her face was tight as she slung her purse onto the dining table. "They're sinners, too," she said. "We're all sinners."

"That's only one way to look at it," said Rob. "What is sin, anyway?"

"This isn't the time for a big philosophical discussion," I told him.

"Whatever you say," he said, and made a reach for the popcorn again.

"Was Ernie there?" I asked, though Daddy frowned at me and pulled an imaginary zipper over his lips.

"At least Ernie knows he's a sinner." Charlene looked at Daddy. "They said he enlisted in the Army last week." She went to the bathroom, and soon the water in the shower was running, as if she could wash off more than sweat or dust.

She never went to another Youth for Christ meeting, not even when they called to ask where she was. Instead, she started driving out to the farm once a week, to pray with Grandma Tattershall. She came home with caps and booties and tiny jackets in patterns I recognized from the crocheted doilies that lay on Grandma's Sunday table. Grandma had clicked her crochet hooks through a lot of trouble.

We could hear Daddy sighing at night again, Marilyn trying to comfort him. "I'm losing both my girls. They've grown away from me. I let it happen," he told her, and, in the next room, Charlene and I looked at each other. "Where did I go wrong?" he asked. He was really asking, if only Mama had still been alive, wouldn't things be different?

In a few weeks, Charlene was going to move out, and at least her life with Marilyn would be over. Daddy arranged for her to live at a home for unwed mothers in Mobile. She could take college credit courses there. Sylvia talked to Daddy about raising the baby, but he wouldn't hear of it. The baby would stay with us, he said. To cheer up Charlene, Marilyn bought baby clothes, white for either a boy or a girl. She arranged them on the kitchen table, the little caps over the sleepers, booties below, so Charlene could admire them when she came home from school. But when Charlene saw them, she burst into tears, both hands over her face.

When she could talk, she said, "I can't be a mother. I thought I loved Ernie, but I didn't. What kind of mother would I be?" She'd never said that much to Marilyn.

A pleased look crossed Marilyn's face, like she could finally be a mother to Charlene. She put her arm around her. "We'll all be the baby's family," she said. She picked up a pair of booties and smiled down at them. "I'll mother your little baby to death."

Charlene was so horrified she stopped crying. "No one's mothering my baby to death. I'm giving it up for adoption. There must be somebody out there who'll be a good mother to the baby."

Marilyn dropped the booties on the table. "I'll help you be a good mother, sweetheart," she told Charlene, but a hurt look came into Marilyn's eyes, as if she needed a mother, herself.

That night, Daddy sat on the sofa next to Charlene. "God gave up his only child, didn't he?" she asked him.

Try to reply to that! said the look on her face, and Daddy couldn't. "But. . . but this is your b-baby, Charlene."

"Yes," she said, "and Marilyn's not going to raise my baby. She acts like it's hers already."

From the kitchen came the slam of a cabinet door, and Marilyn appeared, wiping her hands on a dish towel. "*Somebody* better claim that little baby."

"What do you care?" Charlene stormed out, slamming the bedroom door.

Later that night, when the darkness in our room allowed for confessions, Charlene told me, "I mean, love is what you feel for a baby you're willing to let somebody else raise, because it'll be happier."

"If you'll let me, I'll be a good aunt. I'll be like Aunt Sylvia," I said, thinking of the places I could take my niece or nephew, the worlds I'd open up, the way Aunt Sylvia had for me. I remembered the way Marilyn cradled me during the tornado, how loved I'd felt, but there was no way to explain that to Charlene. "You know, Marilyn might treat the baby all right. She'll love it, I'm sure." But only silence came from her side of the room. "Mama would've raised your baby. She'd do anything for us. She gave up Levi Litvak for us, didn't she?" Still, Charlene said nothing.

During the days, I packed for Berkeley, trying to keep my own life in focus. A new denim jacket, a popcorn maker, I piled it all up in a corner of the bedroom, feeling guilty about my future while Charlene's stomach kept growing. Charlene ignored the pile until she saw me fold a mini-dress on top.

"You won't wear that in Berkeley, will you?" she asked.

"What's wrong with it?" I asked.

"It's too short. Guys'll want to get in your pants. Pack jeans, that's all they're wearing out there, anyway." She pulled the dress off the pile and held it up, her head cocked. "You think rules don't apply to you, don't you?'

"What rules?"

"See? You don't even know rules exist." She folded the mini-dress and put it on my bed. "Take it back to the store. Exchange it." She looked down at her stomach. "This could happen to you, too."

"I've never. . . " I started.

"I know. Just be careful." She picked up the doll I'd rescued from the tornado, and tugged its skirt down. The blue crepe paper dress I'd made for her had faded to purple. She held out the doll. "Here. She'll bring you good luck."

I took it and hugged Charlene. "I'll be back home as soon as the baby's born."

Her arms felt warm around me.

Charlene had to stay home with Marilyn while Daddy and I drove out West. Once he got me settled in the dorm, he'd leave the truck with me and fly back to Mississippi. Charlene thanked God she wouldn't have to look at that truck anymore. He'd answered her prayers again, she said.

PART THREE

BERKELEY 1968

Chapter Ten

Heat rose off the Texas roads, making the asphalt shimmer in black waves like liquid tar. Daddy and I were farther from home than we'd ever been before. For nearly two days, we drove from the green rolling hills of east Texas to the dusty western plains, with boxes of school clothes roped down in the back of the pick-up truck.

It was Daddy's idea to take the back roads rather than the interstates to Berkeley, where classes started in a couple of weeks. You could really see America on its back roads, Daddy had said, eager to get started. He'd never seen anything west of Dallas.

We stopped for gas and rest rooms at rundown, one-pump stations where all you could see on the Texas horizon was the gray of hills so distant they might've been clouds raining on Vietnam. Texas had the cheapest gas I'd ever seen: nineteen cents a gallon. That nineteen cents put Daddy in a great mood. He pulled into a one-pump station with a run-down shack and said, "Heaven on earth! Never dreamed getting across Texas could be so cheap." He bought me a Bit 'O Honey candy bar, and said, with a lilt in his voice, "Here's a bit 'o heaven, hon."

But as I unwrapped it and started to bite, a couple of

fat maggots were burrowing into the candy. I almost gagged. "Maggots!" I said, but Daddy didn't hear, and I tossed it out the window when he wasn't looking. After all he'd been through, did he need to know heaven had maggots?

In the hill country, the truck behaved like a beauty, like a farm nag outstripping race horses in a surprise finish. Every movement when the gears shifted was a perfect purr. Daddy snoozed, his elbow stuck out the window, his head lolling against a pillow wedged between the seat back and the door. When Daddy drove, he arranged a pillow beneath him to raise him high enough to see above the steering wheel. I'd gotten tall like Mama, so I could see fine.

The truck never performed so smoothly with him, I thought, letting the speedometer needle edge above seventy.

It would shimmy and jerk and stall out with Daddy. You just had to have the right touch, like Mama and me.

I distracted myself on that long, hot trip by thinking about the new life that lay ahead: California! At my destination, the Pacific Ocean stretched all the way to Asia. Maybe I'd never go back home, I thought, with a ripple of excitement in my stomach. On the West Texas plains, it began to rain, a hot, steamy splatter that fell in hard drops. "Like a cow peein' on a flat rock," said Daddy, squinting over the steering wheel.

On the passenger side, the windshield wiper was stuck about a third of the way up the glass, and above its slant, for a moment, Mama's face appeared, the drops of rain like pearls sliding down her cheeks, but she was smiling, as if looking at me from the other side of a mirror. Despite the rain, her eyes were so clear that I could see my own reflected there, like a dream so strange you remember it for years. Her face was younger than when she'd died, and she looked like the Rita Hayworth-style picture of her that Daddy had kept on the mantel until he married Marilyn. Mama's red hair was pinned up in a pouf, but this time, in the windshield, her face was relaxed and happy rather than pouty, and her hair lay in waves on her shoulders. I smiled back, the way I did when I saw her in dreams, but then the picture faded into Rob's face and the smile disappeared.

Rob's eyes had been teary when he'd hugged me good-bye. He ducked his head to wipe his eyes on his shirt sleeve, and whispered that he'd call and write every week. I couldn't bring myself to cry. There would be lots of guys in Berkeley, I told myself, people who could make the world a bigger place. He pressed a cassette tape into my hands, the Beatles' "Sergeant Pepper," along with other cuts from *Revolver*. Since the truck had only an AM radio, Charlene bought me a cassette player and FM radio.

With it in my lap, I listened to Paul McCartney sing "She's Leaving Home" while I drove. "I'm puddling up, sweetie," Daddy said, his eyes watery as he reached for the radio dial. "Let's find something else." I was shocked, not that he was sad I was leaving; I already knew that. Daddy never did hide his feelings, and for a long time I thought all men were like that. What surprised me was that he actually listened to the Beatles' words, just like he'd listened to Mama's songs. Somehow, I had always thought rock 'n roll was a secret language that adults couldn't hear even when it was spoken in front of them.

Soon Daddy was snoring beside me and I didn't want to wake him up. You couldn't hear the boxes rattling under the tarp in the truckbed, with both the music and the snoring. Daddy's face looked smooth, reconciled, in sleep at least, to my uncertain future in a foreign place, and to Charlene's new future.

Sitting high behind the wheel, gunning the engine westward toward the spot on the horizon where an orange sun was slipping into a bank of blue clouds and distant mountains, I thought about how Aunt Sylvia told Daddy that people are just people, everywhere. Surely she didn't really mean it. Look at how she'd fled Biloxi. It was just a good argument for Daddy to let me go, I thought. People *had* to be different in California.

As I sped along that West Texas road, my mind wandered with the hum of the engine. In California, no one would know how Mama had died, not if I could help it. The idea was so exhilarating I wanted to push the accelerator to the floor. Daddy was still sleeping, his head against the window, the wind ruffling his hair, a frown now between his eyebrows, as if he were worried even in sleep. Had he known, back then, that Mama was capable of saying "I love you, sugar muffin" to another man? The speedometer needle was on eighty when Daddy woke, stretched his legs, then almost leaped from his seat. "Slow down! Eighty miles an hour! For cryin' out loud, Jubilee Starling!" He clutched the edge of the seat. "Is that how you've been driving this truck while you've put all those miles on it? It's a wonder you haven't had a wreck."

He'd noticed the mileage, then. "But it wasn't even shimmying. See how smooth it rides? And there's not another car in sight." I started to press on the accelerator again, but he grabbed my arm.

"I'm driving." He flapped a hand to tell me to pull over. "It's getting dark, and we've still got a hundred miles to Seminole." That was our destination, the next town Daddy had circled in red on the map.

The truck jerked under his control, and my words came out with a start. "Daddy, what did you know about. . . I mean, did you know anything about, well, what they were doing before it happened?" I couldn't bring myself to say Levi Litvak's name, or to use the word "murder" in the same breath with Mama's name.

The truck slowed more, though there wasn't another car in sight. He shook his head. "No, honey, I didn't have any idea, but if I had, you can bet I'd have put a stop to it."

It was hard to believe those words were coming out of Daddy's mouth. He was actually talking to me about Levi Litvak. I took a risk, scarcely daring to breathe. "But what if she loved him?"

"She might've thought she did. But love's foolish sometimes. She came to her senses, even if it was too late. I tell you, I could've punched him out. He didn't want to take responsibility for anything."

"What do you mean, she came to her senses?" All I could think about was the phone call I'd overheard years ago, Mama telling Levi Litvak she had too much to lose. "What did she tell you, Daddy?"

He glanced over at me, eyebrows raised. "Same thing she told you, I expect."

"Why would she tell me?"

Relief came over his face, and he lifted his chin higher over the steering wheel. "Well, I'm glad she didn't. Some things, well, it's just too. . .intimate for Charlene to be talking about with her little sister."

Charlene! I didn't know whether to laugh or cry. So he'd been talking about Charlene the whole time, not Mama and Levi Litvak. It was the most intimate conversation I'd ever had with Daddy and we'd been talking about entirely different things.

"'Course, you're not so little any more, and you need to know. . ." Daddy cleared his throat. "You need to know things so you won't wind up where Charlene is."

"Mama told me the facts of life," I said, wondering if

153

I should ask, Would you have gone after Levi Litvak the way you went after Ernie Crenshaw and his father?

"I wish Charlene had known a little more," he said. "But she's seen the truth about that boy. I'm a Christian man, but I could punch the lights out of Ted Crenshaw. You look at the father, you see why the son got to be the way he is. An acorn doesn't fall far from the tree."

"Daddy," I said, taking a deep breath, "Did Mama ever eat light bulbs?"

He smiled, like he was remembering something nice. "Oh, your mama could be silly sometimes. When she was young, she loved to be the life of the party."

"You mean she *did*?"

It must have been the shock in my voice that made him frown. "Just once, at her senior prom. She was singing, and it was part of her act. Where did you hear that?"

"I don't remember," I lied, remembering Mr. Langstrom's voice from the teachers' lounge, the nasty laughter.

"It was just one of those little bulbs, for flashlights." He showed me how big it was, holding about half an inch between his thumb and forefinger. "She crunched it up real fine, like sand, so it never cut her." He gave me a sharp look. "Don't you go trying it out, just because your mother did. And don't you go trying any drugs, either. If anybody offers you a marijuana cigarette," he said it like, "marriage-wanna." "Then you say, 'no thank you,' you hear me? If I hear tell of you doing any drugs out there, I'll come get you before you can say 'help me, Daddy.'"

"We've talked about this a million times."

"And we'll talk about it a million times more if we have to," he said.

I thought for a second. "Did anybody offer Mama that light bulb, or did she just bring it to the prom, herself?"

He wasn't smiling now. "Honey, it was just a trick she

read about somewhere. Folks in New York were doing it, I reckon. Don't get funny ideas about your mama. She just did that once, and she was lucky it didn't hurt her."

In the Mojave Desert, we passed through a sand storm so thick we couldn't see anything but swirls of brown sand outside the windows, peppering the glass like gritty sleet. I could even taste the sand, feel it in my eyes and nose. Daddy slid the truck to a stop on what we hoped was the side of the highway. The desert hurled itself at the truck so hard that the hula dancer tipped and bowed all the way to the dashboard, but she stayed on her feet. I looked at her while I prayed, and I thought of Mama and how she would hold me in her arms if she were here. Not now, God, I prayed. Not before California. I thought of pioneers in that great desert, whose wagons would have filled with sand, and whose skeletons would lie buried far beneath the roiling sea that the desert had become in just a few seconds. Charlene would say it was the wrath of God, and I wondered if I deserved this for wandering too far from home. But Daddy handed me his handkerchief to put over my mouth and nose, and then he pulled his shirt up to his face, squinting his eyes shut. Semi-trucks whizzed past us, invisible through that sunless sand, with a rumble that made the pick-up shake even more.

And then, finally, it was gone. The truck shook in only little trembles, and the air got brighter, then the sun came out and the wind stopped.

We saw that we were barely off the asphalt. Ahead, other cars became visible, and they, too, started up slowly as if dazed. "That was scary," I said, trying to spit out the grit in my mouth. Daddy squeezed my hand.

"We got through it," he said. Then we moved on, slowly, though the windshield was so pocked by the grind-

155

ing sand that we could barely see through it. Daddy drove for miles against the blinding sun until we came to a town with a garage that could replace the glass. All those tiny towns looked alike, a main street with dusty storefronts and lazy dogs dreaming on the sidewalks.

Aunt Sylvia's admonition that "people are all the same" came to my mind while we waited for the windshield to be fixed. The kids who lived here survived, just like I had in Biloxi. Someone had painted a bright mural on a grocery store's cinder block wall, showing brown-skinned people eating vegetables. Maybe that was how they passed the time.

Everywhere we went, though, if there was a radio station, it was playing "Hey Jude." It was as if all the small towns couldn't get enough of hearing a song everyone in the big cities was listening to. It made me feel at home there in the barren towns in the middle of the desert, like coming from a small town, whether it was Biloxi, Mississippi or Seminole, Texas, made you part of a bigger community. All those people all over the globe living in villages might be joined together even more than people in New York or Los Angeles. Even in small desert towns and in tiny Mississippi hamlets, in the late-August heat of 1968, people were singing about taking a sad song and making it better. . .

I couldn't wait to get to Berkeley.

Daddy insisted on driving when we neared Stockton. We'd driven all the way from Oxnard, near Los Angeles, but now there was no choice but to hit the main highways. He climbed into the driver's seat and clutched the wheel with both hands. I realized, when Daddy worked his jaws every time he shifted, that the real reason we'd taken back roads across the country was because the interstate scared him to death. I eyed him, and a rush of pity made me put my hand over his. Without taking his eyes from the road, he shook it off.

"I need both hands to drive, sweetheart," he growled. With Daddy jerking at the wheel, it was a harrowing drive to Berkeley. Beyond, the San Francisco Bay was spread out, sparkling under the late sun like a jewelry box filled with precious stones, and you could see what I knew must have been the Golden Gate Bridge. It was like the pictures, except it was brighter orange. The city sparkled under a white light, like someone had waved a wand over it.

On campus, the air smelled different, and trees with long silvery purplish leaves lined the streets. Eucalyptus, I thought. They smelled vaguely like the oils Grandma Tattershall had used on Charlene's and my chests when we were little and sick with colds. It was a good smell, a comfort. Everywhere Daddy turned the truck, there were more buildings than I'd imagined a university could have. We wound our way through narrow lanes that ended in parking spaces marked "Professor Emeritus," and Daddy would have to turn around. "Must be a pretty famous guy," he said, shoving the gear stick into reverse once again.

The eucalyptus trees shivered in the coolness of the late afternoon, and the kids we passed wore jackets with their jeans, and either sandals or hiking boots. My white Keds already seemed out of place, and people stared at the truck while we meandered through the twisting roads up the campus, looking for the dormitory I'd been assigned.

When we found it, the sky was getting dusky, and parents stood clustered, kissing their kids and climbing back into their shiny new cars. We rattled up in the truck. It shimmied and coughed to a standstill, the way it did when Daddy turned off the engine. Two skinny guys in patched jeans and tie-dyed tee-shirts turned to stare. One of them had a scraggly mustache, and the other wore a macramé peace sign around his neck. I jumped out, eager to meet the people who were going to be the friends I hadn't been able to make at Tallulah High. "Are y'all in this dorm?" I asked, picking at one of the ropes knotted onto the truck bed.

The one with the peace sign frowned, like he didn't understand. A disbelieving smile slackened the other's mouth. His eyes tightened as he gazed at the truck and settled on the license plate, with its white magnolia and "Mississippi, the Hospitality State" stamped on it. At least it didn't say "Home of the Two Miss Americas" any more.

"Not real friendly, huh?" Daddy grunted and yanked at a heavy box.

Now the guy was studying Daddy's elevator shoes. "Wow!" He nudged his friend and grinned, showing little pearl-like teeth. "Hey, man, take us all the way up to the penthouse." He snickered, and his friend shrugged and turned away.

What happened to peace, love, and understanding? I hoped Daddy didn't get his lame joke.

He did, but he didn't stop untying the rope. "Nope," he told them, without even looking their way. "I reckon you're high enough as it is."

The guy looked stunned, then burst out laughing and walked back to the dorm. He poked his head inside and yelled up, hand cupped to his mouth just like Mrs. Guest used to do when she'd call Mama over for coffee. "Hey, the Beverly Hillbillies are here!" he called. He came back out, grinning, his hands shoved in the back pockets of his jeans, his elbows standing out like skinny chicken wings.

It reminded me of the way some football players in Biloxi made fun of me once in the hall when I was wearing black eyeshadow and green nail polish: "Hey, it's a runaway from the Addams Family!"

Daddy looked the guy straight in the eyes. "It's a fool who makes the world a little colder, isn't it? Why don't you try not to be so damn cool? You're working too hard at it, buddy." I couldn't believe it: Daddy quoting Paul McCartney!

The guy with the chicken wings couldn't believe it, either. He stared with his head cocked like a bird. All those times "Hey Jude" blared from the radio during the trip, the words had gotten into Daddy's brain. He was listening to every word. It made me wonder what else he might know.

Two girls came out to stare at the truck. "Mississippi!" one of them whispered. She had long, straight hair, the kind I'd envied when I used to iron my waves to look like Jane Asher. They looked at me like I was from Mars, some alien invader posing as a backwoods immigrant to the "love capital" of the world.

Daddy winked at me. "You want to come back home, you say the word, sweetheart. But if you want to stay, you'll show these characters what it means to be a self-respecting human being. They could learn a lot from you." He put his arm around me and kissed my cheek. "You'll teach them some things they never even thought about."

I was proud of him. It was a side of Daddy I'd never seen before, the side Mama must've fallen in love with: he was cool. He was comfortable with who he was, as long as he wasn't driving a truck on the interstate.

As I lifted one of the boxes from the truck, a deep voice bellowed out. "Man, this is what I call a superior vehicle! And from Mississippi, blues capital of the world!" A guy with hair that stood out like amber cotton candy held both his hands before the grille without touching it, framing it reverently. His loose white pants fluttered in the light breeze, and he wore a satin vest embroidered with

159

silver stars but no shirt, so you could see blonde hairs curling on his chest. When he saw me, he strode forward, his hand extended. I propped the box between my hip and the truck and shook hands. "Look at those side vents on this truck," he said. "1948, right?"

"How'd you know?" I asked.

One of the girls looked at me, new respect in her eyes. "It's Cat Heller," she said, as if that answered my question.

"Who's he?" I asked.

"A D.J. on KZEN," she said.

Of course. California was like that, I thought, famous people everywhere. Cat Heller backed off and admired the shiny finish. "Far out. Look at the shape she's in! This is one truck that's been respected."

The two kids in tie-dyed tee-shirts looked sheepish when he lumbered over to them, like a cat would walk, leading with his hips, his shoulders thrust back. He took the skinniest one's elbow. "Now that's your elbow, and that's your ass," he said, nodding to the guy's rear end, where a tear in his jeans revealed a pink square of flesh. "You oughtta stop showing your ass around here. After all, buddy. . ." he turned to me. "Sorry, I didn't get your. ..."

"Jubilee Starling," I said, too eagerly, so I caught myself and put my hand on my hip, trying to look cool.

He smiled, like he was trying not to laugh, and turned back to the two guys. "After all, Jubilee's new in town." He took the box from me, and carried it to the dorm, then went back for another.

"Thank you, sir," said Daddy, and shook his hand when they were both going back for more boxes. I was glad Daddy didn't give him the Shriner handshake. He and Daddy worked silently, while the band of people who'd been sneering began to gather, admiring the truck now that this guy had blessed it. A couple of other guys pitched in

160

to help unload the boxes. With new confidence, I turned Charlene's cassette player to "With A Little Help From My Friends," but before I could click it on, someone in the crowd sang, "Hey Jube, don't be a rube. . ."

It was so soft I wasn't sure I heard it. Daddy and the guy with the silver stars on his vest were grunting and scraping the boxes against the truck, so they didn't hear. I had a second thought. I flipped over the tape and let "Eleanor Rigby" sail out, with the Beatles wondering where all the lonely people come from.

That afternoon was my introduction to the magic of Berkeley. Aunt Sylvia had been right when she told Daddy people were the same anywhere you went.

Everywhere, people thought I was a weirdo. Maybe I was.

Chapter Eleven

Northern California was alternately silvery gray and blue, fog hanging in the air like the veil Loretta Holliday used to wear over her face at Saint Sebastian's, as if she were a bride, still unclaimed. The white rim of the sun glowed through the gray, promising the warmth that nearly always arrived by afternoon, when the fog, like breath blown against glass, faded into blue sky.

In San Francisco, I explored the city streets and then the winding two-line highways that meandered north through redwood forests, listening to the tape deck Charlene gave me, or belting out my own songs – rock 'n roll, hymns, blues, the way I did around the house in Biloxi.

161

With the truck, I learned San Francisco easily, the grid of streets that shifted from Chinatown to the Tenderloin with a turn of the steering wheel. I navigated through whole worlds, feeling as invisible as I was in that Mojave sand storm. On Jones Street, I passed little Chinese girls with long thin braids they would sling over their shoulders like whips. The truck perched at the top of steep streets at an angle when I could see only the blue sky and the spired tops of buildings, and the accelerator seemed to dare me to push, to trust the descent I couldn't yet see. But the brakes held without a single squeal.

Near Golden Gate Park, I parked the truck to watch girls with painted faces dance while a bearded man played a harmonica. People were too busy pointing at the Mississippi license plates to look at me. I was a visitor without a face, only eyes. The westward streets ran straight to the ocean, as if they never ended, continuing beneath the blue waves, deep into secret places where strange creatures lived, into a place of dreams only infants might remember. Maybe Mama was in that place.

Seagulls rose from the beach like scraps of paper, confused but knowing, hurled upward by the whipping wind. I ventured out from the truck, wrapping my jacket against the cold, a bone-chilling dampness unlike anything in Mississippi. Beaches had always been for warmth, but here even the stunted cedar trees seemed to shiver in the cold, bent and gnarled like old women.

My trumpet case rattled gently on the seat beside me, reminding me of notes eager to escape. At Stinson Beach and Muir Woods, I pulled it out and serenaded the tide and the redwoods, playing tunes that wove in and out of the coastal fog and ocean breeze. I played to God and Mama.

Every Saturday when Rob called, he'd find something

to complain about, usually about my picking up hitchhikers. It was a way of finding company, I explained, but he didn't care. "What are you, a taxi?" he asked. "You don't have to help everybody."

I told him it was an adventure, to see where I'd end up at the end of the day, but he didn't understand. I might as well have been talking to Grandma Tattershall. I tried to get off the phone in a hurry so I could crank up the motor. Sometimes I thought I saw Levi Litvak, standing by the road with his thumb stuck out, smiling like he was on television. After all, this was a world where anything could happen.

In October, after a Saturday had come and gone without the usual call from Rob, a letter from him came in the afternoon mail, and I curled up in bed to read it. He was telling me that he couldn't go steady with me anymore. It was obvious, he said, that I was looking for another guy by picking up hitchhikers.

"Go steady!" I said it out loud, and my roommate, Lisa Field, looked up from reading *Who Rules America?*. She always had a book in front of h"er, so we hardly ever talked, unless one of us needed to borrow laundry soap or a quarter for the dryers in the basement.

"What?" She pushed her straight blonde hair behind her ears and squinted at me, as if she hadn't known I was there.

I waved the page. "My friend, Rob, says he doesn't want to go steady anymore. I didn't know we were." My voice shook, and I was afraid I'd cry.

"We all have our contradictions." She went to her desk and pulled out a plastic bag with her marijuana stash. "Here," she said, lighting a joint. She sat cross-legged on my bed, her knee jutting through a tear in her jeans.

I ripped up the letter and sat holding the pieces with

my hands trembling.

"You want to talk about it?" Her words rode from her mouth on expanding wheels of smoke. She could blow smoke rings as easily as kids made floating bubbles by dipping wands into liquid soap.

"Maybe." I took the burning joint. Daddy's words came to me, "marriage-wanna," and my stomach turned a bit. It seemed like everybody in the dorm smoked, but I hadn't tried it. The wet tip stuck to my lips, and the smoke burned my throat so badly I coughed it out.

Lisa looked at me, a curious light in her eyes. "This is your first time, isn't it? Look, here's how." She inhaled deeply, making the joint glow and crackle, and sat with her chest puffed out for a while. Finally, she let out the smoke. "That's it," she said, and handed it back.

She watched, a proud teacher, as I inhaled again and held it. She laughed. "You're funny."

"You know what?" I exhaled and watched the long stream of smoke fade away. "My aunt got a death-threat in Mississippi."

"No way," she said, watching me closely.

I told her the whole story, right down to the letter in the Biloxi newspaper.

"Might have been the Klan," she said. "I wonder what that's like, having the Klan after you."

"I'd leave town," I said, and giggled. Guess that's what I did, right?" I made a face with puckered up lips and wide eyes.

"You're stoned," said Lisa. "Nice, huh?" She took another hit. "You want to talk about that letter now? You're always so quiet."

All around the room, things had a new meaning, as if they'd been holding secrets all those weeks before. A silver coffee pot gleamed on Lisa's desk, shining in a way I'd never noticed. My bottle of green Prell seemed absurd next to Lisa's herbal shampoo, and I realized it should be thrown out. At my desk, the tornado doll stood in one of the cubbies, propped against my philosophy text. She needed a new dress. The crepe paper looked like something the tornado might have left, tattered from the trip out. After all she'd been through, she deserved something nice.

Beneath me, a lump in my bed poked against my rear, and I reached in and pulled out a sock, dangling it between us. "What's this?"

"Your sock," said Lisa, and we giggled. "But, really, do you want to talk now?"

I frowned. "About what?"

"That guy, Rob."

Rob. The sock wasn't funny anymore, and I plucked at the toe. "I'm going to miss him. It's hard to make friends out here," I told her.

She looked surprised. "I'm your friend."

That was the beginning of my friendship with Lisa.

When people asked me to talk just so they could laugh, she'd step in, putting on a heavy New York accent. "What? You think everybody should sound alike and eat the same white bread?" Nobody wanted to seem politically backward, so they would shut up. Lisa was from Connecticut, and she confessed that she was getting away from her own roots, but for reasons different than mine. Her father was a big corporate lawyer with Wall Street offices, and her pictures of her parents and younger brothers showed them in front of what looked like a mansion. "My mom's whole life is shopping on Fifth Avenue," she told me, now that we were getting to know each other. But I still couldn't tell her about Mama. Somehow, knowing what her mother's life was like, the fur stoles and trips to

165

Paris, made it harder. How could she possibly understand my mother?

Instead of talking, Lisa and I went to movies, art films in old theaters, foreign films on campus, black and white Hollywood movies from the thirties that made new ones seem garish. It was a whole new underworld, and the escape into those dark theaters was not so terribly different from my solitary excursions on the road.

After Rob's letter, I started picking up even more hitchhikers, partly for the uncertain thrill of it, partly to get back at Rob, but mostly to make new friends. Most people, though, just told me their first names, as if all they were doing was passing through, so what difference did it make. Once, I asked a hitchhiker who told me her name was Moongleaux (she spelled it for me) where she was from.

She looked at me like I was nuts. "I'm from right here," she told me. A pensive look glazed her eyes. "So is everybody who's right here."

"Good. We've got something in common," I said, hopefully. She rummaged in her backpack and offered me some dried apricots, then a joint.

Live for the moment. The past didn't seem to exist for people. Even the most ordinary questions seem outrageous to them. In Marin County, I asked a hitchhiker what he did.

He eyed me without turning his head. "What do I *do*? You mean, a job?" His voice was an astonished whisper. His shoulders hunched as if he were afraid he'd gotten a ride with an ax murderer or a narc.

I shrugged. "Going anywhere for Thanksgiving?"

He gulped and stared at the hula dancer swaying on the dashboard. *"Thanksgiving?* You mean, like Pilgrims?"

There was silence.

"Think McCarthy has a chance to win?" I'd give it one

166

more try.

"That dude running for President? Hey, I'm no politico, man." He told me about the apple juice fast he'd been on for three days, how the last time he'd gone to the bathroom it was pure liquid. I couldn't think of anything to say, so things were quiet until he bailed out at a Sausalito health food store. The slam of his door was a relief.

Tucked into the glove compartment was a letter from Charlene, written on stationery with "Mobile Home for Girls" printed in somber black letters at the top. She was telling me how good it was to be away from Biloxi's gossip about Mama, and how she had too many other things to think about, like the baby and Art Johnson's letters, to worry about Mama's killer any more. There in the health food store parking lot, I unfolded the letter and re-read it. For me, the ghost of Levi Litvak had grown stronger. On campus, a black-suited man waved a Bible and shouted that anything could happen in California: earthquakes, serial killers, the end of the world. So I still looked for Levi Litvak as I drove aimlessly. It was a habit, even a comfort, a familiar ritual in a strange land.

Unlike Charlene, I couldn't forget Mama's killer just because I was in a new place. Instead, I dwelled on him more, on what might have been if Mama had lived. A grandmother! I saw his face in the crowd at a baseball game on the TV in the dorm lobby, or speeding past me on the highway in a convertible. Maybe Loretta Holliday's rumors that it wasn't him in the burned-out Thunderbird were true.

Even weeks after I'd left Mississippi, the thrill of victory over the grip of Biloxi exhilarated me, but it was never enough to rid my mind of Levi Litvak. The alarm would go off in the morning, and Levi Litvak had been in my dreams again. I'd wake and wonder what I'd do if I did see him, imagining myself seizing his pompadour and shaking him, or asking him, *why?* Then, in my mind's eye, I would see the false teeth that would give an answer, prattling about the forecast for a white Christmas as if the very idea of snow made them chatter.

Now, in Sausalito, the fog was closing in, though it might be sunny at the top of Mount Tamalpais. God could hear a concert if it was, I promised, turning back from the Golden Gate Bridge ahead. As the road wound up the mountain, the fog thinned and the sun broke out, putting a glint on the hood. I pulled into some gravel, took my trumpet, and strolled over to face the ocean, crashing somewhere beneath the fog below. Thin brown lizards scampered through the wheat-colored grass of Mount Tam, still bleached by the dry season, and I played to them, God's little creatures. "Kitchen Man" came blasting from my trumpet, and I let myself float on the notes, eyes closed to the warmth of the sun on my face. When I opened them, the fog was closing in, as if I'd been asleep, dreaming of the turnip tops and chops Mama had sung about. Someone clapped, and I was glad I couldn't see who it was. Music was a way of disappearing into the air, but applause brought me back.

The fog became a drizzling rain as I headed back, and beyond a curve in the road, a tall skinny guy with a backpack and a short red beard was walking along.

"Need a ride?" I asked. The brakes squeaked a little, and I reminded myself to check the pads.

"Thanks. Going to Berkeley," he said, brushing drops from his beard. He was a student, he told me, going back home after meditating on Mount Tam all night. Andy Moore, that was his name. I liked that he told me his last name. One of the first things he said was where he was from: Sacramento. At last, a normal guy. He won my heart by going crazy over the truck.

"You keep it in great condition. What is it?" he asked, running his hand over the dashboard. "Early fifties?"

"'48."

He pulled some goat cheese from his backpack, broke off a chunk and offered it to me. His sleeves were rolled up, and long white scars ran along the inside of each wrist.

Maybe it was the rain streaking the windshield that reminded me of how lonely the dorm was, or the thin scar on my calf where I'd once made myself bleed in the bathtub, but I told him about Mama being murdered there in the front seat. I hadn't told anybody at Berkeley about it. "An accident," I had lied to Lisa when she learned my mother was dead, and she assumed it was a wreck. "Were you in the car?" she asked. "No," I said, and that was the end of it. Since everybody in Biloxi thought it was weird we didn't sell the truck, or have it junked, I wasn't going to tell anyone in California that my mother had been stabbed to death in the truck. They wouldn't understand that it was the one way I kept her alive, putting gas in the tank and keeping it humming along the highway.

But I told the whole story to someone I'd just met, trusting him because he'd told me his last name and where he was from. Andy Moore reached out and stroked my hand gently. "Must be hard," he said. He told me how he'd slashed his wrists after he was arrested for hurling a brick at a police car windshield during an anti-war demonstration the year before. It wasn't that he had hated himself then, he told me. He'd hated the whole world. After he got out of jail, he decided, in a few moments of what he called "looking into the abyss," that the world wasn't worth the trouble of living in it. But the bad karma of killing yourself wasn't worth it, either, and he'd given up what he called the "politics of destruction." "Love, that's the important thing," he said. "That's what teaches you how to live."

I nodded, not sure what to say about such a simple truth.

"What's this?" he asked, nudging my black trumpet case with the toe of his boot. "Clarinet?"

"Trumpet."

"You play?"

The notes wanted to escape again, and for the first time since I came to Berkeley, they wanted an audience. At a gravel spot beside the road, I rolled the truck to a stop, pulled out my trumpet, and climbed out, ignoring the fine drizzle. Andy leaned against the truck, his arms folded, while I pointed the trumpet to the horizon and let the music rage into the gray sky and then dissolve into the peace of the ocean's rhythms. He was silent when I wiped my mouth and put it back into the case. We rode away with only the occasional rumbling of the engine breaking the quiet. He took my hand, though, and never let go unless I had to shift. It took longer to drive, but we finally reached his house, a dilapidated Victorian in Berkeley he shared with a roommate. A mangy-looking yellow cat sat in the window.

"Is that your cat?" I didn't want him to leave. Not yet.

"Nah, she belongs to my housemate, Peter. I'm allergic."

"It's been good, talking," I said.

"Hope I see you again. I'm no musician, but you're great on that trumpet," he said. "I feel like I've known you a long time." He scribbled a number on the back of a movie ticket stub he found in his pocket. "Call me whenever."

Must be women's liberation, I thought, as I drove away with his telephone number.

When we talked that night, he asked me to go to Big Sur. Only he didn't have a car, he said. "Mind if I drive your truck?"

For a moment, I couldn't answer. Was that all he wanted, a chance to drive the truck?

"Or do you want to drive?" he asked.

"Yeah, I'll drive."

"Great. I'll bring the food. And I have two sleeping bags, if you need one."

A sleeping bag? It hadn't occurred to me that we'd be staying overnight. "Yeah, that'd be nice." Sleeping bags kept you apart, I reminded myself when I hung up.

From the height of the cliffs along Highway One, the Pacific Ocean wasn't calm and friendly like the Gulf of Mexico, lapping at Biloxi's sand like a brown puppy. It was as if mysterious gods lived in the deep waters to the west, angry gods who rose up and whipped at your hair or grabbed your ankles as you walked in the sand.

Andy and I had driven all morning, the camping gear tied down in the back. What was I doing with this stranger beside me? He talked about things he saw when he meditated, strange old houses and women's faces, and he even stopped talking a few times to write down lines of poetry. Slowly, he began to seem familiar.

In Watsonville, "The Artichoke Capital of the World," we had a picnic near a plowed-up field. It was an odd place to stop, after passing the Santa Cruz beaches, but we were hungry. The air smelled different in Watsonville, unlike the eucalyptus in Berkeley. It smelled of fresh, sun-baked earth that the farmworkers tended, as if you could scoop the dark brown from the ground and eat it like bread. Andy had packed a thermos full of noodles with a sauce unlike anything I'd ever tasted. That was the way the world felt, full of things I'd never seen or heard or tasted before.

As the truck glided around the hairpin curves of Highway One below Monterey and Carmel, I started to sing, the way I would when I was driving alone. It was one of Mama's old hymns, "Just As I Am." Andy leaned his head back against the seat and closed his eyes till I finished.

"Far out," he said, a dreamy look in his eyes. "You've got a trumpet in your throat, too."

At last, we stood at one of the jutting cliffs at Big Sur, arched out over the ocean where the wind and waters had slowly eaten away the land. Far below, on the little flat plate of land that met the water, a rusted-out car looked as if it had been planted in the grass. "Nobody survived that one," said Andy, and I wondered how the bodies had been recovered, so steep were those cliffs. Then he drew a breath. "A whale! Look!" He pointed south.

Far in the ocean, the waters moved to a different rhythm, a pattern of white spray and a gray hump rising. The most majestic thing I'd ever seen in the Gulf of Mexico was the blessing of the shrimp fleets every spring.

For two hours, we hiked back along Big Sur's mountain trails, backpacks sagging on our hips. I was wearing my white keds, and Andy looked confused when I complained that the rocks on the path hurt my feet.

"Where are your hiking boots?" he asked.

When I told him I didn't have any, he promised he'd find a pair for me. Maybe his housemate had an old pair that would fit, next time we went camping. I said nothing, thinking, next time! He went before me along the steep trails, sure-footed as he picked his way up, then stood to give me a hand over the slippery rocks. I didn't even ask where we were going. It was like the games people in the dorm would play, "trust games" where you would close your eyes and fall backward into someone's arms.

172

The path grew flatter and smoother, and the sound of a stream rippling over rocks joined a bird's song that followed us. Then it came into view: a clear river tumbling through a valley, with a space beside it that seemed made for two sleeping bags. Andy began peeling off his clothes, first his blue jean jacket, then his shirt, and I saw his smooth, hairless chest. Last, his jeans came off, with his thin knees pumping, first one, then the other, into the air.

He wasn't wearing underwear. I stared in wonderment at his nakedness, at the wilderness of his body. He smiled at me and waded into the water, splashing his chest with it, and turning to me as he shivered. "Don't try it. It's too cold," he called, as he dived beneath the surface. His body glided under the clear water like a dolphin, and he came up, slicking his hair back from his forehead and sputtering water. He grinned. "It's great. But it's freezing."

Thin slivers of green that looked like blades of grass wiggled through the water, and I cried, "Look out! Snakes!"

There was a quick swish, and Andy picked one up, holding it squirming by its neck before he gently released it into the water again. I drew my knees to my chest, horrified. Snakes in Mississippi were cottonmouths, rattlesnakes, or water moccasins, and I had learned to be careful of even the garter snakes on Grandma's farm.

"They won't hurt you," he said, wading out when he saw my fear. He bent to pull a towel from his backpack, and then lay sprawled beside me, his arms flung open to the sun, eyes closed. "Feels great," he said, then turned to me and sat up on one elbow. "What's wrong? Really, these snakes are harmless. I'd tell you if they weren't."

I still sat with my knees drawn to my chest, amazed at his body, the first adult male body I'd seen without clothes. I thought of the statues through history, of

Michelangelo's David, of the pictures I'd seen in the text from the art history class I was taking. Andy was beautiful – the red hair, the muscles beneath the smooth pale skin. On his stomach was a freckle, like a chip from Michelangelo's chisel. I couldn't imagine such ease with Rob, all the guilty fumbling we had done through clothes.

He was staring at my face. "This is new to you, isn't it, Jubilee? I'm sorry, I didn't even think about it. You're really young." He smoothed the hair from my forehead, a tender, awed look on his face. "A virgin," he whispered under his breath. He reached for the clothes he'd left in a pile by the backpack.

"Don't." I touched the freckle on his belly, and his body was still cool from the water. "It looks like a sculptor left a spot unsmoothed."

"Well, I'm not perfect," he said, gazing down at the length of his body. Even his toes were long and thin.

"I think you're beautiful."

He threw back his head and laughed, his throat moving under the red hair of his beard. My face got hot. Then he pulled me to him, and whispered, "You are, too."

We stayed for two days, making love by the river in the broad daylight and under the stars at night, listening to the water ripple. The second morning, Andy unwrapped some mescaline as carefully as if it were a sacrament, and the world became holy and hilarious. Indian ghosts rattled the trees with their breath, cartoon faces swirled in the river, shadows of clouds kissed the wind. The snakes in the water were long ribbons of green, undulating and beautiful. Once, a deer nosed its way into the brush, then saw us and stood so still that after a while I decided it was a statue I hadn't noticed before.

"See?" Andy whispered, holding out the palms of his

hands. "Look at your hands." I held them out, and they pulsated with light and energy. "Now you can see what's always there. We're blinded by our sight most of the time." The ache in my heart that was always Mama became more than a puzzle and a mystery. I could hear Mama's voice, and it was pure joy.

At night, after Andy cooked dinner on a Coleman stove, the moon rose over the top of the steep valley walls, a sliver of orange in late October that looked like a scythe, as if, optimistic as new love, it could harvest the clouds that would gather and then pass with the winds. I dreamed of the whale making its long journey in the Pacific, and then snakes slithered through my sleep, like green rain sliding down glass. But I wasn't afraid. Andy had zipped the sleeping bags together, and when I wakened once I felt his arm around me, and heard his even breath. Above, a long cloud moved across the moon in a southward migration, making the lunar eye wink as if this were all a secret joke between the moon and me. Even loneliness didn't seem so horrible, and I slept again.

Chapter Twelve

In his bedroom, Andy had a pin-up on the closet door, not of Brigit Bardot or Jane Fonda, someone you'd expect. It was an X-ray of a woman's torso he had taken from a hospital garbage bin after his wrists were bandaged. "They were throwing it away," he said, stepping back from his closet so I could admire it. "Can you imagine?"

The round outlines of her breasts floated over her ribs like milky-white clouds, and just the tops of her pelvic

175

bones showed. A tease, he said. He didn't know who she was; that was part of her charm, he told me. Then he pulled the X-ray down, folded it, and placed it carefully in the trash container beside his desk. Before Big Sur, Andy had been celibate ever since he'd tried to kill himself, but when he threw away that X-ray, I felt like I'd saved him from something almost worse than death. I would kiss the white indentations on his wrists, feeling the blood pulsing beneath the scars like an affirmation that death didn't always have to win.

In the middle of the semester, I started spending more time at Andy's house than in the dorm room with Lisa. The house stood on a narrow, shady street that ran up into the foothills. As soon as you walked in, the smell of incense and banana bread would hit your nostrils. His roommate, Peter Hoskins, loved to bake bread, and the whole house smelled of it. When I first came over to Andy's house, there was Peter, playing air guitar to Jimi Hendrix, full-blast. When he stopped, he grinned and said, "Oh, it's Jubilee. Andy's girl from Mississippi."

He wore his hair either in a brown ponytail, or wildly loose with a headband to hold it, and he and his earlier housemates had painted the old Queen Anne in psychedel- ic purple and orange. He seemed old, already twenty-two, and he helped organize marches and rallies on campus. "A politico," Andy called him, but then what do you expect when you answer an ad for a housemate in Berkeley?

The first night I slept over, Andy got up and slid out- side the bedroom window at sunrise. I woke to see his toes lightly planted on the sill, then his thin legs disappearing. From there, he climbed on the roof to chant his mantra as the sky lightened. Like a rooster, I thought, putting the pil- low over my head. The more time I spent with him, the more I learned to sleep through the resonating "Ommms".

176

Sometimes, the sound seeped into my dreams, and I saw the blue tiles of Indian temples in my sleep or Oriental tapestries with deepening mandalas that pulled me inside.

You should treat the world with reverence, Andy said, and he folded our laundry or washed the dishes as if the chore might be a meditation on all of life. He took pleasure in turning everyday things into prayers, though when Peter's yellow cat, Che, jumped onto the kitchen table, he tossed the poor thing toward the door and hurriedly washed his hands. But with the food, he was reverent. He gently wiped off fresh mushrooms for a curried vegetable dish he made. The flavor was stronger that way, he said, than if you washed them. It was the way he touched the mushrooms with the dish towel – lovingly, as if they might have been plump babies fresh from a bath – that made me grit my teeth and want to slap them from his hands. Sometimes, I felt like shaking him, telling him to wake up, get in the world. For the first time, I began to miss Rob. Rob had probably never even tasted fresh mushrooms, and I wanted to sauté a big batch in butter just for him, offer him something from the world outside Biloxi.

Behind Andy's back, Peter called him "Andynanda," after some Indian guru.

"How can you stand it?" Lisa asked, over coffee back in the dorm room one morning. Andy's chanting had awakened me at six, and she'd been hearing me complain. "You can do better than that. Is he really great in bed or something?"

"He has good qualities. Except for the cat, he's gentle," I said, as Lisa poured more coffee into my mug. Andy's cooking was the main reason Peter put up with him. Peter paid for the groceries, and Andy cooked, vegetarian meals with strange things I'd never heard of, like tofu and couscous. Then Lisa started dropping by with groceries at dinnertime, and she and Andy would concoct enchiladas or tabouli, delicacies I'd never eaten before. She was there, I knew, to see Peter, laughing at his jokes and nodding at his jabs at Nixon.

On Friday night after midnight, a classic blues show was on the campus station. Peter turned on the radio, listening to Fred MacDowell, Robert Johnson, John Hurt. One night, when Lisa was there, he started singing along with the radio, looking straight at Lisa. "Make me a pallet on your floor." It was Mississippi John Hurt's words, and soon he and Lisa disappeared into his bedroom. Their laughter came through the walls until it dissolved into more romantic sounds that kept me awake while Andy snored beside me, a circle of saliva deepening on his pillow. I was jealous. I lay there wondering how Rob was doing in Mississippi, wondering if he thought about me. I missed the way he cared about the prisoners in the band at Parchman Farm, the way he cared how I felt about Mama.

But Mississippi seemed like another planet.

Charlene wrote, saying she was praying for me, hoping I didn't love Berkeley so much that I wouldn't come back home. She sent me five dollars, asking me to buy some dope, a "nickel bag" for Ernie Crenshaw. Ernie! She wanted to do something nice for the soldiers, she wrote, and since the weed grew out of the earth, it couldn't really be a sin to use it. Charlene could always justify what she wanted to. Ernie had written her from Vietnam, asking how she was doing at the Home, and telling her how terrible the fighting was. He was smoking dope in Vietnam, she said, and since he was turning nineteen soon, she wanted to surprise him by sending him some joints. She felt sorry for the jerk. He might be in Vietnam, but he still wasn't brave enough to admit that he'd fathered a baby.

But what was a nickel bag?

I found her letter late one Sunday evening. Peter and Andy were both home when I got back from the library. My new sandals had rubbed blisters on my heels and across my toes, despite the thick wool socks Andy had lent me to wear with them that morning. "Your toes'll get cold," he said. He was like Marilyn that way, always meaning well. But Peter cheered me up while Andy cooked a batch of vegetarian chili, so involved with his seasonings he barely said hello. I'd invited Lisa over for dinner, so Peter wanted Andy to make it extra special.

Peter and I sat at the table in what we called the "Marakesh Café," where we'd tacked one of Andy's paisley bedspreads from the four corners of the kitchen ceiling for a canopy-like effect. It gave it the feel, we hoped, of Morocco, exotic smells and all. We were talking about the history test we both had the next day when I saw a stack of mail on top of the refrigerator. It was yesterday's, and Charlene's familiar handwriting was at the top of the pile. I'd given my family Andy's address a couple of weeks before, telling Daddy I'd made some true friends off-campus, away from those weirdos who lived in the dorm. I tore open Charlene's letter, and stood reading it, rubbing the sole of my sore foot against the other ankle.

"Who's it from?" Peter looked over my shoulder.

"My sister," I said. I read the first paragraph, then asked Peter if he knew what a nickel bag was.

Andy sighed and tapped the spoon on the edge of the pot. "You can alter your consciousness in better ways." He handed the spoon to Peter. "Hey, keep on an eye on this, will you? Don't taste it yet, it's not done." He left and soon the sound of chanting came from the roof.

Peter looked at me funny while he dipped the spoon into Andy's pot of chili and licked it. "Listen to any Delta bluesman," he said, sticking the spoon in for another taste.

"Don't you know your own roots? Man, you're going to fail that history test tomorrow." He chuckled.

"Are you kidding?" I said. "My mother sang the blues."

"It's not the same thing for a white woman."

He may as well have hit me with lightning. "My mother didn't just sing the blues, she had the blues. Bad," I said, fighting back fury.

"You don't even know the terms." He pulled a bay leaf from Andy's chili and sucked it. "Look, a nickel bag's a Southern term for five bucks worth of grass. Less than a lid. Haven't you listened to John Hurt? Or Robert Johnson?" He glanced up from the spoon of chili and saw my face. "What's wrong? Did I hurt your feelings?"

I folded up Charlene's letter and went to Andy's room, feeling a ball of tears behind my eyes. How could Peter know me so little and why didn't I know more about my own culture? I flopped on Andy's mattress on the floor and read the rest of Charlene's letter while the chants outside rose and fell like a tide. Marijuana was only one of the strange things Charlene was thinking about. She must have been bored, eighteen years old and stuck at the Mobile Home for Unwed Mothers, taking correspondence courses by mail. But good things were happening. The baby was kicking like crazy, she said, and she could feel what she thought was a knee jutting beneath her skin. And Art Johnson was coming to see her every weekend, driving all the way from Mississippi State in Starkville.

On the next page, filled with Charlene's angular, even handwriting, the bombshell dropped. Art had asked her to marry him. She wasn't sure if she would, but she knew she'd keep the baby. No way, she wrote, was somebody else going to raise a baby who could dance in her belly like this one. And she had forgiven Ernie Crenshaw. He was paying for his sins in Vietnam. Tears blurred the words and I had to stop. Charlene was inventing her life without me there to listen. My sister would certainly be a stranger to the way I'd re-invented my own. I sat on the bed and stared at the Indian rug Andy had laid on the bare floor, thinking about all I'd missed back home.

There was no place to go, no home for me anywhere, not where I'd grown up, and certainly not here, where even the real friends I'd finally made, like Lisa and Peter and Andy, didn't seem to understand me. The tornado doll stared at me from her perch on a shelf, still wearing crepe paper, and I took her down and slowly unwrapped the makeshift clothing from her plastic body. The scotch tape had rotted and made powder in my hands, but the tornado hadn't left a scratch on her. I stroked the plastic ripples that sufficed for hair on her head, and a sob choked in my throat. It was all those kids in Mississippi whose biggest Christmas present might have been a doll like this.

Then I was crying for Charlene, being pregnant in Mobile and still wanting to buy marijuana for that awful Ernie Crenshaw, for Marilyn with her game shows and soap operas, for Pearl's daughter, Mary, and how she hated me without even knowing me. I cried for Mama and her Sunday School class, and the confused, earnest women who brought over banana cream pies after the funeral, not saying a word about Levi Litvak, though they had a carload of other pies to take to his house for his relatives. I thought about Loretta Holliday, and the ham and cheese casserole she'd baked for him. What had the rabbi thought? Those women had pitched right in, without thinking of anything but their own customs. Levi Litvak had a regular funeral, and Charlene made an ugly joke about how he'd already been cremated, from the way the newspapers described the body. So I cried for the way it had satisfied me to imagine his dark pompadour burned to a gray frizz on his forehead.

I cried for Deanna, trying to get into a Lutheran college in Jackson so she could teach elementary school, and for the way she'd abandoned me after Mama died, as if my grief might be contagious. That night in Berkeley, I couldn't stop my tears. I cried because Daddy tried to get happiness from such small things now, for the way Marilyn told me he bragged about my grades to the Shriners. Then I cried about how I was ashamed for anyone at Berkeley to know my father was a Shriner. In my mind's eye, I could see the red line across Daddy's forehead that the red cap would leave when he took it off, like either a halo or a brand.

I cried for how sad everybody's lives were, for how locked within themselves people were. On my calf was the thin line I'd once made with Daddy's razor, and I knew now that I would never again be so numb that I'd need to force myself to feel.

On the desk was a copy of *The Tibetan Book of the Dead* that Andy had given me, to help me understand my mother's death, he said. I opened it randomly, hoping for help. "This is the time when perseverance and pure thought are needed," it said, but my thoughts were so jumbled I couldn't make sense of anything. Now I even cried that my purest thought at that moment was that I resented Andy and all his earnest good-will.

Go with the magic, he would tell me, and I'd get mad. Magic was what disrupted the world, created its own mysterious rules. I wanted something more predictable.

Sometimes, I never wanted to go back to Biloxi. At first, I imagined marrying Andy, having a baby. But when he wiped the mushrooms, I saw how he'd take over a baby, and that nothing I'd do would please him.

It surely wasn't because I wanted to spend my life with

Andy, but to make a bridge between two different worlds: one that I created for Daddy in my telephone calls and letters, and the other that I lived. Daddy would write me happy letters about what a wonderful experience I must be having and how much he and Charlene, "and Marilyn, too," missed me. I cried for how disappointed Daddy would be if he could have seen me picking up hitchhikers in Mama's truck, driving all over the Bay Area to deliver them where they wanted to go, or how he'd feel if he knew Andy and I shared the same bed, and that sometimes Peter and I shared the same joint of "marriage-wanna." Then I cried even harder for Rob, for the friend he'd been when I needed someone so badly, and how I'd taken him for granted. I couldn't remember ever having told him I loved him. I'd write him soon, I promised myself. When my nose stopped running and my tears dried, I started writing a poem to Daddy.

When the first glaciers melted and
the flood washed away the seas, Daddy,
you were there with your Bible,
reading your First Corinthians,
lips silently moving as you turned
the wafer-thin pages.
Your eyes were clear holes of water
where I swam, unknowing,
until the fire:
The Baptist preacher would scream
from his Sunday pulpit, pointing
and pounding salvation,
his face red as the Indians in my schoolbook,
dancing half-naked around a fire.

(Daddy I wanna go home
eat roast beef and green peas
and watch TV)

Berkeley nights are foggy and cold
and I have a lover
who once threw bricks at cop cars
but makes love through the afternoon.
We never talk of marriage, or children:
There are certain taboos,
like the scars on his inner wrists.
We walk midnight streets on psychedelics
measuring time by the fading of colors.
and he cooks our supper: in the morning
tofu and beans on a two-burner stove.
The curtains stick to the steamy kitchen windows
and we peel them away from the pane
to watch the sun rise.

But I call you, Daddy,
from pay phones at proper hours,
across two time zones to the Bible Belt,
and never wake you,
never catch you at dinner.
Mostly we are still:
me in a glass booth on Telegraph Avenue,
one hand pressed against the free ear
to shut out traffic and friends
while you let the Sunday dishes soak.

After I studied the lines, I folded the paper up and put
it in my backpack, along with Charlene's letter, knowing
I'd never send it. Then I hunted down Peter in the backyard where he was padding about in the grass, mulching

the plot we called our organic vegetable garden. My tears were gone and now I was furious.

Andy's chants were still vibrating through the air, and he was sitting with his eyes closed, cross-legged, on the flat roof above the porch. I didn't feel any of his peace.

"Hey, Hoskins," I said. "Don't go telling me I don't know my roots. I know all the words to every Baptist invitational in the hymnal, all the plots of the movies that played at the Biloxi Paramount for five years, and I can do sword drills with the best of them. I can *win* sword drills most of the time. I played the best trumpet version of Dixie you ever heard in a marching band. So. . ." by now I was jabbing my finger in his face, "just because I don't pretend to have hung around on sharecroppers' porches singing the blues, don't tell me I don't know my own roots. My Mama sang me to sleep on the blues. You're a cultural imperialist, that's what you are, thinking you know all about a place you've never even been, just because you listen to the blues on the radio. Hah!" I spun around, victorious, ready to march inside and leave him straddling the stakes where the tomato plants had been, the bag of mulch dangling from his hand.

"If my roots were playing Dixie in a Mississippi marching band, I'd have myself transplanted."

I wheeled around. A sheepish look now replaced his usual defiance, and he looked as if he hoped I'd laugh.

I didn't. "If my roots were in L.A., at Beverly Hills High, I'd probably have grown as little as you have."

He looked mortified. I'd known that would hurt him. Lisa had told me he was ashamed of his family's wealth, how it was something they had in common. He tried to say something, but I went on. "You think it's easy to transplant yourself to a place where nobody appreciates your roots? Or even knows them, even if they pretend they do, espe-

185

cially when they're from L.A. like you and don't even have roots of their own?" Peter started to protest, but the words wouldn't stop. "You know what? My mother didn't die in a car crash, like you think. She was murdered. You know who killed her? A guy who was her lover. You know what that did to my father? He married a woman just to have company, and my sister was so desperate to leave that now she's pregnant. You know what she was going to do with the baby? Give it up. You know what that did to my father? My dad's the kind of guy who cries when he thinks no one's around. You know how many times I've heard my dad cry? Hey, here's something worse, at least in your little hip book. Did you know my father's a Shriner?" I was shouting, flailing my arms, ready to throw a punch right in his gut. "He's got the hat and everything. Yeah, it's real far out, man. You should see him on his little bicycle in parades. . ."

"Hey, hey, hey." Peter grabbed my elbow and turned me around. "Your eyes are all red. You been crying?"

I slugged his shoulder. "Let go of my arm. Right now."

"What's going on down there?" It was Andy, awakened from his reverie, glaring at Peter. "Who's watching the chili?"

"What can I say, Jubilee?" asked Peter. "I'm sorry. Your mom was murdered? Really? How come you never told us?"

"I don't know." I couldn't say any more about it. My bones felt tired, but something heavy seemed gone, and I felt an odd happiness.

Andy appeared beside me. "Supper's ready. No thanks to anyone around here."

"She's been crying," said Peter, with a disgusted look at Andy. "You might have noticed if you weren't up there chanting."

Andy looked at me, surprised, and saw the red swelling around my eyes. "What's wrong?"

"I'm all right. Just getting my period." It was too much to explain, and the sound of his chants drowning out my sobs had been another wedge between us.

When Lisa came over for supper, Andy was ladling chili into pottery bowls he'd set on the table. "Jubilee played the trumpet in high school," Peter told her.

Andy's head jerked up. "She still does," he said. "Best damn music I ever heard." He smiled at me, trying to cheer me up.

"How come I never heard you?" asked Lisa. "Where have you been hiding this trumpet?"

"I'm the only one she plays for," said Andy. He was proud, glad to trump Peter and Lisa.

Lisa looked at me, a hurt look in her eyes.

I shrugged. "It sounds better on the beach. I usually keep it in the closet or in my truck."

"Just ask her, she can play anything. Go on," Andy turned to me. "Get your trumpet."

"The Byrds," said Peter. "'To Everything There Is A Season'." There were more interesting tunes, but I pulled my trumpet from Andy's closet and blasted out a jazzy version that made each note twist around the next, weaving a complicated net of loops.

"Wow," said Lisa when I laid the trumpet back in its case. She was looking at me as if I were someone different.

We settled ourselves at the kitchen table, the chili barely steaming now. "You could make a lot of money, if you wanted, playing on Telegraph Avenue," said Andy. "Lots of people do it, and they're not as good as you."

Peter plucked at a hole in the knee of his jeans and gave me a worried glance. "What about your mother?

187

How was she killed?"

Lisa darted a look at him, then at me. "She died in a car accident, right?"

"Not really," I said. Andy started to interrupt, but I stopped him. "No, I'll tell them."

After I finished the story, Lisa said, "Oh, Jubilee, that's horrible. You don't know who killed her?"

"Levi Litvak," said Andy.

"He was in love with her," I said. "Sometimes I dream about him, that he's alive, that he'll be found."

"My god, I'm supposed to be your friend and you don't tell me anything." Lisa looked like she might cry.

Peter put his napkin on the table. "I was being mean this afternoon. She wouldn't have told me if I hadn't made her so mad." He turned to me. "How's your sister?"

"What about her?" asked Lisa.

"She's pregnant," I said. "At first she wanted an abortion or to give it up, but she's keeping the baby now."

Lisa got up and put her arms around me. "Why did you keep all this from me? This is heavy stuff. You never said a word."

"I didn't mean to hurt your feelings. It just felt good to pretend everything was normal, I guess."

It was a relief to release my secrets. But I was still worried about Charlene. How well did she even know Art Johnson? She'd be all right, I told myself. But I sure wasn't going to make her life worse by sending her a nickel bag for Ernie Crenshaw. That Home probably opened all its packages, and the worst thing I could imagine was a baby born in Parchman Prison.

After Charlene's baby was born in November, Daddy sent a roll of pictures of a red-faced, squinty-eyed boy with a cap on his head. In most of them, Charlene was holding him, her face bloated but grinning. I couldn't see much of Charlene in his face, but I wanted to hold that little guy, get him to open those eyes and look at his Aunt Jubilee. She'd named him Lonnie, after one of Mama's favorite blues singer, Lonnie Johnson. The last name would be no trouble: her wedding to Art Johnson was scheduled for June, when the semester ended at State.

Charlene wrote to tell me how beautiful Lonnie was, and what a good baby he was. "Wait till you hold him. It'll be the best Christmas ever," she wrote. "It seems like you've been gone forever."

Chapter Thirteen

Late one night, as I was settling on my bed to study for a philosophy exam, Aunt Sylvia called. After small talk about the finals I'd be taking soon, she said, "We need to talk."

"We always talk," I said. "We're talking now."

"You sound like you've been in California too long," she said. "This is your Aunt Sylvia, remember? We talk straight to each other. I have something important to tell you."

"What is it? Is the baby okay?" I asked.

"He's great. So is Charlene." As soon as Lonnie was born, Aunt Sylvia had broken her vow never to return to Biloxi.

"Grandpa and Grandma?" My breath fluttered like the sparrows that lived under the eaves on the farmhouse.

"No, honey, they're fine." She took a breath. "Remember Loretta Holliday?"

"How could I forget? Is she still in Whitfield?" She had been sent to the state mental hospital not long after the field trip to Parchman. "Black Annie" had turned up in the trunk of her car, goods stolen from the State of Mississippi, which was pretty serious business. But the judge ruled the mental asylum, not jail. Everyone in Biloxi was relieved they'd confiscated her pistol.

"She's been out for a while now."

There was a pause, not at all like Aunt Sylvia's usual conversations, when the words came flying so fast you had to reach out and grab them. "What is it?" I asked.

"She called yesterday. Her husband was killed in a bar fight, shot in the face. The police say it was an act of self-defense, not murder."

"Probably was. I'm not going to grieve that one." I remembered those green and yellow bruises on Kathy and Loretta. "Sounds like the way he was destined to go out." Bad karma, Andy would say.

"Joe Holliday had a lot of bad karma," said Aunt Sylvia, and for a second I thought I'd said it out loud. "Listen, honey, this is important. Loretta wants to talk to you. She says she's coming to Berkeley."

"Loretta Holliday's coming all the way out here to see me? What on earth for?" My Southern accent came back, thick, that's how shocked I was.

"She has relatives in San Jose, says she's been saving money for years to visit them and she'd like to visit you too."

"She's crazy, Aunt Sylvia. She spread awful rumors. Tell her not to come. Please." My stomach ached, and the palms of my hands were sweating. Those knife-high heels and red lipstick – it was unimaginable to think of Loretta Holliday teetering down Telegraph Avenue or accidental-ly wandering into a protest on campus.

"I hope she won't. But be warned, honey. She wanted your address in Berkeley."

"You didn't tell her!" I pushed the notebooks off my lap, my heart thumping.

"You know I wouldn't do that."

"But she's crazy enough to come anyway!" I felt like I'd swallowed a stone.

The next morning, I was up early, drinking coffee while I skimmed the reading for my class on "Philosophies of Eastern Religions," one of the most popular courses on campus. It was the Taoist book, Lao Tzu's *Tao Te Ching.* "Do that which consists in taking no action, and order will prevail," I read. It was comforting advice before a test, and I decided not to worry about Loretta Holliday.

There was an hour before class, so I walked up to the hills east of campus to look at the San Francisco Bay stretched out below, and the Pacific Ocean sparkling beyond the tumble of white shapes of San Francisco architecture. There was something wonderful in those solitary climbs I took. Up there, it was as if I could watch the entire world, including myself.

From my spot in the hills, the campus slowly came alive. The smell of the redwoods and eucalyptus were like nothing in Mississippi. In a little curve in the road, the trees parted so I could watch the campus and bay below. Between patches in the morning fog, I could see the demonstrations begin, people milling about, waving their signs, a speaker with a bullhorn pacing the ledge of a retaining wall.

The morning fog was burning off, and the sun warmed the campus while a Pacific breeze stirred the eucalyptus leaves. If I couldn't have Mississippi gardenias or magnolias, the smell of eucalyptus on the wind made up for it. I breathed it in, thinking about Taoism and the seven paths to heaven.

I wondered what Lao Tzu would have said about the anti-war demonstrations and the dreamy people who performed Tai Chi in the parks while a war raged. Everyone was singing either "Let It Be" or "Revolution." There was a chill in the air that was foreign to my Mississippi blood.

Outside the Bear's Lair, a crowd chanted a mantra as familiar as Andy's by now. "Ho Ho Ho Chi Minh! NLF is going to win!" Pacing the top of the retaining wall was one of the strangest-looking men I'd seen, even in Sproul Plaza. His hair stood out like a giant halo, and the sun shimmered on streaks of silver glitter scattered through it. On his face were streaks of color, like Indian war paint.

Then his voice came over the megaphone and I knew. It was Cat Heller, the DJ who had saved me on my first day in Berkeley, but he wasn't smiling now. Even in the cool breeze, he was naked from the waist up, and a black armband circled the thickness of his right bicep. He paced back and forth, raising his fist, yelling about the draft.

All I could think of was Mississippi, the demonstrations, the shouting, the police; it was Mississippi everywhere.

Chapter Fourteen

After days of steady drizzling rain, a rare December sun emerged that made it hard to study for exams. Andy and I drove to Muir Woods, where the trees sparkled in the new light and the earth smelled of fallen evergreen needles. Christmas soon, I thought, wondering what the holiday would be like in Mississippi this year, a new baby and me with Berkeley on the brain. We brought our books to study, but as soon as we settled beneath a redwood tree, Andy sat in his lotus position and looked at me. "This is a good time to talk," he said. "You spend too much time at the movies. We need to camp more often, like Big Sur." It was not the first time he'd complained about the old movies I liked to watch.

"You missed Greta Garbo last night," I told him. "'I vant to be alone'," I said, imitating her accent.

"That's just it. We don't spend enough time together." He didn't even know Garbo's most famous line.

A squirrel leapt from one redwood branch to the next, showering us with little crystals of rain from the night before. I brushed off my history book and put it away. "You're always chanting, that's why."

"Try it with me," he said, putting his hand on my knee. "Or don't you even care?"

"We care about different things," I said. The sweaty warmth of his palm left my knee, leaving a cool spot.

He rose and pointed to the backpack he had leaned against a tree. "Don't be cavalier with my things," he warned me, and soundlessly walked away from me, across the soft dark earth. Overhead, a hawk soared, dipping and turning, its wings spread so wide that the movements felt like music, and nothing else mattered for those moments.

In the silence on the way back, leaves scuttled down the sidewalks of Marin County like the thin brown lizards when I first gave him a ride on Mount Tamalpais.

When I pulled into the driveway, a woman in stiletto heels stood on the front porch, her hands cupped to the front window, peering inside. She had the highest beehive hair-do I'd ever seen. When she heard the truck, she turned around.

"Who is that?" asked Andy, his first words since leaving Muir Woods.

"Loretta Holliday?" It was an apparition I could barely believe.

All the worst of Mississippi had come to visit me in my new life, and I wanted to turn and run back to the truck. But there she was, waving to me. "Jubilee Starling?"

What could I do but wave back?

The past year had not been good to Loretta. She still wore a scarf around her neck, but it was wound more tightly, like a bandage hiding wrinkles, as close as a noose. Her green eyes glittered through false eyelashes and her lips were smeared with red lipstick. I remembered the way she had scraped the mud off her high heels on the edge of my truck, that day I picked her up on the highway, when she was just standing there, looking lost.

It was Biloxi, Mississippi, back in spades, when Loretta teetered across the porch on those high heels, holding her hand out, the long red nails like ten little daggers. "It's little Jubilee, isn't it?" she said, and took my hand.

Andy whispered under his breath, "Amazing." Loretta extended her hand to Andy, and it took him a second to shake it. His eyes glowed like he was meeting a movie star, or another X-ray of a woman's torso. He had never looked at me that way.

But she ignored him, studying me instead. "Your hair's so pretty and long, I almost didn't recognize you." She reached out and stroked my hair, and it surprised me how good it felt. Nobody strokes your hair like somebody who's been a mother. "You were always so kind, picking me up when I didn't have a ride."

Andy's eyes flicked over at me. "It was nothing," I said, embarrassed.

"I'll never forget your kindness." She pressed her cheek against mine, and the smell of rose water and face

194

powder filled my nose. "Such a sweet girl. I just had to see you again."

I didn't have a choice but to invite her inside. "Subterranean Homesick Blues" blared from Peter's stereo in the living room, his way of getting adrenaline up for an exam. When he and Lisa saw the three of us come in, he turned down the sound and stared.

"This is a friend of Jubilee's from Mississippi." Pride rose in Andy's voice, the same triumph as when he knew that I played trumpet and they didn't.

"It's Mrs. Holliday." My words sounded like the squeak I still occasionally got on the trumpet. Peter and Lisa couldn't take their eyes off her. We all trouped back to the kitchen while Andy heated up the tea kettle. Peter pulled an extra chair up to the table beneath the tapestry hanging from the ceiling. And then no one had a choice but to listen. All those months in Whitfield had wound Loretta up as tight as the scarf around her neck. She gazed across the table at me, one arm slung over the back of the chair, like it was perfectly normal for her to be there. Che crept up and jumped softly into her lap, curling into a ball.

"I make you nervous, don't I, honey?" she asked me, stroking the cat's yellow fur. "But never you mind, you're looking pretty now. That acne didn't even leave a scar. You got yourself a boyfriend." She tipped her beehive at Andy. "And you always so sweet, too. Not like that Charlene. Mean as a cat in heat."

I pushed back my chair and leaned my arms on the table, a battle position. "Don't you talk that way. There's not a thing mean about Charlene." The tea kettle began to whistle, piercing the kitchen like a siren.

"Oh, the girl prides herself on it. Nothing wrong with pride. That's a sweet little baby she's got, though. And you haven't even seen him," she told me, taking the cup of hot tea Andy offered. "Family's important."

"She has finals," said Peter. "We all do."

"Finals?" said Loretta. "Only one thing's final, and that's death. What's this?" She picked a brown sugar cube from the sugar bowl, her fingernails like tweezers.

"Sugar," said Lisa, breathlessly, as if she still couldn't believe the creature before her.

"I like sugar in my tea. You got a little ice for me, and a nice tall glass? That's how we like it where Jubilee and I come from."

"Where I *came* from," I whispered, hoping only my friends would hear.

Loretta stirred the sugar into her cup while Lisa filled a glass with ice cubes. She poured in the contents of the cup without spilling a drop, and kept talking. "I got your address from your stepmother, that Marilyn girl your dad married. Not nearly so pretty as your mama was, but what's a good man like your dad to do? He needed somebody to help him control you girls. And he had his manly needs." The virile needs of a man. Had Mr. Pickens told the whole town?

A smirk edged across Peter's face, and despite the hand he put over his mouth, she spied it with a magpie look. "Maybe you don't have any yet, son," she said, and he reddened while she turned back to me. "I waited for you to come home, but Sylvia said you wouldn't be back till Christmas."

"I don't have many friends in Biloxi, Mrs. Holliday," I said, more for the sake of Lisa and Peter than anyone. Surely Mrs. Holliday knew Biloxi wasn't the kind of place that liked it when you stopped going to church, or painted your nails purple and green. In Berkeley, people said it didn't matter how you dressed or what you looked like. But that wasn't really true. You had to look like it didn't

196

matter, or people would treat you like an alien, like they did in Biloxi.

"No, you never had many friends, did you, darlin'?" asked Loretta. "You weren't popular the way Kathy. . ."

Lisa gulped, gathering her nerve to speak again. "Popularity is false consciousness."

"Nothing false about Jubilee, no, honey. But let me have my say. Lord knows, I've lived with a horrible truth all these years." She folded her hands on the table, like she was about to tell me a story that began with 'once upon a time.' "My Joe died, shot in the neck in a fight in the Drop Inn Grill in Gulfport. I don't know who did it, nobody was willing to say they knew Joe's killer. But of course they did. Wasn't no one sad to see Joe Holliday leave this world."

"I'm sorry," I said.

Loretta's face stretched into a thin smile. "No, honey, you're not. But it's mighty nice and polite of you to say that. Your mama raised you right."

The image of the burly man who used to wear camouflage hunting jackets even when it wasn't deer season came to my mind. I remembered how Loretta was scared of going home that day I gave her a lift, how she looked behind the bushes for Joe and talked about getting the locks changed. I could still see her at Mama's funeral, the thin, penciled eyebrows and green eyeliner, the chiffon scarf with leopard spots wrapped around her neck. When she smiled, she didn't look so different anymore, her mouth filling the boundaries of her lip pencil.

The smile left her face now. "Oh, that Joe was grisly looking, laid out on a slab. Hadn't shaved in three days, I reckon, and you know what they say about how hair keeps growing when a body's dead. . .Oh he looked a mess, you should've seen him."

197

"What'd he look like?" asked Peter, and Lisa's eyes widened at him, horrified.

Loretta didn't seem to hear. "I had to identify him down at the morgue. Now that's something to put a lady through, who's been shut up at a place like Whitfield for nearly a year, for no reason at all, shut up with alcoholics and kleptomaniacs and murderers. But I'm not ashamed of it. That's where they put you if they don't know what else to do with you. Time was," she winked at me, "we thought Jubilee might wind up there, in Whitfield. At least that's what Juanita Kelly used to say." She looked over at Peter. "Juanita worked at the Dairy Queen, you know."

Peter shook his head. "No," he said. "I didn't know. But she's a jerk, if she said that about Jubilee."

That woman at the Dairy Queen had refused to serve Rob and me once because my fingernails were painted with black and green stripes. "Tain't nat'ral," she informed me, swishing her scoop around in a bucket of sudsy water, like she wanted to rinse me away, too. Rob said her ice cream "tain't nat'ral" either, it was full of chemicals. It didn't make a bit of difference to her. She was already waiting on a truck driver, a man with tattooed biceps bulging beneath a thin tee-shirt. We were so mad at Biloxi we drove all the way to New Orleans and ate beignets in the French Market.

Lisa's lips tightened. "No one ever could have thought Jubilee. . ."

But Loretta tossed her hand through the air, as if throwing away Lisa's words. "It was that weird nail polish and driving that death truck, that's all. But tell you the truth? I knew she'd make it." She pointed at me. "And I knew the good Lord would take Joe Holliday from this earth, and I knew it would be by another man's wrath. I was glad to see Joe Holliday dead, and I'm not ashamed to say it. Not that I ever would've done it myself, you know." She lifted her glass of tea and took a delicate sip. "But it was a relief, him lying cold, not able to touch Kathy or me again."

"How's Kathy?" I asked, wanting to change the subject.

She patted her hair. "Did this," she said proudly. "It'll last me at least a week. Best hairdresser in Mobile. She could give you some make-up tips, honey. But I didn't come all the way here to talk about Kathy." She lit a cigarette and blew out a cloud of smoke. "No, I'm free now, and I can talk. Levi Litvak," she waved the cigarette at me. "He didn't kill your mom."

"What?" I spilled my tea, thoughts tumbling so fast in my head that I couldn't even wipe it up. Lisa sponged up the table and I watched, so disoriented that a shaft of sunlight pooling there seemed, for a moment, part of the spilled liquid. "If he didn't, who did?" The room spun, as if the world were changing in a matter of seconds. The paramedics had been in white like moon-walkers that April morning. The sun had been too bright to see clearly and now I felt blinded again.

"Honey, all these years, I been living with the memory of you and Harry working on your Mama's dead body. I was there, darlin', I saw it all. Joe was aiming for Levi with that knife." She closed her eyes, her eyeballs moving beneath the thin lids, like they were looking for something in the darkness. "I dream about it, you there in your slippers and robe, Harry calling Bernice's name."

"You were there?" I was back, in the driveway, over four years ago, but I couldn't see Loretta.

She stubbed out her cigarette. "In the garage, behind the bookcase your Mama was working on. That's where I ran after Joe did the killing. That's God's own truth I lived with. But now I can come clean. Joe's not ever killing anybody else, not even me or Kathy. Levi didn't kill Bernice. He wasn't a murderer, God rest his soul. And God rest your Mama's."

The wind had been knocked out of me, and it was hard to talk. "But what about that letter to the *Times-Picayune*?" I finally asked. "He confessed, all about how he couldn't live without his sugar muffin. Do you remember that?"

"'Course I do, I wrote it. Levi didn't have a thing to do with that letter." She closed her eyes tight again. "I'll never forget it, sitting there at midnight at the WLOX office, Joe Holliday beside me with a gun in his hand. 'Write it,' he said, acting like James Cagney or somebody in those gangster movies he loved. He liked Cagney, except for the dancing stuff. Sissy, he said. Anyway, I typed. My hands were shaking so bad. . ." She held them out and shook them, to demonstrate.

"How did you know they called each other sugar muffin?" I could still see the little "i" jumping above the other letters in "muffin" in the fuzzy newsprint.

"Dahlin', how did *you* know? That's the question." She squinted at me. "I heard Levi on the phone every day. Don't forget, I held down the fort at WLOX. Not much escaped me. It was 'sugar muffin' this, 'sugar muffin' that, every time he'd be whispering on the phone. It was enough to drive me crazy, much as I cared about him, myself."

"But why would your husband want to kill my mother? It can't be true." All those years of dreaming about Levi Litvak, confronting him, couldn't have been for nothing.

Tears welled up in Loretta's eyes, and I remembered the way she'd patted her hair the morning of my mother's funeral, saying how she was going to miss Mama's voice

200

lessons. "Joe was after Levi Litvak. Bernice got in his way that morning. I'm ashamed of it, but I'll tell you this: Joe Holliday was in the Klan, and Levi was on their death list. He was a Jew, you know; they thought he was an outside agitator." She took a long drag on her cigarette. "Besides, your Mama wasn't the only one in love with him, not with a good-lookin' man like him, no sirree. Joe hated Levi because he knew I loved him." She looked around the table at all of us. "It drove me crazy to hear Levi talk about his 'sugar muffin.' Like he did it just to hurt me, to drive a knife right through my heart." Her face blanched. "Sorry," she said, but she went on. "Levi won my heart in an instant and Joe knew it. Killing him made Joe a hero in the Klan. He went up to McComb, a celebrity. He had stalked Levi that morning, all the way to Bernice's house, with me following, a good bit back."

A grim smile stretched across my face. "That was brave. Why didn't you tell the police?"

She ignored my question. "I had practice dealing with Joe. I'd been following him for weeks. He'd been saying he was going to kill Levi. I warned Levi, but he didn't believe me, just like he never believed he was really on those Klan lists."

"Is she for real?" Lisa breathed at me.

"I heard that, honey, but I'm going to choose to ignore it. In Whitfield, you learn to ignore a lot of things. I had a roommate, she'd tear down the walls if she could, tore out her hair and chewed it like a cow on a cud. I tried to do her nails once, you know, try to fix her up, and she came close to pouring my polish remover right down her throat. So I learned some lessons in ignoring folks. Why, even my psychiatrist, he lied to me. Dr. Santamaria, that was his name. You'd think, with a name pretty as that, he wouldn't gaslight his own patients. He told me Joe was probably schizophrenic, but when I asked him about it later, what does he say? He stares at me with his little beady black eyes and says, 'I never said that.' Something wrong with that man. He was crazier than I've ever been."

"I believe it," said Andy. "I've been in a place like that," and Loretta looked at him with new respect.

She stubbed out her cigarette. "Bernice was trying to break up with Levi, and he came to your house to beg. Must've been desperate, risking everything like that. Through the hedge, I could see clear as anything. Levi got in the pick-up beside Bernice, and then Joe yanked open the door and jumped Levi. It would've been him dead. . ."

"The wrong person died." Peter whistled softly.

"Your Mama tried to stop him," said Loretta. "She threw herself at Joe, and the knife hit her right in the heart. She was the hero, not me. Joe ran for his truck, he'd parked around the corner, and I could hear him trying to start it up. I knew how mad he must've been, that truck not starting on the first try at a time like that."

"Levi Litvak just left Mama there?" At that moment, I hated him almost as much as Joe Holliday.

She rested her chin in the palm of her hand and closed her eyes. "Levi was standing in your driveway, staring at Bernice, then in the direction where Joe was cranking his truck, like he couldn't decide what to do. When the kitchen door opened, Levi ran for his own car. Harry never saw him."

A shudder ran over me, the kind that Grandpa would say meant that a rabbit had run over your grave.

"It's hard, I know," Loretta whispered, her voice a thin rasp. "Even now, I can see every detail. It bothered me so much I made up stories to tell myself Loretta and Levi weren't really dead. Got to the point where I believed my own tales."

"Did you lose a scarf that morning?" I asked, glancing at the green silk wrapped around her neck.

"I don't remember a scarf. There was so much happening all at once."

"A red scarf, with orange flowers? I found it in the garage after Mama died. Daddy thought it was evidence, but the police wouldn't listen. We kept it, all this time."

Mrs. Holliday twisted a gold costume ring on her index finger, gazing in the distance. Finally, she said, "Levi gave Bernice a red scarf and some sweet perfume for Christmas. He asked me to help pick it out, and that was mighty hard, I tell you. But I bet she was going to give those nice presents away." She gave me a hard look. "Just like she gave up Levi. She never stopped loving your dad."

I wanted to go straight home to Biloxi and burn that scarf. Daddy had saved the wrong evidence. "You knew who killed my mother and you let us torment ourselves, wondering. You let a murderer go free." I thought of how Daddy insisted Dr. Powell write "accidental death" on the certificate. "Daddy kept telling everybody that what happened in the truck was an accident. It was too horrible to think of anything else."

"Let him call it that," said Loretta. "Who can blame him? No man wants to think his own wife has a lover."

I felt like pulling her scarf tighter, strangling her. "The only man Mama loved was Daddy. She told me so."

Loretta twisted the ends of the scarf into a knot. "I felt bad about you girls, alone with no mother. I used to call you on the phone, just to be sure you'd gotten home from school all right."

The silent phone calls, when I would breathe in rhythm with someone who seemed like my twin, came back to me. "That was you?" My "twin" had been Loretta Holliday.

"It just gave me some comfort, hearing you girls breathe, knowing you were alive," she said.

"Why didn't you tell the police?" asked Andy, his hand resting on my arm. "It's illegal to withhold information about a crime."

She shot him a disgusted look. "You never saw Joe Holliday when he was in a rage, his fists balled up, or waving his gun, and me and my little daughter knowing the thing was loaded full of bullets. He blasted a hole through the kitchen wall once. The whole town knew. Everybody talked about that hole in my wall. Nobody wanted to come fix it. I had to stuff it with newspaper to keep the possoms out of the garbage." She sighed. "He's dead now, cancer would've got him if a gun didn't. Lungs, you know. All those cigarettes, one right after the other, but that's just my idea, just me talking. But nobody can stop Loretta Holliday from talking now." Then, at last, she stopped. She took a cigarette and dangled it in her lips, unlit, squinting as if surveying the damage she'd done.

What was Levi Litvak feeling when he drove his Thunderbird away, leaving Daddy to find Mama? *If I can't have my sugar muffin, no one can. ..* but those weren't Levi Litvak's words anymore, they belonged to Loretta Holliday, her husband's pistol cocked at her head. "What was Levi Litvak thinking," I said, "leaving Mama like that?"

"Nothing," said Loretta. "A man who thinks he's got a killer on his tail, he runs like a bat out of hell. You can ponder that in your heart forever, but the bat out of hell is what you'll come up with every time."

I hoped Loretta had made Joe Holliday suffer during their marriage. I thought about the woman who'd cracked an imaginary bullwhip over Mr. Miller's back at Parchman, and then stolen the real whip, "Black Annie."

Even with all the fear she lived in, she'd stolen that whip to take after Joe.

"Does Dad know about Joe Holliday?" I whispered. "Does he know about Levi Litvak?"

"He was out tending his roses when I told him Joe killed Bernice. 'Live by the sword, die by the sword,' that's what he said. Said he wished he'd been the one with the sword who killed him, and then asked the good Lord to forgive him for that. I told him Levi Litvak was there, too, and he said he was one of Bernice's best bookcase customers. Then he went back to those pretty yellow tea roses without hardly looking up."

I remembered how Daddy had stood on the porch of Ernie Crenshaw's house with his fist drawn back, ready to hit Ernie's father. But he'd stopped himself. Daddy would never have killed Joe Holliday.

Loretta turned to Andy. "Now tell me, young man, is there a powder room in this lovely house?" She rose, a presence bigger than life, like a cartoon character at Disneyland, costumed so thickly the person inside was barely imaginable.

Andy pointed to a door down the hall. My eyes filled with tears, imagining Daddy bending over his tea roses, with Loretta at his side, her words swarming in the air like so many gnats for Daddy to swat. He knew how much Mama had loved him. I wiped my eyes with the back of my hand, but Lisa was there with a tissue.

Loretta came back in to say she'd rented a car to drive down to San Jose. "Been good to see you, honey," she said, and put both hands flat against my cheeks while she pressed her lips against my forehead. "You come see me in Biloxi, you hear? Good girls don't stay away from home long."

We walked her out to the street, where a silver Ford was parked crookedly, one wheel on the sidewalk. She climbed in, arranging her scarf carefully on her lap.

Hadn't seen her cousins in San Jose in a blue moon, she said. I hoped they knew what awaited them. She blew a kiss and cranked the motor. Lisa tissued off the lipstick left on my forehead in the shape of Loretta's puckered mouth.

I managed to wave as she drove off, though my hand felt heavy, as if I were saying good-bye to a lot more than Loretta Holliday.

Chapter Fifteen

I couldn't wait to see Charlene, especially now that we knew the truth. So it had been Joe Holliday the whole time. I shuddered at how close we'd been to him, his boot brushing my foot at the convenience store, his eyes glowing at me on Halloween. At last, he was gone.

The week of finals went past in a blur of calculus equations, historical dates of medieval France, and Buddhist koans. I was reading my history notes one morning when Lisa came knocking at my bedroom door, closed to the sound of Peter's stereo. They were going to a demonstration in Golden Gate Park that afternoon. On the roof, Andy sent his vibrating chants into the morning sky, competing with Peter's music.

"Come with us," said Lisa. "You've studied plenty for that history exam, and this is important."

"But I have a test tomorrow," I said.

"Life is full of tests," she said. "And most of them aren't on paper. What's happening in San Francisco today is history, too."

Andy came off the roof and frowned at me, pointing to his wrist watch. He was the only one in the house who wore one. "Time to study. Your next exam is tomorrow," he said.

That was enough. I closed my book and we climbed into Peter's van and headed across the Bay Bridge. Near Geary Street, we parked and joined the long march to Golden Gate Park. As we got closer, the Jefferson Airplane's music reached us in fragments, the soaring of Jorma Kaukonen's guitar like a beacon in fog. The music pervaded the air in the park like the floating incense of marijuana smoke, intoxicating and euphoric. In the street, throngs of people still marched in a cacophony of color and noise. We had walked the length of Geary, from near the Bay all the way to the Golden Gate Park. Though my feet ached in the heavy hiking boots Andy had given me, my body felt as though as it was detached from the earth. It was that kind of day: gravity-defying.

We followed a path Peter made through the crowd to a spot near the stage and settled in. It wasn't at all like hearing the Beatles on the Ed Sullivan Show in 1964 or watching Elvis movies. The Jefferson Airplane wasn't a collection of god-like stars we worshipped from afar. The Beatles were four human beings totally separate from ourselves, and the Airplane was us. Grace Slick was singing for us rather than to us.

But listening to the music was still about finding freedom, and I'd just been set free from a nightmare that had lasted years. Levi Litvak's face wasn't going to appear in my dreams anymore, I hoped, or show up in the audience at baseball games on television.

For a second, as I watched Grace Slick's face contort and then ease with the flow of the words, I saw Mama's face instead, singing, and she was looking at me, peace

207

glowing from her blue eyes. The guitars and drums receded, and Mama's voice seemed to soar across the acres of people in the Park. Then that strange indigo wave came over me again, that stillness that had been just Mama and me when she died, inside a bubble with all other sound and movement suspended.

"Mama," I mouthed the word, but as soon as I did, her face was gone. It was Grace Slick again. People danced and stripped off their shirts and passed joints. A man with a gray ponytail handed me one, but I passed it along. The bubble had been enough, a secret place of peace, something so mysterious and beautiful I couldn't even tell Lisa. It was just for Mama and me.

We sat cross-legged on the damp grass of Golden Gate Park as the morning fog lifted, and light made prisms out of the drops of water still clinging to the oak trees in the distance behind the stage. Lisa pointed at the branches.

"Looks like somebody put Christmas lights on them," she said, watching the drops flickering randomly. Nearby, a woman with pink day-glo paint on her face swirled about in bare feet, making her thin dress swell up like a tent.

The light made you want to breathe deeply, to hold the crystal air in your lungs as long as you could. Across from us, the San Francisco Mime Troupe had found a small clearing to perform their scenarios in faces painted white. Helium balloons floated up from strings attached to their shoe laces. They were giving out the telephone credit card codes for major corporations so we could call our friends all across the country, courtesy of Gulf Oil or Pepsi-Cola. Peter inked in a number on the worn rubber sole of his shoe. I didn't write anything down. Brother Beeker's sermons about hell were still in me somewhere, and besides, there weren't that many people I wanted to call long-distance anyway.

208

Today in the Golden Gate Park, with thousands of people gathered and the music soaring, the magic was back. When the Airplane stepped offstage, someone leaped up onto the platform, dressed in what looked like a parachuter's jumpsuit, billowing out around him in green silk. His hair, streaked with glitter, blew in a curly circle around his head, and green paint covered his face and hands.

"Cat Heller," Lisa yelled over the noise of the crowd. "He's about to get drafted. He's going to turn his physical into a theater of the absurd."

"What an ego," Peter muttered.

"I've met him," I said, but they couldn't hear me.

"Why are you green?" a girl called up from the crowd. Cat shrugged. "My father was blue and my mother was yellow." He smiled when she laughed, as applause scattered up to the stage. "I'm green because I'm sick of this war. I'm not going to go fight their war! I'm going to the draft board to tell them why! Will you be there? Will you help me?"

Lisa looked over at me. "Ego. This guy's nothing but ego." Then her eyes sparkled, and she cupped one hand around her mouth. "Most heroes have big egos."

It was the first time I'd heard anyone criticize Cat Heller, and I couldn't believe it was coming from Lisa and Peter. On stage, two tall, thin guys appeared with guitars and started to tune up as Cat stepped away and the Airplane began to play again, but this time as I watched the crowd, I began feeling strangely lonely.

We begin life in such solitude, I thought, thinking of baby Lonnie, the nephew I hadn't yet seen. I looked around at the people, rapt in the music, the faces a mask with seven holes connecting to the world, with nothing but love to make us human; love and a little imagination.

We left with the rest of the people, now a stream of

tired individuals rather than the single face that chanted in unison on the march to the park. The Mime Troupe untied the balloons from their feet and they floated into the sky. We filed out with a group of other quiet marchers, first over a green hill, then past a Greek monument and a small fountain with water tumbling over the marble in a constant stream, a tinkling sound like wind chimes. We entered a pedestrian tunnel and, in an instant, the bright light of the park became shadows and cool air.

Maybe it was the peace of the crowd, dispersing the massive energy that had welled up earlier in the day, that had sustained us all for the long hours of the afternoon. Or maybe it was my own fatigue. Somehow, the boundaries of my body felt released, and my eyes seemed to hover above my body, watching the movements of my arms and legs. It seemed as though I could see my footsteps pushing myself forward through the tunnel, see myself there with hordes of others, feeling a singularity of purpose, a oneness with every other soul I happened to be caught with in that concrete tunnel, the light from late afternoon slanting yellow at the end, the sense of the limits of my own physical being giving way to something larger that I couldn't name.

Even my fingertips began to tingle, and my body felt larger, as if it were swelling to allow the rising of whatever it was inside that joined me with everyone, all drawn toward the oblique slant of sun in the same slice of time and light where I walked.

I glanced at Lisa. She was adjusting the strap of her tapestry shoulder bag, looking disgruntled at the buckle that refused to catch. She was bound in her own constraints, as most of us always were. From the speakers, the sound of Cat Heller's voice still came, urging people to support him. Beside me, Peter zipped his jean jacket and

210

rubbed his hands together for warmth.

At home, Andy would be either meditating or cooking dinner for us, gently stirring ingredients while the smells of foreign spices filled the kitchen, saffron and turmeric, coriander and mint.

That, too, didn't matter, that division of who we were by what we needed at a particular moment. I loved them all, including Andy, for being who he was. I felt ecstatic, exhilarated, feeling my own silence like a fullness swelling around me. And back home in Biloxi, there was little Lonnie. The uncertainty of the future seemed a grand adventure, one we all shared, where all our stories would become one.

Someone ahead lit a candle in the tunnel, a flame that flickered with the movement of its bearer, and then another appeared, and another, lots of tiny white fires. I remembered how Mama used to tell Charlene and me, when we were little kids, that, when fireflies flashed their secret codes on summer nights, it was the sign language of ghosts. She would fill the lawn with dead ancestors: an Irish preacher, an Indian princess from long ago, and her own grandfather, the riverboat gambler, their stories flickering in the darkness of the back yard on Mossy Point Drive. Though it was now California, they were here with all of us, still telling their endless tales, weaving the past into the present, to ease their constant parting.

The dark coolness of the tunnel suddenly lifted as we came onto the sidewalk, but the specter of the fireflies in the quiet Mississippi night remained, reminding me of how our stories are all bound together.

PART FOUR

MISSISSIPPI 1968

Chapter Sixteen

It wasn't hard to say goodbye to Andy when I left for
Christmas break. He wrapped up a poetry book for me for
Christmas with no inscription. It was one I'd seen on his
shelves. I gave him some wind chimes I bought from a
street vendor, but the ceramic star that hung in the middle
to strike the chimes had broken when he unwrapped it. We
both apologized, but I had a feeling we wouldn't be shar-
ing the same room when I got back from Mississippi.

At the New Orleans airport, Daddy was waiting at the
gate. He grabbed me so hard my ribs hurt. "Marilyn's at
home, cooking up a big batch of gumbo for y'all," he
boomed, so loud that people turned to look. I cringed. And
then I saw Aunt Sylvia. People were already staring at her
wild hair and sari, and one woman even pointed, nudging
her husband who wore a string tie and alligator loafers. We
were back in the South, all right.

Aunt Sylvia was either oblivious to the stares or
awfully good at ignoring them. She wrapped her arms
around me, and over her shoulder I saw Charlene walking
toward us from the restroom. Her face wasn't bloated like
it had been in the pictures Daddy had sent. She looked like
she always had, except there was a little blue pouch slung
around her chest that she cradled with both arms. When I

got close, I put an arm around her and leaned in to see. The baby opened his eyes, almost as if he'd heard me breathing.

Charlene lifted her son and held out his little red hand to me. "Say hello to your Aunt Jubilee," she told him. Lonnie had a pink rash on one cheek and his ears stuck out beneath the yellow cap he wore, but he was beautiful. Charlene slipped him into my arms, a warm sweet weight. All I could do was stare at him, with a weight in my heart, too, for Charlene. She was happy, but it wasn't the path she'd chosen.

In the station wagon, Charlene and I sat in the back seat, like children again, while Daddy and Aunt Sylvia sat in front.

"So Levi Litvak really did die in that car crash," I whispered to her. We looked at each other like we'd found our way out of a desert.

The baby started to wail, and Charlene jiggled him, then stuck a pacifier in his mouth. He pulled it out and frowned against the sudden sunlight as Daddy turned a corner. Lonnie waved his hands angrily, battling the sun as if it were an attack of bees. Charlene pulled his hat down further over his eyes and he sucked hard on the pacifier, his thumbs tucked into his fists.

"Is he hungry?" asked Aunt Sylvia.

"Well, I'm starving," I said, while Charlene fished inside a diaper bag and came up with a bottle. "I don't think I can wait for Marilyn's gumbo."

"You look like you haven't eaten since you left," said Charlene. "You just about don't have a rear end."

"We'll be home before you know it," said Daddy, looking at me in the rearview mirror. "Robbie's been asking about you."

"Rob?" He must hate me for the way I'd ignored him. "How is he, anyway?" I tried to sound as if I didn't care. Outside the car window, the scrubby pines still bent under the Gulf breezes, as if nothing had changed since the days when I would take the truck out on the highway and see how far I could get away before dinner called me back. It seemed I'd been away for years, that Rob might be different in ways I couldn't imagine.

"He smokes," said Charlene. "Camels."

"Really?"

"He brought a Christmas present to the house. For you," she said. "Looks like a record. *The White Album,* maybe."

"You're messing with my presents?" It was just like Charlene.

"No more than you ever messed with mine. I was making sure it was a real present, not just something he made. You better buy him something."

"Stop it. You sound like a mother," I told her, and hoped she knew I was teasing.

"Get used to it," she said.

"Did Rob like State?" It felt strange to even say his name.

"How should I know?" She shrugged, the same old Charlene. "But he brought Lonnie a present, too. Look." She dangled a pair of embroidered white mittens, so tiny they seemed like doll clothes. "Good taste, huh?"

"He looks like a hippie," Daddy said. "I guess that's what State will do to you. But he's a good boy."

My heart surged; I couldn't wait to see him. How had four months changed him? I thought about Andy, but my guilt was over Rob.

"Art's coming for Christmas," said Charlene. "He's picked out a ring. He asked me to have my finger sized."

She held out her left hand and wagged her ring finger. "Size six."

Aunt Sylvia smiled and reached over the seat to pat Charlene's leg.

"What about Lonnie?" I whispered. "Does Art like him?"

Charlene shot me one of her indignant looks. "How could anyone not like Lonnie? Of course he does. You should see the way he holds him." Her eyes warmed. "He loves him."

The car rolled along the coastal highway, and Aunt Sylvia reached to turn down the radio. As the sound faded, Lonnie cupped his little palms together as if trying to scoop the music from the air as it faded. He cried at his empty hands, waving his fists. "Turn it back up, Aunt Sylvia," I said, and as the music rose, a gummy smile flashed on his face.

Outside the car windows, the brown Gulf waters were calm and flat. A few tourists in swimsuits walked on the beach, and one man splashed in the water, skinny legs kicking up white spray. "Yankees," said Daddy, shaking his head. "Don't they know it's cold?"

This is a foreign place to those people, I thought, maybe even exotic. I remembered Andy, nude, diving into the crisp clear water in the Big Sur Mountains, and wondered for the first time what swimming in the Gulf would feel like in winter. Maybe I'd try it with Rob.

Marilyn was stirring the pot of gumbo when we came in, Daddy lugging my suitcase. She put down the spoon and hugged me, releasing the familiar, slightly sour odor of her sweat. It was the smell of the tornado, of safety. Over Marilyn's shoulder, I could see outside the kitchen window, where Charlene's sculpture of matchbox cars had rusted into a geometry of orange shapes. "A memorial to those God took," Charlene had said then, and now it wasn't funny. It seemed right, like something people in Berkeley might have done.

"It's good to have you back," said Marilyn. She leaned against the counter with one slippered foot over the other, and I realized that she belonged there, in our house, along with the smell of the food she cooked. It would be empty without her.

"I missed you," I told her, surprised at how much I meant it.

She looked pleased and embarrassed, and turned back to stir the bubbling pot. "You don't know how much we missed both of you girls."

"Smells great," I said. It was the old smell of bacon grease and coffee with chicory that the gumbo couldn't conceal.

"Mrs. Guest brought over some of her cornbread. 'Course, it's not the best thing with gumbo, but her cornbread's good on any table."

I remembered how, after Mama's funeral, a plate of that cornbread had sat on the dining room table, wrapped in linen napkins. No one ate it, and Aunt Martha had frozen it. Maybe it was still there, I thought, hearing the freezer chug.

Marilyn went on. "You must be hungry, coming all that way from California."

"She's starving," said Charlene. "Just look at her jeans, bagging. She doesn't have a rear end."

"Get off it, will you?" I gave her a poke in the ribs.

"Girls!" said Daddy, but his eyes shone, like things were finally normal again.

Charlene put plates on the table, and I was starting to help when the doorbell rang.

"Jubilee!" Daddy called. "Somebody here for you."

216

I knew it was Rob before he came in. His hair hung below his chin, not enough to be counted for much in Berkeley, but here it made him either a hero or an outlaw. Or both. A mustache shaded his upper lip, but behind his glasses was the same Rob, his eyes gentle on me. He wore a green shirt I'd never seen before, and the first thing I thought was that some girl had given it to him. I wanted to hug him, but he had changed so much. Even his shoes were different, desert boots that I'd never seen him wear.

"You look different. You've lost weight," he said. "But you're as beautiful as ever." He rubbed my cheek with the back of his fingers, and when I put my arms around him, my head came to the same familiar point on his shoulder. If only that had been Rob hitchhiking in Marin County instead of Andy, I thought.

Rob stayed for gumbo while I answered Marilyn's questions about Berkeley and my courses, how I'd pull all-nighters to study for finals.

"Until you've been up with a baby for weeks on end, you haven't pulled an all-nighter," said Charlene. "You don't even know what an all-nighter is. You try an all-weeker."

"Is that what separates the girls from the women?" Rob asked, and I slugged his arm gently. The muscles were harder, and his jaw seemed more set now, stronger. I hoped he would want to kiss me, when we could get away.

None of us wanted to talk about Joe Holliday, not in front of Daddy. His face shone with delight that both of his girls were back, but in the pauses between conversation, there was a silent knowing among us all. I wanted to tell Rob that I was finally free of Levi Litvak, but all I could do was smile awkwardly at him.

When we finished eating, Rob pushed back his chair and brought his plate to the sink. "Want to go for a ride?"

he asked. At last, I'd have him to myself, and I could tell him how sorry I was. And I'd tell him about Joe Holliday, but I wanted to time it right, let Rob know that I was okay now, that things were as normal as they would ever be.

The troll doll was gone from the hood of his car, leaving a little raised spot of glue where it had been. "Where did the troll go?" I asked.

"Kid stuff," he said. "A lot of things changed after you left." He backed out the driveway and headed along the coast in silence while I waited for the right moment to tell him about Joe Holliday. Some new tourists were on the beach, now, men in wild patterned shirts and bermuda shorts, women in dresses that swirled around their knees as they waded into the cool water. They were laughing and they didn't seem like Yankee idiots anymore, just tourists.

"You wanna go in?" I asked.

He glanced at me. "We're from here, Jubilee. We already know it's too cold." But he pulled into the next parking bay and opened the car door. The wind smelled of salt water and conch shells, and I rolled up my jeans. The sand was cold and hard under my bare feet, and now it seemed silly to go wading. We walked instead, out onto a gray pier with missing planks where someone's crabbing lines were decaying, hanging halfway to the water with frayed ends. Some night, I'd burn the scarf on the beach with Charlene, setting those poppies free, sparks that would disappear over the Gulf waters. I hoped it would feel good, but I wasn't sure. Mama would've given it away, I knew, maybe to Pearl.

"You're awfully quiet," said Rob.

"I missed you," I said, knowing how true it was. "There's this guy I should tell you about. . "

He squeezed my hand to stop me. "We don't have to tell each other that stuff. Not now, anyway," he said. "It's

218

my fault. I never should have stopped calling you."

"I didn't want you to stop," I said, and my warm breath made a little balloon when I exhaled. We sat on a crooked bench at the end of the pier. "Levi Litvak didn't do it."

"Charlene told me."

"She told you?" The balloon of breath expanded on the Gulf breeze, punctured. "You mean, you knew all during dinner?" Leave it to Charlene, I thought.

"I was waiting for you. I didn't know if you wanted to talk about it."

At last, the words tumbled out. "It feels so good, no more secrets. I always wondered how Levi Litvak could've killed somebody he loved. You think he ran into that tree on purpose, trying to kill himself? He must've known Joe Holliday was after him next."

"I think he was just running. He'd have gone to the cops," said Rob. "Soon as he escaped that lunatic."

I imagined Levi Litvak's hair, blowing wildly on the swampy back roads near New Orleans before he crashed. Was he going to the New Orleans' police? Was Joe Holliday close behind? It was hard to imagine his battered truck keeping up with that Thunderbird. "Levi Litvak must have been terrified," I said. "He knew Mama was dying. Maybe he wasn't thinking anything. It was just the Thunderbird and him and the picture of Mama in his mind." *The bat out of hell is what you'll come up with every time.* Loretta Holliday would know, I thought. In my own mind, he was speeding the way I had in the truck, with the accelerator to the floor and the road ahead. Until a curve caught him.

The wind off the water picked up, bringing a salty taste like tears in my mouth with it. I leaned into Rob, and he pulled me into the warmth of his jacket before he kissed

219

me. He smelled different now, of cigarettes and coffee, but his lips were the same.

The White Album was playing on the stereo when Rob dropped me off, and Charlene and Aunt Sylvia sat at the kitchen table, listening. Marilyn had a beer in one hand, her feet up on a chair, dishes still piled in the sink. "Taking a break?" I asked.

"Just waiting for you," said Charlene.

Aunt Sylvia said, "It's none of my business, but Rob seems nice."

"He was always nice, unlike some boys." Marilyn glanced at Charlene with a sad look. "But he looks like a Communist hippie now. Who knows what those professors are teaching up at State," she said. "Evelyn McCarty says demonstrators from up North are pouring into New Orleans for some kind of ruckus this week-end. Oughta send 'em all to Russia." She sounded as if she were tired of saying it, lines rehearsed too often. She sipped her Falstaff and got up.

Aunt Sylvia winked at me.

I smiled and looked out the window again at the sculpture Charlene had created long ago. Now, it glistened in the porch light, an arc of yellow. Rust coated the colors, the little cars indistinguishable now in a beautiful jumble, a coherent mosaic of patterns. Why had it ever seemed so weird?

Marilyn handed Charlene a dish to wash. "You too, Jubilee," she said, reaching for a cup. "Come help wash these dishes. What on earth do you see out that window? You didn't forget how to wash a dish out there in Berkeley, did you, honey?"

As I picked up the plate of cornbread, I remembered Mrs. Guest's words at my mother's funeral, the way she had put her hands on my head and Charlene's, as if making a benediction. "Oh law, what do we know down here, anyway? What do we know on this earth?"

I thought of San Francisco and how time had seemed to dissolve in the Golden Gate Park tunnel, where we were all together in a slice of time, a slant of light. This was something I knew, something beyond words. It was the stillness beneath the motion, the vast vacuum behind the breath.

Levi Litvak appeared in my dreams one last time. He wore Joe Holliday's camouflage jacket, and then he turned into nothing more than a solitary, toothless skull, unseeing eyeballs set into the sockets, the pupils light as bleached marble, like the blind choral group that had sung at our school in what seemed like eons ago.

. . . *Everybody's talking about a new way of walking, do you want to lo-ose your mind.* .

It was the dark side of the moon, a place where justice came, but in strange ways, where there might be something like holiness in the world, a place, I realized, that, wherever I was, I could call home.